The Priest &
The Whistleblower

Gordon Parker

A CIP catalogue record for this book is
available from the British Library
ISBN: 978-1-7393675-0-3
Typeset in **Garamond**

*This book is a work of fiction. Names, characters,
businesses, organizations, places and events are the
product of the author's imagination. Any resemblance to
actual persons, living or dead, events or locales is entirely
coincidental. The exceptions, present and past are:-Karen
Silkwood, Meryl Streep, Vladimir Putin, Richard
L.Garwin, Ted Taylor, Peter Zimmerman, David Kelly
Mikhail Mezentsev, Sergei Shoigu, Georgi Markov,
Alexander Litvinenko, Sergei Skripal, Yulia Skripal*

www.BurtonMayersBooks.com

In memory of my son-in-law Bill Johnston and
my nephew Nick Henry

ACKNOWLEDGMENTS

My thanks to Peter Barker, Neil Campbell and Mark Lyons for their advice and guidance. Also, thanks to William Johnston Jnr for his assistance.

BY THE SAME AUTHOR.

The Darkness of the Morning.
Lightning in May
The Pool.
The Action of the Tiger.
A Waking of Rooks.

There are no secrets about the world of nature.
There are secrets about the thoughts and intentions of man.

J Robert Oppenheimer.

CHAPTER 1

It was raining as he drove her to the train station. There was no sound in the car other than the dull drone of the engine and the steady, soft slap of the windscreen wipers. The silence between them was deliberate and profound, as though to speak would break some edict and set off a chain reaction neither of them wanted. And yet both of them wanted to speak; Clare to say some final words that would terminate their relationship precisely; her husband to choose some soft endearing phrase to convince her that she was making a mistake. Inevitably, somewhere down the line, there had to be a last rounding off of all the bitter dialogue. Before, their acid exchanges had been loud and mutually incriminating; stinging accusations from the past thrown out from both sides. Yet now, in a perverse way a calm finale would bring some strange satisfaction. Like the final lines of a long, arduous novel.

Clare sat staring zombie-like at the stippled colours of the distant city lights. Her lips were tight in a mirthless smile. The silence was heavy and profound.

It took twenty minutes to drive to the train station. At that time of night, roads from their up-market detached house in an affluent estate north of Newcastle were quiet.

Donkley Hall: bespoke residences ranging from mansions to chic bungalows. It was the nesting place for the rich and successful. In some cases, the cash and the success came from the both sides of the law. Clare's father had reluctantly forked out the down - payment, doubting the wisdom of their move especially the cost and a whisper in his ear that the estate carried the old, hackneyed epithet 'all fur coats and no knickers'. Clear of the adjoining village there was little activity on the main road. A couple of spray-spewing lorries with blinding headlights flashed past them. Anonymous cars overtook them, passing through a sizzle of puddles. The airport was bathed in blue-white light with one parked 737 and one bouncing gently past the perimeter fence on its way to the runway and a sunnier tarmac somewhere well south. There was life out in the dark rain-soaked November night but nothing like the snarl of crawling, impatient traffic that would clog all routes to the Tyne and the city at eight in the morning.

"It's one hell of a time to be travelling" Jack Shaftoe barked, then instantly regretted it.

She turned her head with emphatic slowness, exaggerating her inspection of his profile, one second a silhouette, the next caught in the light of a passing street lamp. He needed a haircut. But then he always did. He needed a shave. Ditto. He needed major plastic surgery to get his face looking like it did ten years ago and a gastric band wouldn't have gone amiss.

"It's a good time Jack," she said coldly, "it just happened…it was time."

"So suddenly you can't wait to get rid of me. Want me out of your life."

"Yes. We have no marriage…no kids…nothing. You're married to the goddam Force, Jack. Pimps, pros. and greasy informers are your wife and children. They take all your time – night and day and I've had enough. I had enough in London. And don't tell me you haven't screwed a few of your female confidants in your time, including DC Stella whatshername a.k.a. the Station bike."

He groaned and shook his head slowly. "For Christ's sake don't bring that up again."

"Why not? I've just had a two-hour tirade about my piss poor contribution to this alliance. Journalism and housekeeping don't hang easy together but I tried… I really tried."

"What about your job? Have you informed Bellamy that his ace investigative journalist is off - gone without so much as a wave goodbye?"

"He knows. He knew two weeks ago. I told him I was going back to London."

Jack shook his head in disbelief. "Bloody hell Clare, you knew then and didn't say anything. Don't go. For Christ's sake give us a chance to sort things out."

She shook her head. "It's no good. I'm totally pissed off… have been for weeks – months in fact. I'm going Jack. Accept it and get on with your life and your love affair with the Force...and Stella."

The car moved slowly through the city, still busy as the evening got under way; alive with shops, cafes and innumerable bars. Newcastle: the fun city where men are men and women are thankful for it, so the saying goes. Hard drinkers; hard workers; no nonsense Geordies. When the temperature drops to minus 10 they button up their shirts. Jack loved the place. He was born just up the coast. Clare hated it. She hated the coldness of the winters. She hated the unpredictability of the summers and the damp frets that rolled in from the grey North Sea. She shunned the lush rolling countryside of Northumberland. It didn't bring any enthusiasm or admiration to her mind. The great scimitars of sandy beaches where, on warm and sunny days, a few dozen people might share the endless dunes, did not raise a spark of delight in her. She shrugged at the medieval castles. She was unimpressed by the industrial history of the area that had changed the world: the first railway engine and the first steam turbine. The first sustainable electric light bulb –

months ahead of the American, Edison and the first house ever to be lit by hydro- electric power. Jack was proud of its heritage, its culture and its customs. He had given her a potted history of it all with excited enthusiasm. Clare accepted it with a bored nod. She was a journalist and her mind searched for the new and intriguing. The past was as dull as yesterday's headline. Like a faithful wife she had accompanied her husband north from the endless civilization of London thinking that perhaps… just perhaps she could regenerate a feeling that there was some meaning to her existence; some minor liberation from the intense sleaze, murder and human degradation that had confronted her senses for so long as a journalist in the big city. In that, she was in tune with her husband: a steady cop and a fairly successful detective. He had been promoted to sergeant, but forever ground his teeth at the inadequacies of the Force. His exasperation was always simmering at being handcuffed by protocol. It was endless paperwork usually leading nowhere. It was the insane judicial system that allowed blatant criminals to be released on pathetic technicalities. But somehow, it all became another part of his chosen profession. Somehow, he managed to push it into the neutral corners of his mind and manage his job, where he could, his way. And there were ways. There were wiles that were outside the book and to the rigid mores of protocol, not allowed. But to this detective there were few constraints. Criminals needed to be caught. He understood their mentality and where he could, he mirrored their ruthlessness. Clare reluctantly suffered his frustration and supported his ideals and his dogged approach to the callous London underworld. Jack lived it. She recorded it.

Their life in the big city took on a routine, almost mundane normality immersed daily in the machinations of lawbreakers. Then one day the shit hit the fan. Some nark had decided to spill the beans. Jack Shaftoe stood staring into the bulldog face of Detective Chief Superintendant Church.

"You know why you're here?" he growled, looking over the top of his bifocals, his face twisted in a snarl that had vomit piling up on the inside.

Jack shrugged. He took a quick glance through the glass into the main office. He knew the audience would be loving the anticipated antics of their boss. "The Parkmoor Heist… I know it's slow but…"

"No! It's not the Parkmoor heist," Church barked. "It's the Connie Drinkwater case! And the goddam Percival case! The Charlie Ashley fucking case! Plus a slack handful of others!"

Shaftoe sagged. He knew what was coming. He massaged his brow. "I got results," he whispered.

Church levered himself up from his desk slowly, leant forward and splayed his meaty hands on the array of papers strewn across it. "You got results," he croaked before clearing his throat. He clenched his teeth, his sagging, dough coloured skin turning red then purple as it tried to burst out of his collar. "You got results alright by shagging Connie Drinkwater then blackmailing her to spill the beans on her paedo brother or you'd tell her husband! You got results alright by forcing poofter Percival to shop his partner who was creaming thousands off the Blue Banana night club takings with your little hint at protection… for a goddam slice of the action!"

"It wasn't for me! Christ, you know that! The money went in backhanders for info on the Parkmoor heist. I'll get results."

Church lowered his head. "Fuck results!" he bellowed. "I want my pension!" He raised his head again and a sad, almost painful smile creased his face. "If any of this hits the Press I'll be out on my ear. You know that, don't you?" he whispered. "It won't only be the tabloids that have my head on a pole. The whole shit pile of them will eat me alive. "I want my pension and a few years toasting my backside on some sunny shore. I can't take the risk anymore Jack. You're a good cop…" he nodded reluctantly, "sometimes – most of the time, but I can't take the risk anymore." He slumped down again and rubbed a podgy hand over his mouth. "Look Jack I don't want to sack you. I've had words with Charteris up in your home town. He's DCI up there now. He says he remembers you from your work on the London Newcastle heroin-go-round. He says he'll take you on." His face twisted into a sad pleading look of despair. He closed his eyes for a moment. "Speak to Clare Jack. Think about it. Go home… go back to Newcastle, Jack and shag the Northumbria force up!"

A cold breeze blew through the curved platforms of Newcastle Central station but then it always did. It was ten past seven in the evening and the place was quiet. A few travellers stood with their heads sunk into the collars of heavy jackets. A slow goods train screeched through the arcing tracks heading to an unknown destination. There was the smell of coffee and hamburgers wafting out from a fast-food joint to their left. A drunk sat with his head almost between his legs, a bottle of brown ale clutched in his rigored hand. Jack Shaftoe glanced at the board. The seven-thirty from Edinburgh to London was on time.

He turned to Clare. "Platform four," he whispered. "What about your ticket? You need a ticket."

She nodded. "Got it. Internet."

"Don't go," he said trying to hold her hand.

She pulled her arm away. "It's over the bridge, isn't it?"

He followed her as she strode out over the tracks to the platforms on the other side. The determination in her caused her blond hair to bounce against her shoulders. She was slim, smart; five eight and still stacked nicely for her forty- one years and two miscarriages. Jack suddenly wished all the animosity and friction of their relationship could be instantly forgotten. They stood silently as the train approached, slowed to a stop and a gaggle of passengers spewed from open doors and hurried with an entourage of haversacks and rolling cases up and over the bridge.

"I'll help you with your bag," he said.

"No, I'm fine," she snapped. "'Bye Jack. I'll arrange for the rest of my things. I want nothing from you. The house is yours, but so is the mortgage."

She grabbed her holdall and entered the train. He followed her progress down the carriage until she found her seat. She sat opposite an old woman. The woman was dressed in a black coat buttoned up to the neck. Her matt black hair had a pure white margin close to her skull. Her rheumy eyes stared out at him inquisitively as he stood hunched against the cold, watching Clare. He gazed solemnly at her as she allowed a man across the aisle to hoist her holdall onto the overhead rack. She sat down. Train doors slid shut. A whistle blew and the train started moving. Jack hugged himself. Clare glanced at him. He gave her a painful smile. She raised the middle finger of her right hand as the train slowly accelerated and the old woman opposite opened her toothless mouth in a silent gesture of hilarity.

He watched the train disappear out of the station. He stood for a moment trying to gain a sense of reality. He knew it had happened but somewhere deep in his mind he fought to dismiss the whole thing as a fantasy. She had gone as she had threatened so many times before but the threats were meaningless – just empty words, just angry outbursts that so many married couples deploy but fade as the days pass. He turned and thrust his hands deep into the pockets of his coat. The house would be silent. He would grab a Chinese carry- out near home. It would be nearly midnight by the time she arrived at her mother's house. He would ring her then. She would come back in a few days. She would be stern and cold but she would be back. He tried to convince himself with that thought but as he slouched back over the bridge the prospect hit him that it might never happen. Outside the rain had eased to a light drizzle and the city continued its accelerating evening awakening. Across the road a dozen men dressed in togas and oblivious to the weather shrieked and yelled as they made their way to a bar to initiate a drunken bachelor party. The world still revolved. Life went on. Jack and Clare were nothing; their predicament unknown and irrelevant to the bustling city.

He opened the car door and slumped into the driver's seat. He sat staring through the windscreen, which was a fine curtain of moving colours as the rivulets of fine rain chased each other down the glass. A sensation of loneliness hit him as though he had been locked away from the world for weeks. He took a deep shuddering breath, rubbed the palm of his hand over his mouth and fished in his jacket pocket for his mobile. He hesitated. All of a sudden, he needed an escape from the depression that was settling on him like an autumn fog. He knew where to find some solace and gentle sympathy. It was an act of desperation; a recoil from the abrupt change in his life. He wanted to know he was still relevant and worthy of some affection, however fleeting, from somebody. He punched in a number, sat back and waited as the ring tone repeated itself.

"Hello." That one word stirred something in him. The timbre was milk chocolate. The accent half Geordie, half Caribbean: sexy.

"Hi Stella," his voice was flat and toneless. "It's Jack."

"You don't say. What's wrong, you sound down."

"I am. Clare's gone and left me."

There was a soft phlegmy derisory laugh borne on twenty a day untipped. *"Well, well, well, at last she's come to her senses."*

"Don't take the piss. I think she means it this time."

There was a long pause. *"So, I take it you could do with some…. some, how shall I put it, extra marital activity."*

"You've got such a way with words."

He heard her breathe in and exhale on a low soft growl. *"You're a heartless bastard Jack. Where are you now?"*

"Central Station. Just seen her off to mummy's. I can be there in fifteen minutes."

There was a moment's silence. *"I'm low on gin. Pick up a*

bottle, will you?"

"On one condition."

"What's that?"

"That red negligee. You know the one I mean. Got time to put it on?"

"It only takes a second."

He smiled as he turned the ignition key. "I'll be there in ten."

His mobile rang. A gentle, far-off rendition of 'Blaydon races.' A dozen bars of the Geordie hymn that brought him out of a post-coital slumber. His world swam with warm feminine flesh and the smell of some exotic perfume that promised further mind-blowing distilled intimacies. Stella stirred and wrapped herself around him as he reached for his phone on the bedside table. His eyes focussed on the clock next to it. It was 3.10am. For a second he thought it could be Clare. The phone showed DCI Charteris.

"Jack, are you sober?"

"Just. What's up sir?"

"Get yourself along the A69 Carlisle Road tout suite. There's a lay-by on the north side just before the A68 junction south. Bloke in a car with his brains blown out. Looks like suicide but you'd better check it out. I want you on the job, Jack, for a very good reason."

"What's that?"

"Apparently your address is punched into the car's Sat-nav. It looks like he was on his way to your house for some obscure reason. Find out why and fill Coulson in on what's going on. And I shouldn't have to say this Jack but this suicide better not have anything to do with you. You had better not have been leaning on him for any reason. You understand me? And Jack, I shouldn't have to say this either but I will."

"Yes sir."

"Behave yourself and stick to the rules...y'hear me?"

CHAPTER 2

His mind raced as fast as his car, west out of Newcastle, away from the bright city lights. In no time, he was into the dark countryside of low rolling hills, dry stone walls, bleating sheep and the ghosts of Hadrian's Roman army. He had often surmised they were forever guarding the remains of his famous wall that ran parallel to the A69 and sashayed over the moors on to Carlisle. It had stopped raining but the road was still wet and the darkness only broken by the faint lights of villages that clung to the Tyne. There was a gibbous moon up there that kept hiding for long minutes behind the black clouds. Jack saw nothing but the road ahead caught in the headlights of the car.

He had left Stella softly protesting at his urgent unravelling of her legs from his. Charteris' parting statement had him in a frenzy of imaginings. Who was he? Was he a friend or even a relation? Why was he on his way to Donkley Hall? And in the middle of the night! Or had he been in the lay-by for hours? Who did he know who might top himself? Nobody of consequence came to mind. There were one or two informers who lived on the periphery of gangland, who might contemplate it if their cover was blown, but they were a breed unto themselves. They lived on the edge of life, knowing that one day it might all turn sour and their breathing prematurely terminated.

In the far distance, he could see a faint display of blue flashing lights pulsing urgently into the darkness. A patrol car sped past him doing ninety plus. After a couple of miles, he approached another, straddling the western carriageway, diverting traffic onto a minor side road. He slowed and held his ID against the windscreen. The high - viz officer produced a torch and peered at the document with a look of annoyed curiosity before directing him around the police car. Jack drove on past the illuminated action on the opposite carriageway and turned back on himself at the roundabout. The carriageway east was also blocked by a police car. He stopped and flashed ID at the guarding constable and drove slowly up to the busy activity. Four police cars parked at angles on the lay-by were the cause of the mesmeric cobalt radiance. A police van was backed up near a steel-grey five- door Citroen Picasso. Blinding floodlights poked out from the back. Behind the car stood a large lorry with Spanish livery and an address in Madrid. The cab was in darkness. The cab door was open wide. An ambulance had parked itself in the middle of the road, the two paramedics lounging with folded arms against the radiator grill. The whole lay-by was cordoned off in blue-white major crime scene tape. Six figures fussed around the car, four in white coveralls looking like arctic commandos. Cameras flashed every few seconds. Another was hunkered down talking to the lorry driver. He was sitting, propped up against the giant front wheel of the lorry. Jack could see another uniform leaning over the adjacent dry-stone wall vomiting noisily. His lips thinned as he surveyed the scene. Without viewing the inside of the car he knew the guy hanging onto the wall was young. A rookie. Never seen blood and snots before. He would get used to it. He would harden to the vagaries of human life in all its latent disgusting and irreverent misfortunes.

He ducked under the ribbon. Sergeant Harry Lockwood

seemed to be in charge. A big, hefty man, prematurely grey with his hair Einstein- style. Without his hat he looked like he was approaching out of a cloud. His face carried the pock- marked legacy of a nasty case of teenage acne. He had a prominent brow and a square thrusting jaw. His dour face was permanently locked in the angry expression of 'I hate you all'. He looked menacing and he was. Heaven help any punk who tried his luck with Lockwood. His massive meaty hands had roughly navigated many a speeding drunken driver out of the car and into the Station. And he had cause. His six-year-old daughter had been mown down five years earlier by a nineteen-year-old high on heroin and doing seventy-five in a thirty zone. The judge, looking every bit the caricature of his profession, empathised with the defence sob story. He had been deprived of mother's milk. His father had sexually abused him. He had been bullied at school for having prominent ears. Maybe his predicament resonated with the judge: he got eight years and was out after four. Harry dreamt about their paths crossing again. He relished catching anybody doing thirty- one. He loved to thumb the radar control right down to the thirty zone if his quota looked like it was wanting. It made his day. One more tiny gesture of revenge.

His face broke into a rare, pained smile when he saw Jack. They both worked out of Robert's Hill Station but had known each other from their Army days. Northern Ireland during the 'troubles.' They were both well hardened to humanity without skin. Vicious explosions. Bullet wounds. Severed limbs. A young man with a splintered billiard cue through his neck. A severed head lodged in the branches of a tree and bobbing up and down in the breeze.

"Morning Jack" he growled. "Got a nice one here. Suicide. Blew his brains out before coming to see you, would you believe. What frighteners did you put on him? We managed to extract his mobile. It was half hidden under his left hand but we managed to winkle it out without disturbing the corpse. He rang your landline at eight twenty-seven. I recognised the number. No answer. We're checking other numbers but yours was the last. Your address is on the car sat-nav. The ignition was still on and the engine was running. Seems he wanted to see you, Jack. Looks like something urgent."

Jack shook his head. "Who is he? Have you traced the car?"

"DVLA says it's registered to Albert McManus. He lives... or should I say lived, in Egremont on the Cumbrian coast."

Jack's lips thinned and he shook his head again. "Never heard of him. What the hell did he want me for?"

Harry shrugged. "You're the detective. How's Clare?"

Jack rubbed the back of his neck. "She's... er... gone down to London."

Harry gave a soft, dry laugh. "So she caught you out at last?"

"Don't you start. I took Clare to the station. She's gone to see her folks. She'll be home in a few days. You got a new boy over there?" He gestured with his head toward the young PC now with his back to the wall, his head slumped down on his chest, wiping his mouth with a handkerchief.

"Hah!" Harry grunted. "Only been let out a fortnight ago. Three domestics: one where the guy in the house wouldn't let him in and poked a great big carving knife through the letterbox. A punch-up in the Bigg Market on Saturday night and a flasher on the Town Moor. Tonight he knows what it's all about."

Jack smiled and nodded. He pointed to the lorry. "What's that doing here?"

They turned to where the lorry driver was still propped against the front wheel. He looked to be in his thirties. He was lean and narrow shouldered. A typical Spaniard with short black hair and dark olive skin. Probably from Ceuta with a touch of Algerian Berber in him Jack thought. In the bright lights shed from the investigation Jack could see a thin deep scar running from his hairline to the bridge of his nose. He looked up as they approached, his face wet with tears and twisted with an agonising memory.

"Got him calmed down?" Harry asked the constable.

"Just. Think he's still in shock. He's Spanish. His English is poor."

"I could have guessed. That's a hell of a scar on his face. I reckon the bull outran him at Pamplona. He looks too old to have tried head- butting platform 9 3/4 at King's Cross."

The man wiped his nose with a swipe across his sleeve. "I stop to get the directions," he whispered, "I lose my way. I look for Sunderland… I see *el coche* and I stop to get the directions. I come from Liverpool." He started sobbing. "I come to the driver's window. I knock on the window. I have my map and *antorcha*. No-one answers. I see… I think I see a man… I think I see someone so I shine *la antorcha*. I see him lying over. I see the blood. I see the blood…*Santa Madre de dios porque viesto.*" His voice trailed away to a soft sob. "I ring police like my boss tell me."

Jack nodded and gave a grunt of understanding. He sighed and turned to Harry, "Well, better see the cause of all this activity. What time did Manuel over there ring in?"

"Before midnight. We got here at twelve thirty. I called in forensics. They were here about two."

They turned toward the car. All five doors were wide open. Handles, steering wheel and gear stick dusted with fingerprint powder. Two of the forensic team were in each of the rear doors, only white covered legs on show.

Harry smacked his lips. "Looks like a perfect 'good-bye cruel world job' to me. There's not much left of the left side of his face and most of his brains are stippled over the nearside window and passenger windscreen."

"Anybody contacted his family?"

"The Cumbria boys are on to it."

Jack peered into the driver's space. It was in part shade. "Can I have one of those bloody floodlights over here please?"

A portable light, shining with an intense operating

theatre brightness was wheeled over and positioned near the driver's door. Jack leaned forward. The man was dressed casually. Jeans, leather jacket, checked open-necked shirt. He lay over the passenger seat, his left arm outstretched, his right resting on his lap and holding a pistol. Its shape was instantly recognisable. Brandished in a thousand war movies and probably daily and in earnest during two world wars.

"Christ, that's a Luger," Jack whispered.

Harry nodded. "Yep. Probably 9mm. Common calibre. Plenty floating around when we were mixed up in the troubles."

"Wonder where he got hold of that."

"They're still in use today – all over the world but I'll bet that's a souvenir taken from a dead German."

Jack's eyes roamed over the dashboard then back to the body. The man had short brown hair, with a hint of grey at ear level. There was a bloodied hole just above his right eye where the bullet had entered. The hole had a halo of singed eyebrow hair and black powder burns. A trickle of congealed blood had meandered from the wound down and around his ear. His face had somehow twisted. His top teeth were on show giving the impression of a grotesque smile. Jack studied the right side of his face for a moment trying to raise a memory of where they might have crossed paths but he drew a blank. The corpse was a stranger. A man in his early fifties he guessed. He sighed then something caught his attention. He stared at the man's left hand. It was palm down. He pulled the floodlight closer. He then looked long and hard at the hand holding the gun. Even with the bland pallor of death he could distinguish a difference. The gun hand was white and waxy; the left much darker, weathered and still traceably brown. He straightened up. Harry was talking to one of the forensic team.

"Harry." He beckoned him over.

He broke off his conversation and moved from the back of the car. "Well, Sherlock have you seen enough?"

Jack scratched the top of his head, deep in thought.

"Harry, look at his hands."

Harry looked. "So?"

"The back of his hands seem different...a different colour. One seems...tanned. Never seen anything like that before."

Harry looked then shrugged. "So?"

"A circulation problem?" The voice behind him was rich, lilting and feminine. "Or maybe something to do with work?"

Jack turned, "Stella, what are you doing here?"

"Everybody's got to be somewhere. Charteris sent me. He contacted D.I Coulson and he rang me shortly after you left. He reckons you need some back-up. Says he needs to know the connection between you and the stiff."

"Don't know him from Adam. But I intend to find out. Look at his neck. Below the collar-line it's white. It's darker above. It's November and we haven't seen much sun for months. I'm guessing he's been abroad either working or on holiday."

"With one hand in his pocket all the time?" Harry laughed; a gentle derisory chuckle. "Maybe he's the Cumberland pocket billiards champion."

"Maybe he played with different balls," Stella said, grimacing as she peered in to get a closer look at the body. "Maybe he played golf. They only wear one glove don't they?"

Jack scratched the tip of his chin with a forefinger. "Which hand? Harry, you play golf don't you?"

"I take my clubs for an occasional walk. Yes."

"On which hand do you wear a glove?"

"Left...because I'm right-handed."

Jack shook his head. "Don't tell me why for Christ's sake. But I assume if you were left-handed the glove would go on the right hand. Am I right?"

Harry nodded. "Correct."

"That's interesting. That's bloody interesting."

"What are you thinking?" Stella asked. "You've gone

into your Columbo mode."

Jack stood silently in thought for a moment nipping his bottom lip between his thumb and forefinger. "I'm thinking if this man is a golfer and he's had a spell in the sunshine and if he's left-handed, it could explain why his right hand is lighter in colour. However it could be he has a circulation problem as you say – or something to do with his job. That's a possibility." He shook his head. "Just curious. It's unusual, that's all. Never seen anything like it before. Probably irrelevant."

"You're right there," Harry said as though the statement was a ridiculous flight of fancy. "Could be anything or nothing. But I would concentrate on the hole in his head. That's more important than the colour of his goddam hands. And besides, this golf idea might not hold water."

"Why?

"Because some right-handed golfers are left-handed. There's a couple in our club."

Jack nodded. "Maybe so, but if he is left-handed..."

"What's the relevance," Stella asked, suddenly sensing Jack had a legitimate train of thought.

"The relevance is, if he *is* left-handed, and it is a possibility... he used his right hand to pull the trigger. Surely, the natural thing would have been to use his left. Also, where he was sitting in the driver's seat he would have a problem with the window. He couldn't get the gun to his head sitting up straight because of the length of the barrel and the length of his arm. Just looking at the angle of the sprayed brains he must have been sitting up. Fernando over there says the window was shut."

"Fuck," Harry whispered. "Sherlock *is* alive and living among us."

Jack sighed. "Only a daft theory. Let's see what they find out when they get him on the slab. When they get his watch off, his wrist should have a band of white skin if he has been in the sun. Harry, make sure the forensics get all the dabs, will you. We need to find the bullet. The near side window is still intact so it will be in the car…or still in his head. Don't forget the spent cartridge. That'll be around somewhere. And will you get the Spaniard to the station. I think we need his prints as well as a statement." He paused again. "Yes, we need to get a Post Mortem on Mr. McManus. I want to see his right elbow."

"His right elbow?" What's that got to do with it?" Stella asked.

Jack pursed his lips and scratched under his chin. "Just another daft theory. If he did manage to get the gun to his head with his right hand, the recoil would have banged his elbow hard against the glass… just a thought."

"You're not saying he could have been murdered, surely," Harry said with a soft derisory laugh.

"Just thinking out some possibilities, Harry. Another puzzling thing… if he had a problem getting the gun to the side of his head why didn't he stick the nozzle under his chin or in his mouth. Hardly anything cut and dried in this game, as you well know. Call it a hunch but there's something not right here. I can feel it in my water."

"Bollocks, Jack. He's been on his way to see you about something. Something that's been worrying him to death… and it did."

"Maybe. Maybe you're right. But why me? Where's the significance in that?"

Harry smiled again. "You're the detective."

"Yes Ok," Jack uttered with a bored acceptance of the statement. "For the Press it's a suicide. I need to speak to his family and his work mates. Any idea where he worked?"

Harry spoke into his intercom. There was a brief conversation then he turned to Jack. "The Carlisle lads say he works at Sellafield, that Nuclear place on the coast near Whitehaven. He's the safety manager there."

"Sellafield," Jack whispered. "Sellafield," he said louder, its significance suddenly gelling in his mind.

"Well?" Stella drawled.

"Well?" Harry barked.

"Mr. McManus wasn't coming to see me. He was coming to see Clare! She was over there last week. It was something to do with a leak of some dangerous substance. She told me she had someone sweating but wouldn't commit; that there were some uneasy reactions to her questions, as though they had something to hide. Bet that was our stiff there, having second thoughts. Serious second thoughts."

"So why didn't he ring Clare's mobile?"

"Maybe he tried the land line first… and didn't get the chance to ring her mobile."

"Bollocks" Harry barked again. "Too many C and I documentaries. That's your trouble."

Jack smiled. "Could be. You say the ignition was on and the engine was running?"

"Yes."

"Now why would he do that when he was parked?"

Harry laughed. "He was keeping warm. He didn't want to die in cold blood."

Jack shook his head. The joke lost in his meandering mind. "Possible. Any other ideas?"

Stella turned back to them from another inspection of the body. "He could have been waiting for someone. He pulled into the lay-by to wait for someone."

Jack looked at her and smiled. "Now there's a thought." Their hot embracing seemed a week away yet it was still teasing his body. Bathed in the strong floodlights she was every inch the Amazon. Born in Curacao, her father a Dutch refinery engineer, her mother a direct descendant Arawak Indian. They moved from Curacao to Holland when Stella was six, then to England to join Shell's great oil offensive in the North Sea but she never forgot Curacao. It was ever in her conversation during the cold North East winters. It was a no- brainer that she got her degree at Newcastle University. Most students clamoured to hone their brains there and at the same time pickle them enjoying the myriad of pubs, clubs and wild quayside nightlife.

Harry looked from one to the other, for a moment taking in their soft mutual admiration. He could see the attraction and the sexual chemistry she oozed with a natural unpretentious femininity. At the Station her presence had the boys following her every move with silent lustful imaginings. What attracted her to Jack Shaftoe, the antithesis of svelte, was one of nature's mysteries.

Stella nodded. "It's another line of possibilities. By the way Jack, did you notice something else with his right hand?"

Jack frowned. "What."

"Come see."

All three turned back to the car. Stella positioned the floodlight and shone it on the man's lap.

"Look how he's holding the gun," Stella whispered. "Where should his index finger be?"

"Through the trigger guard… Shit," Jack hissed. "His whole hand is wrapped around the butt! I kid you not, this stinks Harry."

Harry gave a thoughtful nod. "Christ Almighty, you could be right."

Jack turned away. "I'm cold. I'm hungry and I'm bloody tired. I'm going home. I need to gather my thoughts, see a few people over on the west coast and decide on the next move. It looks like a suicide but, then again, there are some unusual bits to it that might need plausible explanations. Let's see what the PM shows and what forensics discover. I'll report to Coulson first thing in the morning. Stella, I'll see you at the Station, OK? Harry, please make sure we get some priority on the PM and a full forensic report on the car. I have a feeling there might be a lot to clarify on this little case of sudden death."

He drove home, his mind racing faster than before. There was a smudge of grey in the sky ahead as the winter morning struggled to let a limp, clouded sun peer above the eastern horizon. He had a case on his hands, he knew that but a key to his investigation was Clare. He would ring her as soon as possible. He had to know if she knew Albert McManus. Was it him she interviewed? Could she know why he would want to see her privately at her home? A trickle of excitement ran through him. A weight lifted from his mind. It dawned on him that such a juicy bit of mystery bait might just stir something in her journalist's natural curiosity to bring her home and he could begin to sweet talk her into staying.

CHAPTER 3

The house was cold, dark and still as he entered. There was a sombre silence to it. The stagnant atmosphere seemed to wrap itself around him. Clare had been gone for just twelve hours but there was already a sense of finality to it as though the place had been empty for an eternity and would never recover. He wandered into the bedroom and opened the wardrobe door. All her dresses were in a neat row. He ran an index finger along them with a sickening regret that they had allowed their relationship to deteriorate into such profound emotional inertia. He slid the wardrobe door shut and glanced at his watch. Five after seven. He decided to wait until eight. He knew the Pritchards would have stirred by then. He imagined Nigel Pritchard would be the one to pick up the phone: Clare's father. Jack grimaced as the thought of him went through his mind while he waited in the kitchen, listening to the kettle fizz on its way to a boil. Nigel Pritchard, ace Hedge Fund manager. A portly little man, bald except for a horseshoe of greying black hair that ran from one ear to the other around the back of his puffed neck. He was a dead ringer for the mayor of any small town in a TV comedy. Officious; short bristly moustache; mournful pouches under his eyes; head tucked into his shoulders. All he needed was a waistcoat and a giant gold Albert hanging from it to complete the picture of a pompous Victorian martinet. He treated anyone with a lower intellect and north of the city with bored tolerance and subtle dismissal. Their house was in the three million bracket. Four storeyed Georgian terraced. Thornhill Square, Islington. He couldn't hide the distaste from his face when Clare introduced Jack as recently out of the army and just into the police force. His eyebrows went up when he heard the northern accent and with a dry, mocking growl and his chin pressed hard against his chest said, 'Newcastle? Isn't that where they eat their young?' From that day on Jack topped up his new career whispering in his ear discreet fairy tales about the corrupt finance industry. How the police were on to them all and Armageddon was at hand for anyone moving money. Nigel took it all in, bowing reluctantly to Jack's inside knowledge and twitching visibly as his mind ran riot.

They say opposites attract. So it was with Clare's mother, Eve. Taller than her husband and probably half his weight, she was the epitome of a wealthy suburban housewife exiled in the city. Always smartly dressed. Forever in twin-set and pearl necklace. Never a hair out of place at any time of the day. It was as though it was expertly styled each morning while she was still in her nightdress. Her round, flushed face always broke into a smile when she saw Jack. She had relatives in Durham. She was forever recounting her visits there as a girl. What she never mentioned was her early life in Ipswich and that she had been jilted at nineteen by an American airman. Nigel caught her on the rebound. Fresh with his degree from Cambridge and back home, he was, it seems from Clare's telling, ready to conquer the world and take himself a wife. They married in haste, as they say, but leisurely regret had not materialised. She had, with typical female wiles, managed the nuances of Nigel's character and gently controlled him without him realising it.

He made himself a bacon sandwich while the tea bag

brewed in his black and white striped mug. He glanced at his watch again: half past the hour. Time for a shower and a change of shirt if there were any Clare had ironed. He felt drained mentally and physically. The trauma of Clare's departure and the mystery of the McManus death had him weary and emotional. He bit into the sandwich but it was tasteless. The tea was merely hot and without any lift. His mind struggled to co-ordinate all the urgent tasks that were crowding into his brain. First he must get Clare home. He must find the link to McManus. He had to recount his suspicions to Coulson. He had to get the Post Mortem report and the forensic report and find out what Ballistics had discovered. "Fuck it," he hissed, dispensing with the formality of allowing his father-in-law to wake up naturally. He swallowed a mouthful of tea and picked up the phone.

As he expected after a dozen rings Clare's father croaked out a sleepy "Yes, what is it?"

"Nige, it's Jack." (He hated being called that.)

"Oh it's you," he grunted.

"I need to speak to Clare. It's urgent."

"She's still in bed. I don't think she'll want to speak to you, Jack. She's come home."

"Look, please wake her up. I'm not kidding, this is important. She needs to know something."

"What?"

"Confidential, Nigel. She'll thank me. Please wake her up."

He could hear a muffled conversation then Eve answered. Her voice was low and slow. "Hello Jack. Sorry about things... really sorry."

"Eve, please get Clare to the phone. This is business...but I'm positive we can sort ourselves out. It's all a bad mistake."

He heard her sigh and there was silence for a moment. In the distance he heard Nigel bark, "Let the bastard stew."

A door banged. Another muffled comment from her father then Clare spoke. Her voice an icy dismissal as though she was replying to a far eastern con man telling her, her computer password had been hacked. "Jack I said all I had to say yesterday. We're through. Believe it and get used to it."

"Clare, listen to me."

"No."

"Clare for Christ's sake listen! Does the name McManus mean anything to you? Albert McManus."

There was silence.

"Clare, do you know this man?"

"Why?"

"Just tell me."

"What's that got to do with our situation?"

"You'll find out and thank me for it. Mr. McManus worked at Sellafield. You were there last week. Am I right?"

There was now a cautious interest in her voice. "Yes... yes I was. I got a lead from a relative of our office cleaner. Some leak of a dangerous substance. Her nephew was working there. Got himself contaminated."

"So you spoke to McManus, the health and safety manager?"

"Yes. I did. But he didn't have much to say."

"Well he won't say anything anymore. He's dead. He shot himself."

"What! He killed himself!"

"Right in one. And guess what, he was coming to see you. And something else, I'm not certain it was suicide. I'm on the case and something stinks. I thought you should know, Clare. There could be a big story here."

There was undisguised scepticism in her voice. "How do you know he was coming to see me?"

"His last call on his mobile was to our landline and our address was programmed into his sat-nav.

He was found dead in his car."

"Shit," she whispered.

Silence for a moment. Jack crossed his fingers. He heard a loud intake of breath. "There's a train every hour. I'll catch the noon express. Meet me at the Station, will you at about three o'clock And Jack, if this is a load of nothing you're really for it…understand?"

Jack punched the air with his free hand. "It's something big Clare, I'm sure of it. I'll see you at the Central Station."

D.I. Wilbur Coulson had a sinister suspicion in his face that was a permanent fixture. Everyone was a suspect in every case that landed on his desk. It appeared that even his staff were on his list from his attitude to their reports and investigations. He was a thin, willowy man in his early forties, seemingly plagued with some duplicitous notion that everyone and everything was conspiring to undermine and unseat him. He had bushy eyebrows that hadn't seen scissors for years and cascaded over rheumy eyes that darted suspiciously whenever he was in thought mode. He listened intently to Jack's resume of the overnight events and rubbed a hand nervously over his mouth, then vigorously across the back of his neck.

"Forensic report?"

"Waiting for it."

"Ballistics?"

"Same."

"P.M?"

"A.S.A.P."

Coulson thought for a moment and juggled his false teeth. "OK Jack, if the reports come back with anything that doesn't add up to suicide get cracking on the who's, why's, where's and whatnot. I'll fill in Charteris with the details. In the meantime for the Press it's a straightforward case of taking his own life OK? I need a comprehensive report on this, Jack. I don't want *him* at headquarters giving me a bollocking for some spurious investigation. They're just waiting, you know. Charteris would love to bust my balls. And there are others. So don't you go and fuck it up Jack. If it's murder we want a killer tout suite OK?"

Jack made to get up. "I'm on it now, boss."

"Good." He gestured for him to sit down again. His voice took the low tone of a conspirator. "That D.C. Stella, er, whatshername. I can never remember."

"Stella van Kirk."

"That's her. Is she...er...is she competent?" His eyebrows shot up. "How shall I put it... and accommodating?"

Jack nodded. "Yes and maybe."

Coulson sat back in his chair and smirked, showing nicotine-stained teeth.

"Good to know. I'll put her on this case with you."

Jack nodded and rose again.

"And leave something for somebody else... know what I mean?"

"I know exactly what you mean. Good luck."

Coulson grunted, gave a weak smile and began studying some papers. "Mum's the word, Jack," he mumbled without looking up.

Newcastle Central station was busy. It was a cold, drab afternoon with an arctic wind in a frantic hunt to barge past bodies on platform two. It was Friday and all the platforms were crowded with hunched commuters intent on a weekend away or people like Jack waiting to greet travellers from the south. He glanced at his watch. Ten minutes late. He thrust his hands deep into the pockets of his padded jacket trying to subdue the mixed feeling of delight that he would have the chance to speak to her again and dread that she might change her mind and quickly depart again for the Capital. He tried to persuade himself that the potential news story that the McManus case could evolve into would have her hooked. He knew Clare. He knew her voracious appetite for reporting the sensational and anything that would have the readers slack jawed with surprise and awesome possibilities. He had left Stella to cajole anybody and everybody into swift conclusions on the car, the gun and the body. Stella: he had a twinge of conscience about his recent infidelity but dismissed it with the counter thought of his non-existent sex life. For almost a year Clare had been cold and distant. He knew why. He knew the vagaries of his job had him out at all hours of the day and night. She had barely tolerated it in London. In Newcastle it had taken her to breaking point. It was a necessity for him to mix with low life that came alive when darkness gave them some cloak of security. Rumours had to be checked and subtle actions taken. Tales whispered behind a hand. Bonhomie with the dregs and dubious. Bargains struck for smatterings of information. It was all part of a symbiotic process alongside the endless examination of files, phone records, C.C.T.V footage and interviews. All had to come together to form a case that would convince a jury and twist the judge's arm into passing a meaningful sentence. He had tried hard to conform since his lecture from Church in London. He had reined in some of his actions that matched the criminals he was stalking, but it was not easy. The conventional way did not always produce results. And results were the mantra that echoed through his head on every case.

The train arrived, motivating the travellers to pick up bags and grab suitcases as it came to a halt. Doors slid open and people began to spill out, manoeuvring luggage past the eager crowd waiting to find their seat. Berwick next stop; then Edinburgh. His eyes hunted frantically for Clare then he saw her at the far end of the platform; no mistaking her blonde hair, her red coat and carrying her holdall. He rushed to greet her, a feeling of relief and pleasure that she had really arrived. Clare had a different mood. She wore the pained look of bored anger. She took a step back from his outstretched arms knowing they were intent on hugging her.

"Jack this better not be a wild goose chase."

His arms dropped and he grabbed her holdall. "It's not – I promise. There's something that just doesn't add up with Mr McManus, Clare. Let me crack this and I'll make sure you get the scoop."

"And what do I do in the meantime. Christ, it could be months."

He led her to the car. "Do what you've done so well for the last few years. Tell Bellamy you've changed your mind. There is plenty of other stuff to get your teeth into. What about that Triad lead I gave you. All the names in China Town who were suspected of torching the 'Pearl Palace'."

"I got started but certain other things got in the way…like me making arrangements to jump ship."

The car lock beeped and he opened the boot and threw her holdall in. He eased himself behind the wheel and waited until she opened the passenger door. She flopped down heavily and folded her arms.

"Forever the gentleman," she said with exaggerated sarcasm.

"Sorry," he whispered, "My mind is just full of this so-called suicide. Tell me about McManus."

They threaded their way north through the growing weekend city rush hour. Horns blared. Traffic moved then stopped. Exhaust fumes meandered upward and were snatched away by the wind that blew down the streets and had litter waltzing and tumbling ahead of them. Clare sat back and thought for a moment.

"Well, the office cleaner has a nephew, works for an engineering company in Wallsend. N.N.S. Neutron Nuclear Services. Seems they specialise in the installation of nuclear equipment and repair and refurbishment of anything that might be radioactive or in a controlled zone. They've got a team of experts who deal with the mountain of paperwork that goes with such projects. You know; safety aspects, permits, security and the like. Jim Melrose, that's the cleaner's nephew and some sort of engineer, was working with a team at Sellafield a few weeks ago. The job was to install some large tanks in a building. Metal tanks I presume for some weird and wonderful process that they do there. Anyway, the tanks were delivered outside the perimeter fence. N.N.S had to move them into position in the building and connect them up. They were raised up on wheeled jacks and pushed a short distance along the perimeter fence. It's a narrow tarmac road. It starts to rain and puddles form in the road. The road is outside the perimeter fence, mark you. A public highway. The boys in coveralls get their leg bottoms wet. They get the tanks in position and finish the job. So far so good. Next job, Hartlepool nuclear power station. You know, down near Middlesbrough. In they go, working in a so-called controlled zone. No problem getting in. Big problem getting out. Everyone that goes in has to go through a radiation contamination sensor to get out. All the alarm bells started ringing. A crowd of health physics and safety men descend on them with Geiger counters. It appears that the bottoms of their coveralls were contaminated. Coveralls were confiscated and the hapless inhabitants scrubbed raw. Big investigation. It didn't happen at Hartlepool. It wasn't from the new building at Sellafield. It had to be the pools outside the perimeter fence."

Jack gasped. "Ah, so it could be that something inside the fence has leaked outside."

"Exactly. I thought there's a story here that needs to be told. I made an appointment to see the health and safety manager, Albert McManus. I had to be escorted to his office and there sits the overall site manager, the publicity manager, and Albert McManus looking twitchy and nervous and not saying much. In fact the other two laughed off the whole thing while Mr McManus glanced from one to the other with a sickly look of guilt and sweat on his face. When I did get a reaction from him it was forced amusement and a half -hearted explanation that such minor leaks were not rare and all well within safety limits. I knew the place had history. I tried hard for one of them to really open up but...they didn't. I knew I wasn't going to get anywhere so I left. McManus escorted me to the main gate. I could tell he was troubled. He had that look of a man with a conscience. I gave him my card. I told him to ring me if he could remember anything relevant. He said he would but I could see he was fighting against the urge to tell me something there and then…but he didn't. Wasted trip, really. But now it's a different matter. He was about to spill the beans about something. Something big enough to get him into his car and drive one hundred and odd miles."

"Did he look as though he'd come back from holiday. I mean did he have a tan?"

"Come to think of it, he did. But it didn't trigger a question about it."

Jack shook his head. "God, Clare, the plot thickens. I knew there was something amiss. Suicide is getting more remote by the minute. Coulson's put Stella van Kirk on the case with me… and before you jump to conclusions it's purely business. Please believe me."

Clare grunted. "I don't."

'Blaydon races' struck up in the car, muffled in his jacket pocket. He rummaged to find his phone and stuck it to his ear.

"Watch the road!" Clare barked.

Jack drove with one hand. "Right…right. Yes. I'm taking Clare home. Nearly there. I'll be at the Station in twenty."

Clare couldn't hear Stella's soft mocking laugh.

The ballistics officer was waiting at his desk with Stella. He was a small, frail man with a soft apologetic voice, limp brown hair and sad cautious eyes. From his demeanour, it was hard to imagine that killing machines were his forte. Butterfly collector would have been a more accurate guess. He held a sheet of A4 in his hand and passed it to Jack.

He spoke as though he was embarrassed to report. "Well, the gun is a Luger P08 Parabellum. 9mm.World war two. Serial number filed off. A typical villain's weapon. Could hold eight rounds but it only had one…the one that went through his head. Modern cartridge casing. Out of that sort of gun, the casings eject upward. It was found under the car. They also found the bullet. It had ricocheted off the central pillar of the car and buried itself in the headrest of the back seat. It's been checked. It's the one out of the gun."

"So the shot could have been fired outside the window if the cartridge was under the car?"

The ballistics officer gave a pained smile and nodded. "Most probably."

Jack clenched his teeth together. "I fucking well knew it," he whispered.

Stella took the report out of Jack's hand and thanked the man. He nodded sadly at Stella, turned and shuffled down the office.

Jack rubbed at his neck. "Jesus Stella that was quick. How did you manage to get priority out of that old fogey?"

Stella propped herself against his desk. She folded her arms and winked. "It's a miracle what some sweet talking can do."

Jack gave a dry laugh and shook his head.

He took the paper from Stella's hand and glanced at it. "Well, what do you know? The shot looks like it came from outside the car. It's brewing up Stella. So where's the other info?"

"On its way. Should be anytime,"

It took another half hour for the details to arrive. The post mortem was delivered by a woman who looked to be just out of high school. Dark hair. Slim. The fresh, innocent face of someone who should be with wholesome live company, Jack thought and not spending her working days slicing into cadavers.

"Cause of death most definitely a close-range gunshot to the head," she said with a keen satisfaction. "There would be no powder burns if the shot had come from a distance. Stippling or tattooing as we call it usually occurs if the shot is fired closer than a couple of feet from the target, and this shot was as close as hell. No other obvious causes. Death probably occurred at about eight or nine last night. Maybe a little later. The full report will take a few days. We understand the corpse has a brother. A priest, would you believe, here in Newcastle. Saint Cecilia's in Jesmond. He's coming to do the official identification tomorrow. It seems his family back home are in no fit state."

"Saint Cecilia's!" Stella said with surprise. "That's next door to my house. Father McManus, so that's what they call him. I've seen him wandering in and out as though all the troubles of the world are hanging around his neck."

"Well I hope tomorrow's viewing doesn't choke him all together. Mr McManus... the late Mr. McManus is not a pretty sight."

"Did you check his right elbow?" Stella asked before Jack got the thought into words.

"Yes, Sergeant Lockwood made it clear it was important." She shrugged, "Nothing unusual. No skin laceration or contusion. The remains of bursitis that's all. Maybe a year or so ago."

"What's Bursitis?"

"It's a common problem. Inflammation of the olecranon bursa in the elbow. It can be caused by constant pressure on the elbow or a repetitive sports action. Can be painful at first. Takes a good while for the swelling to disappear completely. Maybe a few months after it appears."

"Golf?"

"Could be," she said, eyebrows lifting; surprised that he might know a possible cause.

Jack slapped a fist into his other hand. "I knew it! I bloody well knew it. Any hint that he might be left-handed?"

She smiled. "Sorry. Miracles take a bit longer than an eight-hour examination."

"What about the colour of his skin. Had he been in the sun?"

She thought for a moment. "Well, yes, I would say so. It looks like he's had a good dose of it. We've done a rush job here. You'll get a full official report by probably Thursday. O.K.?"

Jack glanced at Stella. It was all coming together. Forensics would clinch it. If he hadn't shot himself, who had… and how… and why? "I'm sure he's been murdered Stella and from what Clare's told me I think we have an answer to stage one of the investigation. I think we have the embryo of a motive. Someone didn't want him to speak to Clare. Someone wanted him stopped so badly they had to kill him."

The girl from the morgue looked from one to the other, a frown of fascination on her face. "Well now, I'll leave you two sleuths to unravel it all."

"OK yes, thanks for the early info."

The girl nodded. "Good luck." she said cheerfully and left to go back to her chilled examination room to tidy up.

It was time to check his wife had not changed her mind and galloped back to London. He punched their land line number into his mobile. Her voice was cold and toneless.

"Sorry Clare, there's been a bit of a hold up. I just need the forensic report to stick in front of Coulson then we're off and running. It looks like it's going to be something big, Clare. I told you so. Everything's starting to point to a possible homicide. I should be home by seven or maybe half past."

Clare had heard it all before. *"Yes. Right. OK. You'd better be."*

Jack felt a tiny surge of pleasure at her relatively gentle reaction. In the past such bulletins were met with anger and animosity. "Listen, Clare, don't cook. I'll get a Chinese for us at the carry-out in Ponteland. OK? Your favourite…with noodles."

He waited for an amiable reply. There was none. The phone went dead.

"Well, well, well," Stella whispered. "Am I witnessing a heart-warming reconciliation here or the sugary words of a poxy philanderer?"

Jack tried to muster some assertive response but he couldn't. The long day previously and the night without sleep were telling on him. There was the soft satisfaction of having Clare home mixed with a twinge of guilt in giving Stella a not too subtle cold shoulder.

"Sorry Stella," he said, smoothing the hair at the back of his head. "It's just, well, you know…it's just…"

She stared at him. She knew him well enough to know that when he got himself immersed in a case he was like a terrier. His teeth lock in and won't let go. But somehow now, he had taken on the manner of a dowdy, defeated mortal that would not have looked out of place selling the 'Big Issue' in the main streets of Newcastle. His limp apology emphasised his demeanour and Stella railed at his sudden duplicity both with her and his wife.

"Just fuck off," she barked, folding her arms and turning her back to him as a woman approached.

She was a fashion model nightmare. She had a weird hairstyle parted down the middle: a pasty face with prominent ears and perfectly round eyes. Her fifty-year-old body outline challenged imagination. From the neck down she arced out into a perfect symmetrical pear shape, supported somehow on two spindly legs. Jack knew her. For all her strange contours she produced brilliant forensic work that had sent many a criminal to jail on microscopic and obscure evidence.

"Well, hello Bridget. What have you got for me?"

Bridget wasn't amused. "I'm tired and it's late and it's Friday night. I want to go home." She slapped some A4 sheets on his desk. "There's your info. We e-mailed all the prints to Cumbria. There were three sets. Seems your victim had a wife and a son. They've checked them out. Both match, along with the driver."

"What about the gun. Any dabs you couldn't identify?"

"None. Nothing even on the trigger guard or trigger itself. Just the victim's on the butt. Otherwise clean as a whistle other than a few fine traces of nitrile on the butt which could have come from a glove. Maybe a surgical glove. That in itself stinks. There should always be something in the way of prints all over the thing. It seems like it was nicely wiped. And besides, if it was a surgical glove who the hell wears one of those for a shooting." Her eyebrows lifted. "Pretty clinical event if you ask me."

Harry gave a low whistle. "If that's right whoever pulled the trigger didn't want to leave a calling card. Anything else? What about the angle of the gunshot."

"Well, judging from where the bullet hit the central panel and where it went into his head I'd say he was sitting upright with his head turned toward his window. Can I go now?"

Jack smiled, his theory gaining credence by the minute. "Thank you Bridget. That's a good job done. Did you find anything else?"

She shrugged "Nothing to write home about. A crisp packet in the boot. A receipt from a Whitehaven supermarket dated last month and a couple of golf tees. We're still looking. Might take a few days."

"Golf tees. D'you hear that Stella? Golf tees! The man played golf. If his prints were not all over the gun, Mr. McManus was bloody well murdered."

Bridget made to leave. "Goodnight all and happy hunting."

Stella came out of her huff in an instant. "Jack, you were right. I reckon he was sitting in his car waiting for someone. When that someone appeared, he wound down the window. Mr. Someone shot him, through the open window, opened the door with gloves on, put the gun in his hand, wound up the window, shut the door and skedaddled."

"Spot on. But I'm guessing it was an amateur job. A pro hitman would have taken the time to push his dead finger through the trigger guard and taken the time to research whether he was left or right-handed."

"Even a pro might have overlooked that one. You can't be sure he was left-handed but it looks like it was a good try at faking a suicide. But not good enough."

"Correct. Whoever wanted him dead, wanted a straightforward uncomplicated decision and the event forgotten quickly. I've got to get over to Sellafield on

Monday after I've seen Coulson. I need to speak to his family and his boss."

"Come Monday will I get some background from…er N.N.S. at Wallsend? We might get some leads on how McManus ticked."

"Good idea. We'll get together Tuesday. Now I'm off for a Chinese carry out. What are you doing tonight?"

She shrugged. "Three quarters of five eighths of fuck all."

"Sorry, Stella," he said with genuine regret. Then added, "I needed Clare's bit of the story. I didn't think she'd come back." It seemed a plausible lie.

She stared at him. "Sorry, my black ass. You want a strictly business relationship? That's fine with me, bwana. Just don't think I'll be here to catch you when she heads for the hills again."

She strode away from him. "Enjoy your meal…no…I'll rephrase that. I hope it fucking chokes you."

He watched her go. The stragglers in the office, intent on their own investigations, looked up and with solemn imaginings followed her rhythmic movement as she slung her handbag over her shoulder, threaded her way past them and slammed the glass door. He looked out of the window. He saw her stop and light a cigarette before her car unlock lights flashed. Even then, he regretted the situation and hung his head for a moment. He looked at his watch. It was ten after seven. He was hungry. Clare was at home and waiting. Two portions of Number 49 with noodles suddenly swamped all of his senses.

CHAPTER 4

He had to scrape the ice off his Volvo windscreen on Monday morning. He had to call in at the Station, shove the report in front of Coulson and pick up an official car. The weekend had turned into constant clear skies and frost. It had been no better in the Shaftoe household. As much as he bombarded Clare with eager conversation about the McManus case, she wasn't thawing. Her answers were clipped and trite. Her favourite Chinese had done nothing but send her into a doze in front of the T.V and then bed in one of the spare rooms. Sunday wasn't a great example of co-existence either. He explained his intentions to interview the McManus family and his co-workers at Sellafield. Clare asked if she could attend but he had to refuse. His explanation that he couldn't have an uninvolved civilian on official police business didn't convince her.

"Your female partner going along to hold your hand?"

"No, I've sent her to get some background info at that engineering outfit. I'll be there myself."

"Then I'm going to the power station at Hartlepool." Clare snapped. "I need some background intelligence as well, for when the story breaks. I've spoken to Roger Bellamy and I'm back on the books." She sniffed and grunted. A look of disdain wrinkled her face. "He says I was never off. He expected me back anyway. He says the leak at Sellafield is still worth chasing."

"Christ, Clare, don't print anything about McManus until I get my head around some facts about the whys and wherefores. What they say at the power station will be useful. That leak of contamination or whatever could be the key to this whole thing. If I can link the leak to the McManus death then we're off with a bona fide motive."

Clare shrugged. "Don't worry. As far as Bellamy is concerned, the whole thing is merely some form of radiation leak and its consequences for the workers and the locals. I'll wait, but don't lose any time on it. You know what an impatient cow I am. Don't let this get to the cold case state, Jack. Like you say, there could be something big to break here. If we get the story first there's a chance we could syndicate it…put the paper on the world map. A murder tied to a radiation leak is big international news."

Jack sucked through his teeth. "Hold on, Clare. We're talking local, north of England news here. It won't be like the Martians have landed on the Town Moor."

"Listen Jack, I've done some quick checking on this sort of problem. There have been a multitude of nuclear incidents all over the world. Some big, some small. This potential scandal at Sellafield reminds me of the Karen Silkwood case in America in the early seventies. You heard of that?"

Jack shook his head. "No."

"I read all about it years ago. Karen Silkwood was a nuclear operative for an outfit called Kerr McGee. Somehow… and it was never explained just how, she got herself contaminated with plutonium. The company made nuclear fuel pellets. She became an activist campaigning for stricter health and safety issues. And guess what?"

"What?"

She died in a car crash on her way to meet a reporter from the New York Times. Cause of car crash… still unresolved. Ring any bells, Jack? The story was so big Hollywood made a movie out of it. Meryl Streep played the part of Karen Silkwood."

Jack blew a quiet whistle. "I see what you mean."

"I've been to Sellafield. You haven't. I've met some of the men McManus worked with. Call it intuition or what you like. Wait till you interview them and then tell me how big the story could be."

Stella sprayed the windscreen with de-icer, cursed the winter weather and thought about Curacao, sun and palm trees. It was on such dark, cold days that her mind was flooded with memories of balmy air, the colour of the sea and sky and the pastel rainbow of Dutch style bungalows. She regretted not clearing out the garage to make way for her Mini as she had promised herself in the summer. There was four years of accumulated junk in there; a bicycle with flat tyres that hadn't been ridden since the spring; sundry decorating paraphernalia with accompanying half used paint tins and general detritus that once had a use and was now discarded and blocking the way in like a barricade. Her small two bedroomed detached bungalow sat around the corner from the main road, with a broad gravel drive and was snuggled up against a row of high bushes that formed the boundary to Saint Cecilia's church, Jesmond. Jesmond, a chic suburb of Newcastle packed with eclectic dining spots, hotels, boarding houses and Victorian homes. Stella's house was pre second world war, with one gable end facing the side road the other into a small garden ending in a stone wall with the edge of the church graveyard behind it. Compared to the surrounding buildings it was relatively new. She had modernised it and added a garage without it losing some of its inherent country cottage appearance. She loved it from the moment she saw it. At the time it was part of church property, probably the home of the priest's housekeeper or a church warden maybe. It was a two-horse bidding contest. Her grandfather, a Dutch flower merchant had willed her enough money to keep her almost independent and perpetuating a loving memory of him. Her rival to the property was a small housing association with plans to demolish the house and build six small houses for needy families. They topped her bid but she managed to up hers. The poker game went on. After five rounds of increases the association caved in and she won…so did the church.

The drive to Wallsend took twenty minutes. She opted to use her own car because of the short journey. Most of the morning traffic was slow and heading west into the city but she was down to the Tyne in ten minutes and on the road heading east along the river where a few decades ago industry swarmed and now presented little more than a pastoral view on both banks. Neutron Nuclear Services was housed in an unimposing fabricated building on the edge of a small trading estate. A large sign on the wall broadcast its presence with the iconic logo of a planetary atom at each side of the name. A few years ago the land was the car park for a shipbuilding company. Just beyond the gaggle of small workshops, the derelict rusting remains of a company that had designed and manufactured giant offshore oil rigs reared into view like a sombre ghostly scrap yard. There had been a string of quality shipyards as well, but the collision of metal and the blue sparks of welding with all the skills that go with them had been snuffed out by the ever-changing imposition of commercial demands and the internal inability to master them.

Stella rang the bell at the side of hinged glass doors. The girl at the desk inside looked up, stopped chewing for a second, pressed a button and the door unlocked with an audible buzz.

She flashed her I.D. "Good morning. D.C. van Kirk. I'm here to see Mr. Nicholson. I rang him earlier."

The girl seemed in awe of the visitor. She quickly punched the phone dialling pad, looked guiltily at Stella and whispered reverently. "Mr. Nicholson, there's a policewoman to see you."

Stella heard a door slam and heavy footsteps from a corridor on the left. Nicholson appeared, beaming as though she was his long-lost sister. "Good morning, good morning," he sang, holding out his hand. His head moved gently from side to side, examining her face as though her position and her colour were somehow incongruous.

"Well, this is a surprise. A detective eh? What have I done wrong? It's a fair cop. Heh…heh…heh." The laughter was forced, an act Stella had seen a thousand times before. He held out his arm and ushered her down the corridor. He was tall, slightly hunched; a round, fresh cheeked face with a nose just short of a ripe strawberry. Thinning fair hair hung limp over his brow. He looked to be in his late fifties and dressed for the part of a boss man. Grey suit with a trace of cigarette ash on the lapel and a dusting of dandruff on the shoulders. Sky blue shirt and spotted tie. A flower in his buttonhole would not have looked out of place.

The establishment did not reflect the dismal vista outside. Modern; all glass, polished tiled floor and pale green walls. He showed her into his office. "Sit, sit please. Coffee?" He didn't wait for an answer. He waved through the glass to the adjoining office, mimed the order for two and eased himself into a seat behind a large paper strewn desk. He took a deep breath, "Well now Miss…er…"

"van Kirk. Detective van Kirk, C.I.D," she said flatly, putting on her serious interview manner. "I'm here to just ask a few questions about a Mr. McManus at Sellafield; the health and safety manager. You know him?"

His eyebrows shot up. Alarm opened his mouth and widened his eyes. "Why yes, Albert McManus, the health and safety manager. Yes I know him, or should I say I and we as a company have had dealings with him. Hell, what's he done?"

"I'm sorry to say, Mr. McManus is dead, Mr Nicholson. A suicide. I need to get some background details on him. That's why I'm here. Just a formality."

The coffees came in. Two cups; separate milk and sugar. Nicholson sat back and covered his mouth. "My God," he muttered from behind his hand.

"Have you any idea why he might have done such a thing? Last time you saw him did he seem worried or troubled about anything?"

He shook his head. "Not that I recall. Oh my God. I can't believe this."

"How about when your men got some contamination on their coveralls? How was he then?"

There was another look of shock on his face but he quickly composed himself. "Ah, so you know about that. Yes, I suppose he was really concerned then. There was a formal enquiry at Sellafield when the proverbial hit the fan. Everybody and his aunty got involved. The International Atomic Energy Agency, the Health and Safety Executive...you name it."

"What was the outcome?"

Nicholson gave a weak worried smile. His voice was low and had a fragile solemnity to it. "The conclusion was the escape through the boundary fence was within safety limits... yes he was certainly not happy with that outcome, but don't quote me on what I'm going to tell you now. There are some deep storage tanks at Sellafield. Concrete tanks. Water fifteen metres deep. Just like swimming pools. In fact seagulls love to swim in them. Legacy ponds they're called. Why are they called that? Because they contain a legacy of past cavalier nuclear operations. In the fifties and sixties any old radioactive rubbish was thrown in the ponds as well as spent fuel rods from nuclear power stations...no records... nobody knows just what's in them. That's fine until you have to decommission them or... until one of them leaks. Like legacy pond five. That pond developed a big crack and started leaking. The crack had massive steel bracing fixed across it to stop it getting any bigger. If the water drains completely the nuclear rubbish in there could heat up and there would be one hell of a radioactive release.

There could be serious contamination over a massive area. It's got to be constantly topped up."

Stella shook her head. "Wow, so that must have been a big worry for McManus. Is that where your men picked up the contamination?"

He shook his head. "I wouldn't swear to it. Depends on how far the leak has travelled underground. If that wasn't the cause, God knows where."

"How far were your men from this… this legacy pond five?"

Nicholson blinked rapidly, his chin up as though deep in thought. "Probably two or maybe three hundred yards."

"Sound like a long way. Is this information out on general release?"

Nicholson smiled. "Some. Just enough to keep the local public and the environmental anoraks from sleepless nights. But listen, the nuclear industry is not all scary. Radioactivity gets a bad name." He pulled open a drawer and produced a small clear plastic box. Inside there was a sausage sized piece of dull silver metal. He passed it over to her. "Here, what do you think that is."

Stella held it up and turned it around in her hand. "It's heavy. Lead?"

Nicholson gave an exaggerated grin. "Uranium. Depleted Uranium. Perfectly harmless unless you eat it, breathe it in or get it in a body wound. The radioactivity was largely spent creating uranium 235 for weapons or fuel rods. This is uranium 238. They make bullets out of it. Most aircraft have it in the tail for balance. You feel how heavy it is. It's much heavier than lead."

Stella returned it quickly. Nicholson left it on the desk. "The whole world is radioactive Miss van Kirk. Your smoke alarm has a source in it called Americium 241. You like Brazil nuts? Radioactive. The trees have really deep roots and reach down through the soil and pick up natural radium. The latest fad – granite bench tops… radioactive."

He sat back and put his hands behind his head, a wan

look of satisfaction on his face. It was his party piece astounding people with his knowledge of the mysterious and fickle world of nuclear science. Then the news about McManus brought him back to a solemn blank face. "Christ…Albert McManus…dead. I can't believe it."

"Have you a good business here?" Stella asked, unimpressed by his revelations and ignoring his return to shock.

He shrugged. "Well, yes. I suppose so. We're specialists in an exacting line of engineering. We bid for most projects that crop up in the industry. We produce all the necessary mountains of paperwork that go with working in hazardous nuclear areas and the skilled men to carry out the work. But of course we could do with a lot more. Sellafield is a good steady source of business."

"Did you know Mr. McManus has a brother. A priest, here in Newcastle. Well…Jesmond. St. Cecilia's."

Nicholson frowned. "No…no I didn't. A priest, eh, good God."

"He identified the body on Saturday. His immediate family across in Egremont didn't come. They were, naturally, distraught, to say the least."

Nicholson frowned and nodded his head. "Yes…yes they would be."

"Aren't you going to ask me how he died —or where?"

"Of course… of course," he said quickly, scratching at his brow. "Hell, I… it never occurred to me. I was just trying to get my head around the fact that he actually killed himself."

"He shot himself. In his car. In a lay-by on the A69. That's why the Northumbria force are involved."

"He shot himself," he repeated. "With a gun?"

"What else?"

Nicholson nodded, blinking furiously. "Yes… yes… what else," he whispered.

"Is there anything else you could tell me that might help us understand why he killed himself?"

He shook his head, brow furrowed in thought. "No, no sorry. I can't help you there."

"What about the people he worked with. Do you think they could pinpoint a reason?"

He shrugged. "Maybe. I just don't know. Sorry. He never gave me the impression that he would do such a thing. The state of the site got his blood pressure up but… but, hell, not enough to…to shoot himself."

Stella sighed. "Ok. Thank you. Mr. Nicholson. That'll do for now. We might need to contact you again."

She made to get up, her coffee untouched. He gripped the knot in his tie and wriggled his neck out of his shirt. "Is there something funny about his suicide."

"Funny ha, ha, no. Funny strange, no. He just shot himself. This is just a routine enquiry."

He was silent as he led her to the door. The girl behind the reception desk stopped chewing again and the door buzzed. Nicholson held it open for her, smiling broadly. "Sorry I couldn't be of more help."

Stella nodded. "Thanks anyway."

He waited behind the glass until the mini disappeared. The smile on his face disappeared at the same time. "Open the door again, Jemma."

He stepped outside and lit a cigarette. He fished in his jacket pocket and pulled out his mobile, dialled and held it to his ear. "Terry, it's me, Henry. I've just had the police here about Albert. They believe it's suicide but we can't afford to have the law sniffing around us. It's too close to home…you know what I mean?"

There was silence at the other end for a moment then the voice was calm. "*Yes, that's the word going around the town. I knew he was bloody frantic but not enough to do that. London was going to deal with it. Whether they got the chance, I don't know. You know what we discussed. When you speak to Billy, you're totally shell shocked…OK? So we leave it like that. He could have done us a big favour. So don't panic Henry, I'm on my way. I'll be over there in about an hour or so. We'll talk it through. There's no way now he can spill the beans about our project."*

Clare's visit to Hartlepool power station had been just as unproductive. Driving north back along the A19 she began to wonder if the potential for a major story was really there, hiding somewhere among the labyrinth of everyday incidents experienced by the nuclear fraternity. The station director seemed only too willing to see her and, like Stella, she got little information of any relevance to her husband's theory.

Hartlepool nuclear power station loomed out of the morning mist, hugging the broad mouth of the river Tees. An enormous oblong box of grey aluminium cladding. Silent: without chimneys or the grotesque, squat cooling towers that blighted the landscape on most other conventional power plants. Only a trace of steam, climbing languidly from some hidden vents and merging quickly into the mist and strings of pyloned cables, fizzing energy, showed any sign of life or activity. She had already read that the monolith churns out enough electricity to power almost two million homes and over five hundred souls help it in the task. Yet the man directing it all was young, Nordic looking, fresh faced and quietly spoken. There was suspicion in his attitude as though he knew journalistic prowess in exaggerating the most nebulous of half-truths and rumours.

Clare quizzed him about the coverall incident and he just shrugged and smiled. "It was nothing. There was no danger to anyone – including the N.N.S workpeople. It was minor contamination quickly dealt with. The sensors here are incredibly sensitive, you know. Remember Chernobyl in the Ukraine? You'll have definitely heard about it if you can't remember all the facts. All of thirty or so years ago. A major nuclear incident. Of course the news of the explosion did not filter out of the Soviet Union for days. Here, everything was working as normal until every alarm on the station went off. Panic and more panic. Where was the source? The source was a radioactive cloud from Chernobyl. That was verified by Sweden who analysed the fallout. So you see, here, even the slightest leak would be dealt with immediately. People get all hot under the collar and suspicious about what we do here. All we do is produce electricity. Instead of enormous boilers burning fossil fuels to produce steam, we use the heat from a nuclear reaction. The steam drives turbines like any other power station and out comes electricity. Years ago a woman in Middlesbrough accused us of creating an enormous smell of sewage." He smiled. "That's the sort of prejudice that we have to field."

Clare became fascinated in the gentle amusement of the man and his obvious eagerness to dispel any doubts about danger.

"It certainly is a weird and wonderful business."

He nodded. "Do you really know what we're dealing with? Do you know how small an atom is?"

"Small... very tiny."

There was a jug of water on a table to the side of his desk. He slowly filled a tumbler and placed it in front of himself. "You see this tumbler of water. There are more atoms in this glass than there are glasses of water in all the oceans on the Earth. That's what the amazing scientists of the past had to understand and harness. To me it was a miracle. The fact that they also sussed out how to make a bomb was the down side to the whole phenomenal saga."

He sat back and sighed. "So there you have it Mrs... er... Shaftoe. Would you like to look around the site. I'd love to give you a quick tour to prove there are no weird shenanigans going on."

Clare looked at her watch. "I'd like to get back to the office by eleven."

He stood up. "I'll give you the twenty-minute special."

Clare's thoughts as she drove see-sawed between what she had seen at the power station and why McManus might have found what seemed to be a minor incident, so profoundly catastrophic that he wanted to speak to her alone and across on the other side of the country. The other bit of the jigsaw was Jack's theory that he had been silenced before he could speak. Nothing seemed to fit. She had been led around the maze of the power station, in awe of the latent energy stored within its workings and released in controlled and measured amounts. The cavernous pile cap area underneath, which was the hive of silent nuclear activity, so clinically clean: the turbine hall housing great horizontal beasts giving out a low, powerful growl as they spun in their lair and relentlessly produced their formidable end product. And then the compulsory full body scanner. It all seemed in order. It all seemed so natural and without controversy. Maybe Jack was wrong. Maybe McManus in a deluded way thought he had a sensation on his hands which was really newsworthy but to a hard -nosed journalist was nothing more than half a dozen lines on page five. So why did he kill himself? And if he didn't, who did? Her mind raced between a hotchpotch of possibilities as she headed back to her office. She mulled over her departure back to London and her immediate return on the premise of a good news story. Then she wondered if that was the real reason or just an excuse to convince herself that she had left in haste. She thought of Jack and his devotion to the cause. He would see a case through come hell or high water to get the outcome he wanted. Maybe she had been hasty and blind to his enthusiasm to put the cruel world to rights. They had a marriage of sorts that needed a joint consensus of how it should work. Maybe neither of them had paid attention to that. Maybe without giving that credence they had expected it all to meld into a harmonious workable partnership. Maybe his intuition would prove to uncover a callous murder and the reasons why. Maybe she should forget about giving up on him and the whole thing and just see what developed.

CHAPTER 5

The journey from Newcastle to the west coast is a pleasant one at any time. On that November morning the crisp, clear air and the powder blue sky made it take on some magical liberating quality that had Jack Shaftoe feeling glad to be alive. The A69 follows the course of the river Tyne, past the spot where Albert McManus had died and past the ancient market town of Hexham, voted England's favourite. There are a string of villages, small towns and the remains of Roman forts and milecastles on the route. They are now mostly bypassed by road improvements but still cling to the rural lure of a more innocent and serene lifestyle. He threaded his way through Carlisle, a two-thousand-year-old city and the northern frontier of the mighty Roman army, where the famous coast to coast wall, seventy-three miles long started and ended at the aptly named Wallsend on the Tyne. He skirted the North side of the English Lake district heading for Cockermouth, another ancient market town before turning south to take the more scenic fell road past Ennerdale Bridge, as he had been advised by Clare. The view as he navigated the twisting narrow lanes turned into broad, wild rolling hills with a scant veil of snow clinging to the summits. It was this landscape that Jack loved. It took him back to his days before the army and weekends fell walking in Northumberland and the Lake District. Aching legs and blistered feet. Nights in front of a blazing log fire with endless pints of real ale, bawdy jokes and a belly full of Cumberland sausage. If only Clare could have taken to it, he thought… if only.

Ahead he could see where the road peaked and when he came to it, the vast view seemed to shrink him into total insignificance. Off to the right was the blue Irish Sea and a smudge on the horizon, the Isle of Man. Through the windscreen he could see the descending route waltzing down past dry-stone walls, green fields and impassive feeding sheep. Then in the distance he saw it. Sellafield; an incongruous metal city perched on the edge of the sea and circled by rural greenery. Two square miles of an eclectic mix of over a thousand aluminium and brick buildings, chimneys of varying heights, and a mysterious metal sphere more than forty metres in diameter. So this is it, Jack thought. This is where the work begins.

Coulson had scanned the reports from Forensics, Ballistics and the brief post mortem. His face twisted into a look of doubt. "Are you sure Jack? It looks like there could be a homicide here but it could be just…" he shrugged, "a good old-fashioned suicide."

"It's murder. I'm sure of it. He didn't kill himself. A suicide just doesn't fit the picture. He was shot. He drove a hundred miles to see Clare. He had something important to tell her and he was stopped. I'm sure of it."

Coulson thought for a moment. "OK Jack, go for it. Find out where the gun came from for a start, and for Christ's sake come back with evidence. Charteris and Co. are after my balls. You know that don't you? Where's Stella?"

"She's getting background info in town. Then she's going to trace McManus' phone calls."

He nodded. "OK. She coming back here?"

"Yes, she'll be back before eleven I would think."

Coulson gave a quick smile. "OK. Better get going."

The country road brought him out at Calder Bridge and a smattering of civilization. He turned right, skirting Sellafield and headed for Whitehaven. He had to establish some form of liaison with the local police before visiting the McManus household and his place of work. Then there was another body whose cooperation would be useful and possibly the key to the whole investigation. Sellafield had its own security. An independent police force, part of the Civil Nuclear Constabulary. Firearms trained and firearms worn during working hours, these men and women existed to keep such sensitive places free from subversion, sedition, sabotage and the occasional saviour of the world who might try to scale the high fence and razor wire to haul up a skull and crossbones on some prominent building.

The Inspector at Whitehaven was a burly rugby player with a blue chin, scarred face and ears that broadcast years of scrambling for the oval ball. He listened intently to Jack's information and his theory. He blew a low whistle. "Wow, a possible murder. The community officer has been to the family twice, but shit, this news is going to set them back a bit." He shook his head. "I can't give you much history about McManus. When you get to Sellafield, Bob Driscoll, a CNC sergeant will have all relevant info on him. Everybody that works there is on file with all their misdemeanours. You know, not paying their TV licence, shagging their sister- in- law and the like. You'll probably put a smile on his face when you tell him the news. I play rugby with Driscoll and he's told me he's had a few run- ins with McManus in the past. He hated his guts."

Jack sat back. "Why?"

He shrugged. "Irritating breaches of security involving working practices I think. Nothing too serious but Bob would descend on him and McManus would get all uppity and start laying down his own law as though he had the royal prerogative to do as he liked. There was also some bad blood between them about McManus' son and Bob

52

Driscoll's daughter. Something to do with money I think."

Jack stood up. "Well thanks for that. I need to speak to the family and then speak to some of his work colleagues. Hopefully there'll be some hint of a motive I can work on."

They shook hands. "Let me know if I can give some help on this. If we've got a murderer on the loose I want him caught."

Jack smiled. "Don't we all."

Egremont is a small market town dominated by a wide main street and overlooked by the remains of a Norman castle. Thriving on iron ore mining in the past the place now lived mainly on the earnings of Sellafield workers. The McManus house was a three-bedroom detached on the south end of the town in what looked like a recently built estate on the banks of the river Ehen. Jack steeled himself for what he knew would be a sombre if not hysterical interview. The agonising reactions as the shuddering reality of a sudden violent death hit the family, were all too familiar to him.

The door opened and a man, muscular and probably in his late twenties stared at him. He had bright ginger hair and eyebrows to match. His face was round and smooth with thick pink lips and puffed cheeks. He observed Jack with a sullen wariness that Jack had seen many times before. He knew what to expect. The sullenness was masking the mix of anger and despair at the situation and he well remembered his own feelings when they came to tell him his father had been rushed to hospital and diagnosed with a major stroke. He remembered his mother's wailing anguish. He remembered his own harrowing helplessness and the anger he felt at not being able to restore him to his carefree self and dismiss the dreadful finality of his condition.

He flashed his ID. "Detective Sergeant Shaftoe. It's about your late father."

The man stood silently to one side. "Go through to the living room," he whispered. "Mother's in there."

The room reflected the convictions of a good catholic

family. A large crucifix hung above the fireplace and a posturing Virgin Mary entangled with a rosary gazed out with a benign smile from the top of a bookcase. The woman was late forties, short auburn hair, small and painfully slim; pale and red eyed. The shock of it all was still in her. She held a handkerchief to her nose and looked at him with her face pulled back into hunched shoulders as though she was expecting more devastating news. And she got it. Her son sat and put his arm around her. His attitude changed. He gazed at Jack with a belligerent smirk. "Another cop, mother. Another do-gooder. Should be out catching murderers not bothering us."

Jack sat down and returned his smirk. He felt a surge of anger but controlled himself. "That's exactly why I'm here, sonny," he said as a slow, cold pronouncement. "Mrs McManus my name is Jack Shaftoe, Newcastle CID. I'm very sorry to tell you we have reason to believe your husband could have been the victim of foul play and not suicide."

The bottom jaw of the son dropped in shock. "You mean some bugger killed him? He didn't shoot himself! Somebody shot him!"

His mother let out a high-pitched whine and covered her face with her damp handkerchief.

"I need to ask you both some questions, I'm afraid." He nodded at the man. "Why don't you get your mother a glass of something…er?

"Billy…Bill McManus," he said on a slow exhale.

Jack studied him as he reluctantly got to his feet. He gave him a quick once over honed on years of confronting both suspects and victims. What he saw he didn't like. The man's smirk did not disguise the look of alarm in his eyes and he could sense a vulnerability there; someone who could be manipulated. He knew natural leaders when he met them. He also knew who were the workers. Billy McManus seemed to fit into the latter.

Jack leaned forward and spoke softly. "Have you any

idea why Mr McManus might have wanted to end his life? Did he have any enemies that you knew about who might want to hurt him?"

The woman started sobbing softly into her handkerchief. Her son returned from the kitchen with water. "There were few on site that didn't like him," he said ruefully. "Dad was a stickler for the rules and it upset some people. That's right isn't it Ma?"

His mother hesitated, then nodded.

"What about Bob Driscoll?"

"If you've been talking to that prick don't believe a word he says. He's had it in for him for years. Dad could never do anything right in his eyes."

"What happened between you and his daughter?"

"She's a bitch," his mother spat out suddenly. "They had a joint bank account. They were going to be wed but she cleaned him out."

"What for?"

"Gambling. Gambling debts. Internet gambling… Bingo… horses…you name it… thousands." Her voice trailed away to a deep slow shuddering sigh. Her son stayed silent.

"Any idea why Mr McManus decided to travel across country last week? Why was he heading for Newcastle? Was he worried about something? He has a brother who's a priest over there hasn't he?"

Billy nodded. "My holy uncle. He said he'd identify the body. Ma's in no fit state and me," he rubbed a hand across his brow, "me… I couldn't see him dead… just couldn't." He looked up and sighed. "If he was worried it was no more than normal. There was always something at work that he moaned about but never something that he couldn't handle. He went to see his brother a couple of weeks ago. No reason really, just a family visit. He hadn't seen him in months. But after tea on Thursday he just got up and said he was going to the golf club to see somebody or other. There had been a man at the door earlier. They spoke for ages. Don't know who it was. I never bothered to look. Probably something to do with work. There was always somebody at the door… always something to do with work. He was quiet though. Had been for a few days. He'd been quiet, hadn't he Ma? It was nothing out of the ordinary. He was… he had been quiet off and on for months. Just got back from Cyprus. We'd been playing golf for a week. He seemed OK."

"Ah, so that's where you've been. Was the weather good?"

"Fabulous. As always"

"Where's your tan? Your father had some sunburn. Yours looks like a good nightclub tan."

There was no disguising the fluster in Billy's voice. He pointed to his red hair. "Oh… oh well you see I burn easily. I slap the sunblocker on. Er… Dad never bothered."

Mrs McManus nodded her head. "They all love their golf," she said in a faltering whisper. "And Cyprus. That was their third time since June. I'm a golfing widow and no mistake. They never took me. They always just left me, and yes, and I'm a real widow now."

"Third time?" Jack said with surprise. "Very nice if you can get it. You say all. Who're your golfing mates?"

"Oh… er, Dad's deputy, Terry Seaward and his pal from a company in Newcastle. Henry Nicholson."

Jack thought for a moment. "Is that company Neutron Nuclear Services – N.N.S? Is Nicholson the boss?"

Billy frowned as though he had let slip some great secret. "Yes, that's the company. Henry Nicholson, yes that's him. He's the boss," he said mustering some smattering of nonchalance. "N.N.S are always on site doing some job or other."

"Do you work at Sellafield?"

He nodded.

"What do you do?"

"I'm a glove- box operator."

"Glove- box! That sounds like something from an on-line warehouse."

"They're for handling radioactive materials, but of course you wouldn't know anything about that," he said with sarcasm.

Jack smiled. "Yes, you're right. Each to his own. Your father was involved in health and safety. Correct?"

He nodded. "He was the boss."

"Was he worried about the leak of some substance that had managed to get out under the perimeter fence? The N.N.S. workmen had problems with that I understand."

Billy looked shocked. "You know about that. How do you know about that?"

Jack shrugged. "We have our ways but then you wouldn't have the faintest idea about the workings of the police force, would you. Do you think that could have had a bearing on his mood...made him depressed perhaps?"

Billy sighed again and shook his head. "No...no like I said, he'd had plenty of safety problems in the past and sorted them. For Christ' sake don't tell me he riled somebody from around here enough to kill him. It must've been robbery or something."

His mother moaned into her handkerchief.

"It's possible but I'm covering all angles. Such as can you account for your movements that night?"

Billy slumped in his chair. "Oh for Christ's sake, am I suspect number one? They've already been here and taken our fingerprints."

Somehow Jack enjoyed watching him squirm." Do you know that nearly all murders are committed by a family member, or relative, or close friend. A statistic...but relevant."

"Well stuff your statistics. I was in here all night. Right Ma?"

She nodded. "He was here all night."

"Did your father own a gun? Or do you know anyone who has a gun collection?"

Mrs McManus covered her face with her hands. "No, he had no gun," she wailed. "Did somebody *really* take a gun

57

and deliberately shoot him?"

"It's possible...probable, I'm sorry to say. Are you sure you don't know where a gun could have come from?"

Billy thought for a moment then shook his head. "No, but that bastard Driscoll is into guns. They're all armed at Sellafield."

"Are they now? Well I will certainly speak to Driscoll. Are you sure you can't think of a reason anyone would want to harm him?" He looked from one to the other, "Billy? Mrs McManus?"

Billy bit at his bottom lip. It looked as though he was about to say something relevant. His plump face creased and he scratched at an eyebrow. "No... no not even Driscoll. Even that prick hasn't got it in him to do that."

Jack stood up. "Well I think that will do for now. Thanks for your help. Investigations will proceed and I'll be in touch. I might need to see you both again and rest assured the body will be released for a funeral just as soon as possible."

Mrs McManus wept silently into her handkerchief again. Billy showed him to the door. Jack turned.

"Just one more thing. Did your father have a computer...a laptop or the like?"

"Yes, but it'll be in his office. It's not here so he'll have left it in his office."

"And was your father left-handed?"

Billy frowned. "Yes...yes he was. He did everything left-handed."

It took him almost thirty minutes to drive to Sellafield. His mind mulled over the McManus family and their attitude to the event. McManus' wife displayed the usual shock that rendered her in a world of unreality fighting against the awful truth but her son was a different matter. He seemed to have accepted his father's fate with unusual composure, yet although there was a nervous fear in his eyes, he didn't broadcast any textbook subtle guilt, or hidden knowledge of the crime. Early days Jack concluded.

The main road took a turn right at a roundabout and skirted the three-metre-high perimeter fence topped with tight coils of razor wire. The enormous sphere that conjured up weird and dangerous alchemy dominated the view to the left; strange concrete chimneys, over one hundred metres tall with equally bizarre concrete boxes perched on top, stood near it. There was no mistaking he was driving toward an area of activity. The entrance to the site was divided off with large low yellow and black striped concrete barriers. They were arranged in a chicane to halt any vehicle deciding to accelerate in past the armed guards or out from the place. The car park had the look of a London traffic jam. Cars, lorries and vans were in tight random formation. People milled around the entrance, coming and going. Two policemen with high-viz jackets stood weighing up visitors, cradling black intimidating Heckler and Koch G36 rifles. Handy weapons ready to fire a magazine of 30 rounds in two and a half seconds into any terrorist anxious to take a shortcut to the promised land.

He managed to find a parking spot and walked toward the entrance past the poker-faced gun-toting policemen. At the reception desk, he produced his I.D. to another member of the Civil Nuclear Constabulary. He was a giant of a man, at least six two, a Tyson neck, shaved head, a round face and small bright eyes that seemed out of proportion to his broad pock marked doughy skin. In any other guise, he could have been head boy at Durham jail. He glanced at the I.D. then stared at Jack's face.

"Newcastle C.I.D eh. Come to see Butterworth I take it… about McManus?"

"Right in one."

He turned his head to the left and shouted into the adjoining office. "Hoy Bob, he's here."

Bob Driscoll walked in slowly, a look of curiosity on his face. He didn't appear to be the rugby type. He was only up to his colleague's shoulder. He was slim but the way he moved there was a sense of solid muscle under his sergeant's uniform. He had a narrow face with a pointed chin that turned slightly to the left while his nose, broken at some time in the past, tended to go in the opposite direction. He made an exaggerated inspection, slowly looking Jack from head to foot. His face twisted into a mocking smile. "Well, well, Royalty from Geordieland. Whitehaven said you'd be on your way. Not often we have a murder on our hands in this neck of the woods. He pointed toward Jack's stomach. "What do they feed you on over there? Looks like too many pies and pints of Newcastle Brown." He laughed silently, shoulders jumping up and down.

For a second Jack looked down at his open padded jacket and at the noticeable fold of fat hanging under his shirt and over his belt. Then he looked into Driscoll's smiling face. "Blame your wife. Every time I screw her she gives me a chocolate biscuit."

Driscoll's face changed instantly. He frowned and blinked as though trying to believe he had heard the words. Then he laughed and his colleague laughed. "Nice one. I'll remember that."

Jack looked at his watch. "OK, can I see the boss man now? There's a pie waiting for me in Newcastle."

Driscoll turned to his partner, still smiling. "Sign him in George, and get Butterworth's secretary to escort him over."

"Just one thing," Jack said on his way out. "What small arms do you gunslingers use?"

"Glock 17 pistols. Why do you ask?"

"9mm calibre?"

"Yes."

"Any Lugers?"

Driscoll shook his head. "I've ever seen a Luger here. Is that what killed McManus?"

"Could be. I'll let you know."

Butterworth's secretary showed him into the office. It was a short walk from the main gate to a brick building that looked its immediate post second world war age. She said "Please follow me," in an unusual childlike voice, her head bowed, her steps quick and determined. He followed her.

"Mr. Butterworth will just be a minute," she said. "Please take a seat."

Jack looked around. It was a typical working office. Paper strewn desk; two iconic green metal four- drawer filing cabinets; a whiteboard covered in meaningless scrawls and diagrams. On the wall behind his desk was a pseudo-Victorian needlepoint sampler. Neatly framed it read 'In case of a nuclear incident, sit down, place your head between your legs and kiss your balls goodbye.' Next to it a small glass case held an orange box. The label said 'Potassium Iodate Tablets. For use only in the event of a nuclear accident.' Suddenly Jack had the cold sensation that he was surrounded by latent and invisible danger. He shuffled uncomfortably in his seat as the office door opened and Roger Butterworth swept in, a sheaf of papers in his hands; spectacles balanced above his eyebrows.

He dropped heavily into a swivel chair, threw the papers on the desk, his spectacles dropping as if by magic onto his nose. He held out a hand. "Detective Sergeant Shaftoe, pleased to meet you. This is a terrible business about Albert…a terrible business. Sorry to keep you waiting. I'll do everything I can to help."

He was a small man, probably early fifties, smooth black hair parted at the side. His face had the flustered look of someone under pressure, as though there was a major deadline in the offing. He unconsciously shuffled papers as he talked and fidgeted in his chair.

"Do you run this whole site?"

"For my sins…yes. It's the largest nuclear site in Europe and has the most diverse range of nuclear facilities in the world."

"I need some background to Mr McManus. You know

there's a possibility of foul play. It could be suicide but...there's also the possibility it was murder."

Butterworth nodded. "Yes there're rumours already... a gunshot. Somebody shot him."

Jack looked around. "What exactly do you do here?"

Butterworth sat back. "We reprocess spent fuel from nuclear power stations."

"Is that all? I'm surprised."

He smiled. "We do other things."

"Like?"

"Try to decommission the beasts that are under those big chimneys that you would notice outside. Piles one and two. Way back in fifty-seven we had a major fire in Pile one. They were plutonium factories. You know, in those days we were desperate to be a world nuclear power. The fire was contained but there was a hell of a release of radiation. Wigner energy was to blame. It's too complicated to explain how that works but getting the things down to ground level without contaminating the world... now that *is* a big job. The year 2040 might see us getting toward a satisfactory conclusion. There are other things which I can't go into."

"What the hell is in that big sphere?"

Butterworth smiled again. "Looks intimidating, doesn't it. It's nothing scary. It's known as WAGR. Windscale advanced gas cooled reactor. It's just the prototype for the second generation of nuclear power stations. We've got them up and down the UK now. Had them working for years."

Jack shook his head in wonder. "There've been a number of accidents and incidents over the years I take it."

Butterworth pursed his lips. "Quite a few, unfortunately. There's always an accident waiting to happen."

Jack nodded to the glass case behind his desk. "Is that what those tablets are for?"

"Yes," he said ruefully. "A release of radioactivity into the air would contain radioactive Iodine. Would go straight to your Thyroid. Those tablets flush the Thyroid and stop it lodging there."

"Nasty. What about the recent leak that strayed outside and affected the workmen from N.N.S?"

"Ah, you know about that. There was a full enquiry. Acceptable within safety limits."

"McManus was the health and safety officer. Would you say the incident caused him a serious problem?"

Butterworth thought for a moment. "He didn't take the findings as gospel. In fact he instigated a full survey of the whole site... but he didn't have time to submit it officially."

"What did he find?"

"Don't know. I was waiting for his full report."

"Do you think he could have discovered something that was so critical it could have cost him his life? That somebody shot him to keep him quiet?"

Butterworth leaned forward and folded his arms on the desk. "Mr Shaftoe," he said softly. "Let me tell you something. There are over ten thousand people working at this site. Take an average husband, wife and two kids. That's forty thousand mouths to feed. On top of that, you have Egremont and surrounding villages...even Whitehaven and Workington depending on it to some extent. If this place dies, half the county goes with it. On top of that, we reprocess fuel from installations as far afield as Japan. We earn the country billions in revenue. If McManus found a major problem and the word got out, we would be surrounded by Friends of the Earth, Greenpeacers, and sundry other nuts who want us back using horses and carts. There's no one on this site wants it to close Mr Shaftoe. Staff, Unions, workforce in general. As long as nobody is dropping down dead... I exaggerate of course... we want to keep it up and running. We can't have the outside world forcing us to close down. Do you get what I'm saying?"

"You're saying McManus could have died because his report might have caused this to happen."

"That's exactly what I'm saying. You have over ten thousand suspects Mr Shaftoe...take your pick."

"If I told you that he was shot in the head and someone tried to make it look like suicide would that narrow the field?"

Butterworth thought for a moment, he pursed his lips then shook his head slowly. "Mr Shaftoe in this day and age everybody has had a good dose of TV 'who done its'. I imagine anybody who plots to murder somebody would try to disguise the act if they could. A fake suicide is a good option I suppose for shortening any investigation. I'm sure you know that."

"I do, but you just watch me Mr Butterworth, if it's one of your flock, I'll winkle him out of the ten thousand, rest assured on that. Now is it possible to speak to his assistant and golf partner I believe...er Terry Seaward isn't it?"

"He's not here today. Got the day off to see Henry Nicholson of N.N.S at Newcastle. They're golfing friends and had been away with Albert and his son to Cyprus. He'll be really cut up about this."

"Do you know McManus was on his way to Newcastle when he died? Any ideas why?

Butterworth blinked then shook his head without conviction. Then his eyebrows shot up. "Probably to see Nicholson. Other than that I haven't a clue."

"Maybe to see his brother. Do you know he has a brother, a priest in Newcastle?"

Butterworth looked surprised. "A brother...in Newcastle...a priest. No, didn't know that."

"Could he have been going to speak to the Press about the situation here?"

"Christ, I hope not. I very much doubt it. His report...his report wasn't finished. We intended to take all appropriate action when his report *was* finished. That seemed to calm him down."

"In that case can I have a quick look around Albert's office before I leave? Just routine."

"Be my guest."

He picked up the phone. "Millie, can you take Mr

Shaftoe to Albert's office please." He put the phone down. "Millie will escort you back to the gate. I have a meeting in five then there's things to do for Albert's widow, but feel free if there's anything else I can help you with."

Millie appeared, solemn faced. She was an incredibly frail looking fortyish with tiny mouse like features and a greying head of hair in tight curls. Jack followed her down the corridor and up some stairs to the next floor. She stopped and opened a door. As he passed her, she looked up at him. There was pain now showing but she said nothing.

Jack looked around the office. It was similar to Butterworth's. "Thank you Millie," Jack said softly. "Did you know Albert well? You know we think somebody shot him."

She nodded and made to speak, but stopped. Then after a breath said with a voice matching her appearance "Ring me on 205 with the white phone when you've finished."

Jack looked around. There was a desktop computer beside a tray full of assorted documents. He flicked a switch and brought it to life. Nothing but meaningless tables and calculations. He scanned a few papers on the desk but they might as well have been in a foreign language. The desk drawers were full of stationery junk that looked like it had accumulated over many years. The filing cabinet revealed files with puzzling titles like THORP, HALES, MOX and EARP. He knew the letters would stand for something but he let the curiosity go past him. He opened the bottom drawer. It was empty except for a grey laptop. He spent another ten minutes casually glancing at technical magazines and scribbled notes but there seemed to be nothing of relevance. He placed the laptop on the desk and rang for Millie. She appeared after a minute with four A4 sheets folded in half in her left hand. She looked up at him and took hold of his coat with her tiny right. Her faint voice had a soft frightened tremble to it. "Mr Shaftoe, I've copied Mr McManus' preliminary report for you. It's not finished but there will be information you will want. Please hide it now.

I do most of the typing for the managers. There's something funny going on here Mr Shaftoe. There have been a lot of meetings in this office. Mr McManus and his son, Mr Nicholson, from N.N.C. and Terry Seaward. They were all in here on Thursday. They were arguing. There's some of us here frightened Mr Shaftoe."

"About what, Millie?"

"About…about everything…our lives."

Jack picked up the laptop. "Millie, I'm going to sort this out. I'm taking the laptop. Say nothing to anybody, Millie. I'll contact you again. I need full details of what's scaring you but not here. We can meet off site…would that be best? Give me your phone number. Here's my card with how to contact me. Ring if you need me."

She nodded quickly as though her actions had been an act of absolute treachery. There was a pad on the desk. She scribbled her number on it, folded it quickly and stuffed it in his hand. "I'll take you to the main gate." she squeaked.

He slipped the papers into his inside pocket and followed her out. Driscoll would see the laptop but there was nothing he could do to stop it leaving the site. Official police business. Official investigation. Maybe the official exhibit number one. Jack had the upper hand.

He was almost back to Carlisle when 'Blaydon Races' rang out in his pocket. Until then his mind had been swirling with possibilities. He sensed some form of conspiracy; at least with four players now down to three. Was Butterworth involved? Where had the gun come from? Driscoll was obviously well used to firearms and supposedly had the capability and some motive, however nebulous. But the opportunity to take a gun off site was remote. Nicholson was an enigma. He was an outsider but on his way out Driscoll had confirmed his regular presence on site, and Jack assumed, only a cursory entry and exit security check. The radiation leak seemed to be the catalyst for the whole shebang. There was a cover up…a big cover up, he could now be certain of it. Now he had an ally in little Millie and papers to study. He felt the day had not been wasted. He had made some forays into what appeared to be a jigsaw of possible clues and to assemble the whole would be an onerous task but the prospect was not daunting, it excited him.

He answered his phone. It was Stella. *"How's it going? Anything positive?"*

"Yes. It stinks, Stella. On my way back now. I'll give you all the details in the morning. Any joy at N.N.S?"

"Well, the boss man, Nicholson's a bit of a prick, but nothing worth getting orgasmic about. But wait till you hear this, forensics have found some papers tucked into McManus' car service book. They look official. Lots of figures. The symbol PuO2 crops up all the time. Turns out from our learned contacts at the physics department at Newcastle University that it means Plutonium Oxide. And not only that, forensics have sussed that a lot of the entries have been altered."

CHAPTER 6

He was in a good mood as he drove to Robert's Hill the next morning. He had arrived home at seven, hungry, having realised that he hadn't eaten all day. His mood following Millie's potential revelations had a tingle of exhilaration rising in him. Then Stella's news raised a further possible hint of dirty work afoot and had his mind racing wildly. He was convinced his initial suspicions were gaining ground at a pace. Altered facts and figures on official documents smelled of corruption and cover up and he felt empowered to railroad his investigation past any lingering doubters. The papers passed by Millie contained a site map with prominent red dots shown inside and outside the perimeter fence. There were twenty in all and fifteen had a large cross over them. Beside each were scribbled chemical symbols, percentages and what looked to be measurements in metres. It would take an expert eye to decipher that and the other pages of figures, he imagined but he knew there was damning evidence in there somewhere. There had to be, otherwise she would not have thrust them to him with a look of terror in her eyes. The laptop could also reveal something to add to his growing cache of clues. His mood blossomed when he opened his front door. There was a smell of rich cooking; his favourite chicken Kiev he guessed immediately as Clare leaned backward at the kitchen door to greet him with the hint of a smile on her face. It was a small gesture but it gladdened his heart to see a chink in her armour of cold tolerance. They talked over dinner and well past eleven. Clare caught his mood and her enthusiasm matched his. She also sensed that a major and convoluted unravelling of the facts would enhance the story and when it broke the world would be clamouring for a breakdown of all the heroes and villains. The usual guff; marital status; sexual orientation; mistresses; political allegiance; past criminal record. Everything to satisfy the public's curiosity and their ability to judge their own lifestyle against those in the limelight.

Jack got into bed, sat up and waited hopefully. He heard the toilet flush and water run in the bathroom washbasin. His nose caught a whiff of scent, probably some cream or lotion he knew she regularly massaged into her face before bed. He heard her soft footsteps on the landing and he breathed in a slow expectant breath. Then he saw the landing light go out and heard the adjoining bedroom door close gently.

Stella was waiting for him. She had already taken four copies of the papers from McManus' car.

"Coulson's got a copy and so has Charteris. The originals are getting analysed and these two are for us. What happened over there?"

Jack glanced quickly at the document. There were various chemical symbols arranged in columns with dates and weights that seemed to be in grams. He needed to speak to Coulson; fill him in on the scene over in Sellafield and plan his next move.

"Wait till I see Coulson then I think we need to visit Nicholson again and I think the priest might throw some light on what his brother was up to. I'll fill you in on the way."

Coulson glanced up as Jack entered his office. There was sour look on his face. Either his piles were acting up or Stella had given him the bums rush, Jack surmised.

"Ah, Jack," he growled. He picked up a sheet of paper and threw it across the desk. "What's all this bullshit."

They're documents found in McManus' car. Certain figures have been altered according to forensics. Could be somebody was cooking the books…"

"Or could be somebody was just adjusting mistakes," Coulson snapped. "What books and what's been cooking?"

"They're getting analysed now. On top of that, I've got some documents given to me yesterday from a potential informer. The site manager's secretary. They need analysing as well. Looks like a site survey of sorts. Could be that McManus was scared of what he found and was going to pull the plug."

Coulson sat back in his chair. He listened intently as Jack recounted his day across on the other coast. He leaned forward, his arms resting on the desk, documents fanning out in all directions. "Too much maybe and could be, Jack. Let's have some hard evidence before Charteris twists my knackers. OK? I'm counting on you to crack this one, Jack."

"There are some possible suspects, Boss, every one of them capable and with a motive for rubbing McManus out."

"What…who?"

"There's a whole site of ten thousand plus men under suspicion and that's a fact."

Coulson grunted. "Well, get them sorted and get back to me as soon as all this paper crap is making sense. Lean on that woman informer. She could know more than you've got so far… and Jack, Stella whatshername…"

"van Kirk."

"She's a bit of a bitch."

He immediately picked up a folder and held it to his nose. Jack smiled. Stella had given him the bums rush.

Stella rang Neutron Nuclear Services. Nicholson was out but expected back at lunchtime. Jack found the number for St. Cecilia's church. The voice that answered sounded old and frail. There was a clearing of the throat before he spoke but even then, the sounds came from a larynx coated with phlegm.

"Ah, the police. My brother. I thought you might want to see me. I have a mass at noon but I can see you anytime this morning."

"We'll be there in half an hour."

The rectory of St Cecilia's was a large ivy-covered house, situated up a narrow curved, red-gravelled drive that lead away from the church to the right. Large old sycamore trees made it almost invisible from the road in the summer but in November the trees shedding the last of their leaves showed just a glimpse of its frontage among the naked branches and the graveyard of leaning headstones behind.

Their car crackled loudly on the broad gravel drive as they passed the church and approached the house. The imposing gothic-looking door opened before they got their feet on the ground. The priest stood in the entrance, the epitome of Catholicism. Black cassock buttoned from top to bottom; dog collar and a large silver cross hanging from a chain around his neck. He was a slight, round-shouldered man with rimless glasses and thinning grey hair. He looked to be about sixty but his sallow sunken cheeks could have disguised a troubled shorter life. He greeted them with a sad smile and ushered them deferentially into a house that had a strong sterility in the atmosphere and a whiff of incense that somehow lent itself to the ambience and sanctity of the place.

He led them to a room full of dark wood and books that looked to be unopened for a century or two.

"Sit...please sit," he whispered.

They sat; the priest behind a desk in a large swivel chair, smoothing the back of his cassock as he copied them.

"You came about my brother. Albert, my younger

brother," he croaked, then cleared his throat.

"Yes Father," Jack whispered, as though to speak louder would fracture some long-established religious edict. "I am D.S Shaftoe and this is D.C van Kirk. We need to ask you some questions about your brother. You did the formal identification last week."

He nodded. His face creased in pain as the image of Albert came back to him.

"We don't think your brother killed himself, Father. We have reason to believe he was murdered."

The priest hung his head. "Dear God, suicide is a bigger sin than murder. I thank him for that." He crossed himself. "In a way I knew something…something evil was coming."

Stella stirred. "What makes you say that?"

"Albert came to see me the day after he returned from Cyprus. I took confession from him. He was a troubled man. There was fear in him. He had a tortured soul. There were demons after him."

Stella glanced at Jack. "What did he confess, Father?"

The priest shook his head slowly. "It is apparent that you are not catholic or you would know that I cannot divulge his confession. I am merely a channel to the Almighty. Only He can, in his mysterious way, reveal it to you."

Jack leaned forward. The term 'sanctimonious prick' shot through his mind but he controlled himself. "Father McManus. We are looking for a murderer here. Your brother's murderer! Surely you can help us…get special dispensation from the Pope or something. Give us some hint of what or who was scaring him."

The priest shook his head again. "All I can tell you is that Albert had financial problems. He was deeply in debt, sergeant. He had a weakness…a weakness for business deals and investments that weren't kind to him… among other things."

"Like?"

"I cannot tell you… desires…temptations."

"Other women?"

"I cannot say. You know, sergeant, the act of confession is a sacred thing. It cleanses the soul. In this day and age sadly the confessional is used less and less. When I was a young priest, it was a place of importance. I took many confessions from my flock...young...old, but now it seems as though only the old and deeply troubled find any value in it. Many young people would come to unburden themselves. You know... desires of the flesh... perversions... infidelity... self-abuse."

"You mean masturbation?" Stella queried.

The priest eased himself slowly back in his chair. A sad smile creased his face. His hands came together, fingertips touching. "Such an ugly word for...dare I say it... such a delightful pastime but a mortal sin in the eyes of the church."

"So your brother was deeply troubled then," Jack said trying to control his agitation at the priest's prevarication. "Surely you can help us catch the person who committed this crime. Can you tell us if problems at Sellafield came into his troubled confession? Did he mention anyone by name?"

The priest shook his head. Then he thought for a moment. "Can I suggest you speak to Henry Nicholson, his so- called friend."

"So- called. Why do you say that?"

"I think they had a falling out."

"Did they now," Jack snapped, sensing some progress. "Fell out...why?"

The priest suddenly sat upright, as though some trance had left him. "I'm sorry. I have said too much." He glanced at his watch. "I have a mass in fifteen minutes. I must prepare."

"Father, I just live next door," Stella said. "If there is anything you can think of that might help us just let me know."

His eyebrows shot up. "Ah, my neighbour. Amen cottage. Yes, I thought I recognised you. Yes...yes I will. I'm sorry I cannot be of more help. But you must understand… the church…we have rules. But let me say this. I pray your investigations bear fruit because…because." His voice trailed away in a phlegmy croak.

"Because what, Father?" Jack said urgently.

"Because if Albert was murdered I want justice and also… also there is the devil's work to be overcome."

"What devil's work, Father? If you want justice tell us what your brother confessed, for Christ's sake."

The priest tutted and shook his head slowly, but said nothing. He stood and held out his arm guiding them from the room. There was silence. He followed them out and closed the rectory door behind him.

They sat and stared silently through the windscreen, watching the stooped, careworn figure enter his church.

"Jesus Christ," Jack muttered. "Fucking religion. The cause of all the troubles in the world and always has been. Now that bugger knows what the score is here and won't say because of some crap church rules."

Stella nodded. "Devil's work. What exactly did that mean? I think if we put pressure on him he'll crack."

"He'll crack alright. I'll wring the truth out of him. I'll make it my business to find out how many choir boys he's rodgered. Meanwhile our little trip to see Nicholson is even more important. Then there's that Terry Seaward, McManus' second in command. He was straight over here from Sellafield to see him yesterday. Maybe this leak at the site is more dangerous than they're all making out. There seemed to be four players in this little plot. Maybe McManus started to have a righteous fit and came over to get his soul given a clean bill of health… maybe…maybe… fucking maybe. But it didn't work. He decided to come to see Clare. For a proper confession."

"And now there are three," Stella said. "But for how long?"

He flicked the ignition key and the engine came to life. He glanced at his watch. "It's nearly noon. Nicholson's due back. We'll grab a sandwich then let's see if we can catch the prick out."

Nicholson's bonhomie was revealing. He was too friendly; too gushing; too excitable. Both Jack and Stella recognised the symptoms; they had seen it all before. It was a strange psychological phenomenon. Probably Freud could have fully explained it but to police investigators it was a weird defence mechanism that was borne out of a fear of being somehow threatened with exposure or confronted rightly or wrongly with an accusation of guilt. He made a flustered gesture ordering three coffees through the office glass then sat down, his face suddenly changing and draining of what colour it had, as though he realised his exuberance was a give-away.

Stella's voice took on a deliberate ominous tone designed to unnerve Nicholson even more.

"We have had some developments since I saw you yesterday. That's why D.S. Shaftoe has decided to attend. We suspect Albert McManus was murdered, Mr Nicholson. This is now a serious crime investigation. Can you tell us anything more than you did yesterday?"

Nicholson closed his eyes. His face crumpled into meandering wrinkles before he covered it with both hands. "Oh my God," The words came muffled through his fingers. "You said he used a gun on himself now you say someone shot him… no…no, I don't believe it."

"You'd better believe it," Jack snapped. "Yesterday you said last time you saw him he didn't look worried."

"Yes."

"When was that?"

Nicholson shrugged. "A few weeks ago."

"When you were in Cyprus playing golf."

He made to speak, stopped, swallowed, and nodded weakly.

"Not when you were in his office on Thursday morning?"

Nicholson leaned forward, resting his forearms on the desk and hung his head. The office door opened and his secretary entered with a tray. She gazed at him, a look of concern on her face as she lowered it.

"It's OK Mary, he whispered, "That's all for now."

Jack moved forward and copied Nicholson, resting his forearms on the desk, their faces only two feet apart. "Right, let's stop all this bullshit Mr Nicholson. We've got a murder inquiry here. I want the truth, OK? For instance, where were you last Thursday evening around seven or eight? You were at Sellafield, that day we know that. You and McManus and his son and Terry Seaward, all good golfing buddies were arguing. What about?"

Nicholson sat back and shrugged, a sickly grimace on his face. He shook his head. "It was nothing…nothing really, just some permits that had been overlooked. You know on that site you can't break wind without a method statement, an environmental certificate and a waiver from the noise abatement society. He complained that Driscoll, he's a sergeant in the C.N.C, would delight in jumping on him for any breach of security. He gets stroppy when he thinks that's going to happen."

"Was it a breach of security?"

"Well, yes it was. Some forms hadn't been signed off for us to enter a controlled zone. That's all. After we sorted it out, I left for home. Check the book at the main gate if you don't believe me. I was home about sixish."

"Now why didn't you tell me all this yesterday?" Stella asked. "You gave me the impression that your relationship with McManus was… well, casual to say the least. Now we find out you were just about blood brothers. Golf in Cyprus three times since June we learn, my…my…lucky you. Why did you try to mislead me? Have you something to hide, Mr Nicholson?"

"No! No, I swear I didn't mean to… to…" His voice faded to nothing.

"Then why do it? There has to be a reason. It seems

strange you would not want us to know about your friendship with the deceased unless you have something to hide."

"It was just…just shock I think and I felt a bit vulnerable, you know. When suddenly you're confronted by police."

"So when did you fall out with McManus? We understand from his brother that you were no longer friends," Jack whispered with menace.

"You've spoken to his brother?" Nicholson's voice took on a high tone of surprise.

"We've had a long chat. He came to see his brother the day after you all came back from Cyprus. Can I assume something happened over there? What happened between the pair of you? Come on Mr Nicholson, let me have some facts then we can leave you in peace."

Nicholson took a deep shuddering breath. "Christ officer, it was nothing. Nothing but a dispute over a few golf shots. We often fell out on the golf course. He takes a five I took a four. Big recount of shots down the fairway. He coughs as I lined up a putt. Big moan from me when I miss. He hated to lose as much as I loved to beat him. It happens all the time in golf…it means nothing. We were fine afterwards."

"And that was it? He took the huff over a game of golf. So much so, he had to race over here and confess to a priest. Sounds fishy to me."

Nicholson tried to wriggle his neck out of his collar. "What did he confess?"

"We don't know. Some religious rule of confidentiality says he isn't allowed to divulge any confessions. But we're working on it. Sooner or later we'll find out. What he *did* say is that his brother had demons in him, that he was a very troubled man. Now why do you think that was, Mr Nicholson? What brought him racing across here on two different occasions? If I tell you that on the second, that is Thursday last, he was on his way to speak to a journalist in

Newcastle. Would that surprise you?"

Nicholson reached slowly for his coffee. There was a visible trembling in his hand as he grasped the white plastic cup. "I don't know…I honestly don't know. All I can think of is that leak of cooling water from legacy pond five. Yes!" he said on an excited breath, "Yes! that's it. That's got to be it. It was on his mind all the time. He initiated a full site survey. It wasn't finished but he told me the readings he got were worrying…really worrying. That's what was troubling him, Mr Shaftoe. I'm certain of it."

"Why would he want to tell the Press," Stella said. "Wouldn't he have conferred with his boss." She turned to Jack. "What do they call the site manager?"

"Butterworth. Roger Butterworth. You know him I presume?"

Nicholson nodded quickly. "Yes...yes, we've had meetings with him about various projects."

"Did McManus think Butterworth wasn't taking the situation seriously?"

"Probably…I think so. Maybe he worried so much about it he thought if it got into the newspapers it would force some positive action."

Jack took a deep breath and scratched under his chin. "And get him into deep shit with his employer. But it's a possibility. I've heard of whistleblowers but that would be a siren and a half."

"I'm intrigued," Stella said, picking up her coffee and staring into the cup. "Cyprus three times in five months. That must have cost a packet."

Nicholson thought for a moment. "Not as much as you might think. I can take as many holidays as I like as long as I keep the wife sweet. Molly's," he shrugged… "Molly's glad to see the back of me. At Sellafield they can split their annual leave into individual weeks or days even. And other than the air fare we get free board and lodgings."

"How come?"

He hesitated. "My sister. My sister and her husband have

a small hotel just south of Paphos. We stay there. It's a short walk to Aphrodite Hills golf course. My sister's husband is a great friend of the course manager. We get cheap rates." He nodded as though pleased with his explanation.

"Is your brother-in-law a Cypriot?"

A cloud of concern came over Nicholson's face. "No, no… he's not." He hesitated again, took a noisy breath and sighed as though it was an act of defeat. "I will tell you something but I beg you to keep it confidential. "My brother-in-law was a refugee from Russia… no …no, sorry, he would kill me for saying that. He's from Chechnya. My sister met him in Cyprus on holiday way back in 2007. He had fled there after Putin's second Chechen war. He was classed as a terrorist and Putin vowed to track down all terrorists no matter where they were hiding and wipe them out. He managed to get to Turkey then Cyprus, crossed the border and became a Greek citizen in 2012." He sighed again. "He has made a new life for himself. Changed his name. He is now Alessandro Dimitriou. He keeps his past close to his chest for obvious reasons."

Jack nodded. "Understandable." He made to rise. "OK Mr Nicholson, I think we'll leave it there for the time being. We'll probably have to see you again. In the meantime, if there's anything…anything else you think can help us nail his killer make sure you contact me. Anything… however minor you understand. Here's my card."

Nicholson's head twitched which Jack took to be an agreement, a wan smile creeping across his lips. The interview had been an ordeal and he slumped visibly before rising to his feet, his hands resting on the desk and his arms forcing himself upward.

At the door Jack turned. "Just one more thing before I forget. Where's your tan? You and Billy McManus are like milk bottles, Albert was well toasted."

Nicholson sighed. "Mr Shaftoe, I love the sun but it doesn't like me. Have you heard of Basal Cell Carcinoma? It sounds frightening but it isn't. It's a type of skin cancer.

Non-malignant. Just looks like dermatitis, but it can spread.
I had it on my nose and a patch on my forehead. I use factor
fifty all the time now. In my younger day, I would lie in the
sun covered in coconut oil and fry myself. Not now. Billy is
a carrot-head. He burns easily."

"And what about Seaward?"

Nicholson shrugged. "He browns in no time."

He watched them as they walked to the car. He noted
their heads turned toward each other and their lips moving
in conversation. A sickening surge of fear ran through him
as he forced a wave to the moving car. He turned and
stepped quickly back toward the open reception door,
closed it and gestured to the girl at the desk. It buzzed as it
locked him out. He pulled out his mobile dialled 00357, the
area code for Paphos, 26, and the number.

"Hello."

"Brenda, it's me, Henry."

"Henry who?"

"Brenda, don't fuck about. Put Al on."

There was silence for a moment then a thick guttural
voice blasted at his ear. *"Henry. Yes Henry hallo to you."*

"Al, we have a problem. Albert McManus has been
murdered."

"What…what you say! McManus… murdered. Who done this?"

"I don't know. I've had police crawling around here
yesterday and today. They know all about our golf trips. Just
got rid of them. They're asking a lot of questions, Al.
Questions too close for comfort. And something else.
McManus was a bloody catholic and his brother is a priest,
here in Newcastle. Now get this, the stupid bastard
confessed to his brother the day after we got back home.
What he confessed God only knows but the police are
expecting him to tell them. You know the state he was in
when we left. He could have blown the whole goddam
project. And Al, now we're down to three."

"Bloody fucking hell. It'll mean extra visits."

"I think something needs to be done Al or we'll all land

up doing life. We can't have the priest blabbing anything significant."

There was silence for a long moment. Then the voice came with a growling determination. *"Leave this to me, Henry. I get Khasan to fix it. He is in Sheffield."*

"Can he get here before the priest decides to cooperate?"

"Hmm. I'll ring him. Give me all the details and I'll sort this out. Leave it to me… and Henry, don't… how you English say?… get knickers in a twist. It will be all right. Everything will still be on programme, yes?"

Nicholson's mouth had dried and his tongue felt thick and heavy. "On programme, OK," he managed to say.

"Well, what do you think?" Stella asked as they drove away. "I think he's hiding something."

"So do I."

"But what? I get the impression that he wasn't involved in the murder. He seems to have a good alibi."

"So did MacManus' son, but Nicholson's answers were too exact…too precise. They had been rehearsed. Either Billy McManus or Seaward tipped him off."

"Seaward. You didn't see him?"

"No, I need another trip over there. He was here, seeing Nicholson."

"He didn't mention he was expecting anyone from Sellafield when I was here yesterday. You didn't bring that up for Nicholson to explain."

"No I was waiting for him to say something. That little trio are guilty of some skulduggery, I'm certain of it. When we get back fill me in on McManus' phone calls. I'll try to make sense of what's on his laptop. Let's get some explanation about those papers. Stella, can you get a financial report on N.N.S. McManus was in debt and his son had been cleaned out cashwise by his girlfriend. Seaward might be short of cash and if N.N.S is in financial trouble there might be a motive for some dirty dealings. Just a thought. Oh, and another thing. That guy who works for

Nicholson. Clare's office cleaner's nephew. I think we need a word with him. We might get a better picture of the real Nicholson."

"And what about McManus?" Stella said gently with mock sarcasm.

"Don't worry we'll catch our man for that but I get the feeling we might have bigger fish to fry. Another thing on the agenda is this Chechen cum Greek, Dimitriou. Any link, however nebulous between Russia and western nuclear affairs doesn't sit comfortably with me, Stella. We need to find out if he's kosher or not."

CHAPTER 7

It was mid-afternoon when Coulson breezed up to Jack's desk and threw a folder down.

"Came while you were out. The boffins have run their expert eye over that survey document and come up with some answers. The red dots are obviously survey points. Where they are crossed off, the symbols show depths below ground level and, it appears, radiation levels. Alpha, Beta and Gamma contamination, whatever that means but they say it needs urgent checking out. I think we need some experts in on the whole scenario."

Jack felt a prickle of excitement. "I thought as much. Looks like that whole area is riddled with nasties. But I can't understand why he suddenly decided to take in water before he had finished surveying the whole site. I don't think we should involve anybody else at this stage. Not until we get some hard facts on the McManus death. If he was murdered it could muddy the waters."

Coulson shrugged. "Looks like McManus could see what was happening. Just took a decision to blow the whistle and someone didn't like it. Now you, Jack have to find out who, and make sure Clare doesn't break the news until it's all set in concrete...OK?"

"She won't. We've got it sorted. You would see the Press article. Twelve lines on page six. Suicide. Nothing out of the ordinary as suicides go. Same with the Cumbrian media. Clare gets the scoop when it's juicy enough. What about those papers found in McManus' car?"

"They're in that folder. Looks like an inventory of sorts. Dates; weights; all referenced to Pu02. Plutonium Oxide. Whatever that is. Could be just a list. They've got all sorts of chemical crap over there, so they tell me."

"With alterations?"

Coulson put on his traditional bored expression. "We all make fucking mistakes, Jack."

Jack smiled to himself. Coulson had made a big one trying to lay Stella.

"What's your next move, then?"

"Stella's getting the phone calls traced. I need to get back over there. There are a few loose ends to clarify and there's another route I need to follow up. The whole rigmarole has a line to Nicholson, the boss man of N.N.S in town here and maybe, would you believe... Cyprus."

"You can forget that sunny Jim! If there's something to chase up in Cyprus, I'll be there."

Jack smiled. "It won't come to that I don't think. Just some wild idea that need to be discounted."

"And what's that?"

"I don't really know. Just a niggle. The main players in this case, including McManus have been to Cyprus three times since June. Seems Nicholson has a sister over there married to a Greek who used to be a Russian or a Chechen... same difference I think."

Coulson juggled his false teeth. "Hmm, not if you're from Chechnya. There's been a hell of a lot of trouble there over the years. Even I know that. But listen Jack, don't go off on a tangent. Keep focussed on your latest pet...and I don't mean Stella, I mean McManus. OK? Charteris was on his high horse this morning. He's screaming for developments on that drug surveillance operation that's been going on for three months – and only five miles from his office at Force headquarters at Wallsend. He's got it in for me."

"OK boss. It's coming together. The motive is plain now. I just need to nail who was where and when then I can winkle out the budding Al Capone."

Coulson grunted as he walked away which Jack assumed was his approval of his intentions.

Stella appeared with two coffees and eased her left buttock onto his desk. "Got the list of phone calls traced for the last four weeks. Nothing of much interest. Mainly local; people and shops in Egremont. A few to Seaward's office and one to McManus from Seaward at six fifteen last Thursday. It was the last call on his phone before he tried to contact your land-line. Also last Thursday there were two to N.N.S and one to the Ministry of Defence in London."

"The MOD. That's interesting. What time was that?"

"Eight seventeen in the morning. The day he died."

"That's really interesting. Can we find out who he contacted?"

"I'm working on it. I'm busy running a business check on N.N.S. I should have info before we leave or first thing tomorrow at the latest."

"Good. Coulson's piling the pressure on. I need to contact somebody at M.I.6. Remember that bloke who came up here from Vauxhall Cross when we nobbled those two amateur bomb makers. You know who I mean? He came with a couple of his M.I.5 mates. That pair of Syrian immigrants were running a food bank in Scotswood, bless their cotton socks. They might have wound up with a gong from H.R.H if we hadn't sussed out that they were collecting bags of fertilizer, wires, fuses and the like, at the same time. What was his name, Colin somebody or other?"

"Forrest...Colin Forrest." Stella whispered as a vague but pleasant memory passed through her.

"Yes, that's him. I need to find out if they have anything

on Nicholson's brother-in-law. See if you can find out if he's still lurking in the shadows down there."

Stella finished her coffee and slid off the desk. Jack watched as she smoothed the back of her skirt as she walked away. The rhythm going on under the cloth was mesmerising. It seemed an age since he had felt the hot urgency of her body against his and a surge of lust stirred in his loins. Then Clare swamped the flame. She was still distant but the coldness that had been so pronounced on her return, seemed to be thawing to a state of sterile friendship. And he was grateful for the improvement however scant. He had to ring her.

He got the ringing tone and it repeated five times. Her voice was flat, the words slow and impersonal. *"Hello, Jack. What's new? I'm doing a piece on council corruption. Any contributions?"*

"We won't live long enough to get it all down. Can you get me the address of your cleaner's nephew? I need to speak to him about his boss."

"Jim Melrose. Yes, I'll see Betty shortly. I think he lives in Gateshead but I'll get his address. What time will you be home?"

"Probably six. That OK?"

Her voice went colder. *"Suppose so. I need you to tell me the latest. I want to be kept in the loop. Don't you dare keep anything back."*

"Don't worry. I'll fill you in on McManus' brother and N.N.S boss man, Nicholson. Now there's a slimy prick if ever I met one. And McManus' brother. Oh my God, a typical bible puncher. See you later."

There was a click as the phone disengaged.

He opened the laptop and cursed. The screen was locked. He tried a few random guesses but nothing worked. He picked up the phone again. "Hello, Bridget it's Jack...Jack Shaftoe. I've got a laptop here I need to get into. Anybody in your Frankenstein department that can crack the code?"

Bridget's voice held the usual tone of bored supremacy.

"Hmm. So it's another miracle you want. Well I suppose we can give it a try. I'll send someone to pick it up. I suppose yesterday is soon enough?"

"You've supposed right."

"Thought so. By the way, those sheets found in the car. The alterations seem to be in some form of order."

"What do you mean?"

"Well, they're all one or two or three days apart. There are several items on some days but only one alteration on any given day."

Jack sensed a revelation. "What are you saying, Bridget?"

"Could be a case of one for you and one for me."

"You mean someone's been concealing something?"

"Possible, I suppose. But I doubt it. Could be a coincidence. Could be just amendments."

Jack nodded to himself. "Thanks Bridget, the laptop's on my desk. ASAP please, sugar-bun."

"Don't try to flatter me. Another crack like that and you can have it within the hour."

"OK gorgeous, that would be great."

"Piss off," Bridget said softly.

Her smile carried right down the line.

Stella returned with a sheet of paper. "We've got the financial low down on N.N.S."

"And?"

"Dodgy. Massive overdraft. Sky high interest rate. Late filing accounts to Companies house. A few red flags and big cash flow problems."

Jack studied the paper. "Well, well. Would you believe it. Looks like Neutron Nuclear Services could do with a large cash injection."

"And here's Colin Forrest's direct line. I've also got his mobile number. Took a hell of a lot of security checks but I managed it."

Jack picked up his desk phone and rang the number. He remembered the voice that came down the wire. Soft. Suave, with a faint Bristolian accent. *"Hello, Forrest."*

"Hi Colin, it's Jack Shaftoe Northumbria C.I.D. Remember me?"

"Why yes…yes Jack. How's that lovely county of yours…and how's Stella?"

Jack glanced up at the hovering Stella and smiled. They're both still delightful."

"Great. It's about time I brought the family up there. Show them what unspoiled beauty looks like."

"You do mean the county I take it."

Forrest laughed. *"But of course. What can I do for you, Jack? You still sniffing out the lawbreakers?"*

"As always. But today I need some of your vast international knowledge. I need some info on a citizen of Cyprus. A nationalised Greek by the name of… hold on."

He shuffled some papers on his desk. Stella, with a disapproving frown found the name and held it in front of him. "Here it is…Alessandro Dimitriou. He runs a hotel near Paphos in Cyprus with his English wife. Apparently he's a refugee from Chechnya. Been there since about the early 2000's I suppose. Have you got a file on him?"

There was suspicion in Forrest's voice. *"What interest is he to you?"*

"Not much really. We've got a murder case here and a suspect is related to this guy's wife. Just trying to tie up all the loose ends."

"Hmmm…Off the top of my head I couldn't say, but I'll get the computer stoked up and ring you back. Alessandro Dimitriou you say. How urgent?"

"Just when you have time. I appreciate your help."

"All in the service of the Crown, old boy. I'll be in touch."

The phone went dead.

Jack turned to Stella. "Next in line is that Jim Melrose. Clare's getting his address. I'll pick it up at home tonight. I might give him a call this evening if he's home. Fancy joining me?"

Stella shrugged and sniffed. "Might as well, nothing better to do."

Jack nodded. He looked at her and a wave of sympathy came over him. The fact that men used her seemed to place her in a forlorn cloud of helplessness. He inwardly cursed his own involvement yet he suspected that her easy virtue somehow gave her a smattering of power; the ability to play the catch, albeit until the panting prey flopped to one side. Someday, someone would sweep her off her feet and appreciate her for not only her beauty and her body but for her mind and personality.

"OK Stella," he whispered on a sad smile. "I'll check with you about sevenish and pick you up."

"Sure Clare won't have an attack of the vapours?"

"No, she'll be fine." He said it but he didn't mean it.

He had one last thing to do before he left for home. He had to ring Millie at Sellafield. He needed to see her off site where she might relax and give out some relevant information even without realising it. He found her number in his wallet and dialled her mobile.

He recognised her frail voice instantly. He guessed she was still at work by the nervous tremble in her whispered words when he said his name.

"Hello Millie, It's me, Detective Sergeant Shaftoe. Can you talk?"

There was a moment's silence. He could almost see her looking furtively around before answering.

"Yes sergeant, I can talk."

"Good. Millie I would like to see you again tomorrow. Say, in the afternoon, off site. Could you manage that, maybe just twenty minutes or so?"

She hesitated. *"Well, yes I could, but where?"*

"Can you suggest somewhere. A pub...or a café."

"There's the Cat Inn in Egremont, but I don't know who might get in there. I could meet you at home... no, The Cat Inn would be handy for me. You know it? In the main street. It's not far from my house."

"I think so. I'll find it. Say two thirty, Millie. I'm bringing a colleague, Detective Constable Stella van Kirk. Ok?"

The voice at the other end was doubtful. *"Well, yes OK sergeant. Tomorrow you say…at two thirty. I think I'll take the day off."*

"Fine Millie, but before I see you I'm going to see Terry Seaward and then Butterworth again. I take it they'll both be on site tomorrow?"

Silence for a moment. *"Yes, as far as I know. They don't know I'm meeting you do they?"*

"No Millie, you'll be all right. Are you sure the Cat Inn is OK?"

"Yes…yes, that will be fine."

Jack put down the phone and smiled at Stella. "We're off early in the morning. See you here at seven o'clock sharp. I want to check something with that C.N.C security sergeant and the site manager, Butterworth but most of all our elusive missing link, one Mr. Terry Seaward. You can make the appointments while I drive."

Stella nodded "OK, what about tonight?"

"Pick you up at about seven thirty."

The earlier cold drizzle had stopped as he drove toward Jesmond. He could see the bars and restaurants were busy despite the weather and it still only Tuesday. He often wondered where all the prosperity was coming from considering the area's backbone of shipbuilding and coal mining were long gone and it's great innovative engineering prowess only fizzing like a damp squib.

He had a surprise for Stella. When he had arrived home, Clare was back to her aloof aura of tolerance. She gestured to the kitchen. "Sausage and mash out there. It needs heating up. I've had a busy day," she snapped.

"I've got to head out again after this," he said gingerly, expecting a tirade.

"Back to normal. Just as always."

"I'll only be an hour or so then I'll give you all the day's developments… It's really hotting up now Clare," he added, hoping to cool down her mood. "I need to see that engineer from N.N.S. whatshisname… Jim Melrose. Apparently the company's in the shit money wise. Coulson's breathing down my neck. He needs some positive movement on this case, Clare…sorry."

She brought her handbag to the table and produced a torn piece from a jotter. "There's his address but you won't find him there. Betty says he left N.N.S last week. He's got a part time job pulling pints in a bar on the Pink Triangle. The 'Back Door Inn'… need I say more?"

Jack nodded. He knew the area well. For all the macho image of Newcastle it has a thriving gay centre. A stone's throw west from Central Station, it's a hive of bars and night clubs where people of all persuasions meet to socialise, flirt, dance and generally relax in the comfortable atmosphere of like minds. Beer and wine flow. Acts of affection are uninhibited. Music bashes against the eardrums. Male strippers get the audience whooping in delight. Drag queens flaunt themselves on waves of unfettered crude jokes. And Jack found it a gold mine for information when needed.

"Thanks, Clare. Promise I'll be home by…say," he glanced at his watch, "Nine?"

She gave a reluctant nod. He found the plate of sausage and mash and gave it three on high in the microwave. He sat at the kitchen table and after a long squirt of brown sauce, started eating. He didn't mention Stella in case it set her off on another biting round of accusations.

Stella was ready at Amen cottage when he tapped the car horn. Even with the car window still up he could hear youthful singing from the church and wondered if Father McManus was standing in rapture at the sounds while harbouring secret confessions that could allow crimes to go unpunished.

"Guess where we're off to?" he said as she slid into her seat.

"Cyprus?"

"I wish. The Pink Triangle. Would you believe Jim

Melrose is a barman there 'The Back Door Inn'…ouch!"

He parked in a side street just opposite the train station and they walked. Like Jesmond, the area was alive with punters. They passed 'Rockies', brightly lit and noisy. Then 'The Eagle' three levels of jollity with the basement bar mysteriously for men only. There was a gap before the next bar, a disused building with a rendered wall on either side of a blistered blue door. The wall had once been white; it was now grey and plastered with posters, most shredded with edges flapping in the breeze. Someone with a marker pen had written 'My mother made me a homosexual' and underneath in a different hand it read 'If I give her the wool will she make me one.'

The 'Back Door Inn' was in the middle of a long line of eight establishments, small, with the décor reminiscent of a French boudoir. White walls and sparkling chandeliers. Mirrors and red velvet cushions. Scented candles burned but the light they gave off was dimmed by incongruous spotlights that glowed pink. There were thirty or so people in the bar when they entered. There was a moments silence as conversations stopped and faces turned to the arrivals. Most recognised Jack, he'd been in many times before. They walked up to the bar. What appeared to be a woman with long blond hair smiled at him. The face was heavily made up, carrying a poor attempt at disguising a blue shadowed chin. Long eyelashes fluttered and a bright red handbag moved along the bar from where he stood to make room for them.

"Well hello, Captain. Nice to see you again. Is it business or pleasure? This your girlfriend?" The voice was plainly deep and masculine.

"Hello Lily, it's business. You keeping out of mischief?"

"But of course, don't I always?"

"No."

Eyelashes fluttered again and he turned away with a petulant flourish.

"His name is Magnus but he prefers Lily," he whispered.

The barman walked up from the far corner. He was a slight figure; short dark hair and sharp features. Early thirties.

"What can I get you," he said sullenly.

"Pint of real ale and…" he turned to Stella.

"Red wine." She had her back to the bar surveying the scene. She had been in a few bars gay bars in Newcastle, mostly on police business and once in some gay café in Canal street Manchester. The scene never failed to amaze her. She had no problem with gays and it was their unreserved exuberance when together that fascinated her. She had tried to analyse it but could only put it down to the exhilaration of a life now mostly without prejudice, something she was no stranger to herself.

The drinks came and Jack paid. "I'm looking for Jim Melrose. Is that you?"

The barman hesitated, looked left then right then nodded quickly.

Jack gestured with his head to the far end of the bar, away from Lily and ears. The barman followed.

Jack flashed his I.D. "DS Shaftoe, this is DC van Kirk. Jim, I'd like to ask you some questions about your boss at N.N.S…or should I say your old boss. You've left the company we hear."

"Nicholson! What's the twat done now," he growled.

"Don't know. Thought you might tell us."

He glanced furtively around. "Look, I'm on my own here. The mob'll be screaming for drinks. I've got a break in fifteen. Can you wait?"

"OK, understood."

They found a table and sat down and surveyed the crowded scene. There were frequent glances in their direction. Broad smiles, little finger waves and blown kisses. The mix was eclectic. Young men, fresh faced with glowing excited cheeks and bright eyes; bare arms sprouting out of coloured vests wrapped lovingly around a companion. Butch females with short, parted hair and pint glasses held high above the huddled, bustling throng. Men dressed as women. Women dressed as men. Every hue and tone of gender seemed to be fused into a homogenous mass of enjoyment.

"Looks like we're popular," Stella whispered through a returned grin.

"They love it when straights wander in," Jack said folding his arms and sitting back. "They get a kick out of the puzzled faces that suddenly realise where they've landed for a drink."

The barman walked up to them. "Fred's taken over. There's a room at the back. Bring your drinks."

The room was full of bar junk. Unopened boxes of glasses. Beer mats. Spirit fixtures lying on the floor. There was the smell of old fried food, stale beer and disinfectant. Melrose unfolded a card table that was propped against a wall. There were four spindly garden chairs behind some boxes and stacked one on top of another. He placed them around the table and ushered them to sit down. The dull thud of music suddenly came through from the bar. He turned and slammed a door that once had been painted but was now chipped, stained and forlorn.

"I hope I can help," he said as he sat. There was curiosity and concern on his face. "Nicholson's a prick. What's he been up to?"

Stella got in first. "We don't know. We want you to tell us about him."

Melrose thought for a moment. He sniffed. "Well he's a villain. A robbing bastard."

"How do you mean? What's he been stealing?"

"I don't know but what I do know is the company's going to the dogs. He's been penny pinching on equipment. Reduced our lodging perks and the like. Cut our travelling allowance and overtime. He would give us great lectures on what he would do for us, then we realised anything he did for us meant it was twice as good for himself. The whole place knew we were going downhill but he got us all together the other week and said it would be all hunky dory early in the New Year."

"What did he mean by that?"

"He wouldn't say. All he said was that there would be a big cash injection into the place that would put us back on an even keel. And with him swanning around in a top of the range Jag. in the meantime. I...most of us, didn't believe him. He never got his arse from behind his desk unless it was to go to Sellafield. He left the staff to do all the donkey work then deigned to show himself when contracts were placed as though it had all been his hard work. I got sick and jacked in." He shrugged. "My mate runs this place. Got me in until I find some other engineering work."

"What about Sellafield, Jim. You worked there didn't you?"

"Plenty of times."

"Tell us about Nicholson and McManus. You know McManus is dead?"

His jaw dropped. "You mean McManus senior... not his son?"

"That's him."

Jesus, Nicholson didn't kill him did he?"

"Why would he do that?"

"I don't know." He scratched at his brow. "Jesus...McManus, the health and safety manager...dead... How?"

"He was murdered, Jim and we're trying to find out by whom." Jack said. "We understand they were big buddies. Golf mates. Those two and McManus' son and Terry Seaward."

"Murdered! Fuck! I never thought it would come to that. Huh, the four of them were always in McManus' office. I was often past his office when I was heading for the projects section. Heads together. Papers passing from one to the other. Arguing...they were always arguing."

"About what?"

"Don't really know, the door was always shut but you

could tell by their faces and raised voices. Nicholson rarely came to see progress on the contract we were working on. He was always with McManus, either in his office or wandering around the site somewhere."

"How long was this going on?" Stella asked.

He shrugged. "Well we've had a few jobs there over the last few years. Most went really well but this year Nicholson never seemed to be interested...in the job that is, just in getting together with McManus, Seaward and McManus junior."

"We've got to see Mr Seaward tomorrow."

Melrose suddenly sat back. "You don't think that one of them really murdered him do you? Christ I know they argued but not to that extent."

"That's what we intend to find out, Jim. Now put your thinking cap on and try to give us some lead on why he got himself shot. Or anything else however minor that might have some relevance."

"Shot! He was fucking shot!" He shook his head in amazement. He chewed at his lip for a moment. "There's nothing really... except one day I passed them as they were coming out of the MOX plant; all four of them. McManus son works in there... they were all deep in conversation..."

"What the hell is MOX?"

"It means mixed oxide fuel. They reprocess spent uranium and separated plutonium into new power station fuel."

Jack felt a prickle of alarm. He glanced quickly at Stella. Her frown showed the same. "Just what did you hear, Jim?"

"Not much, other than Seaward said 'Book the flights for January.' Something about delivery and then Billy shouted 'No! too early.' Nicholson said 'no it's not.' then they clamped up as I passed them. Albert McManus looked worried. Nicholson gave me a watery smile, asked how the job was going and they all walked on. I assumed they were organising another of their poxy golf jaunts and McManus thought the weather might not be good in January. That's all I can think of other than their meetings and shouting matches. But it did occur to me from their sudden silence they might be cooking something up."

"What made you think that?"

"Dunno, just the way they looked as I passed them…you know, guilty, as though they had just been caught stealing apples."

Jack took a deep breath. "OK Jim, I think that'll be all for now, bu…"

He was cut off in mid-sentence. The door burst open. Loud heavy metal, courtesy of Led Zeppelin came in with Fred, a wormy looking pale faced individual with a line of silver trinkets bored through the side of his left ear. He yelled into the room. "For fuck's sake Jim, get back behind the bar! They're about to lynch me out there. They all want topping up before the drag starts."

All three stood up. "OK, we'll get out of your hair Jim. Thanks for the info. I might need to get back to you."

Jim nodded and followed them out. The crowded bar whooped and cheered as they appeared.

A shrill voice yelled "Let's have a look at your truncheon big boy." More laughter. Stella gave them a flamboyant wave as they threaded their way through the throng and managed to get to the door without any groping hands and playful assaults on their nether regions.

"Well, now we know for sure, they're up to something," Jack murmured as they walked away.

"But what? We've only got theories. Coulson wants hard facts on his table. And we're still no farther forward on McManus' killer."

"We're getting there. Someone needed to silence McManus because he was about to blow the whistle on the site contamination. But is the conversation Melrose heard anything to do with that? More trips to Cyprus. Deliveries and disagreements on timing… that's if Melrose heard right. What the hell was that all about?"

The drizzle had started again as they got to the car. The

doors slammed and the engine caught. Windscreen wipers swept away the beads of colour. "Tomorrow we might find out." Jack said.

At Amen cottage they sat for a moment staring forward and mulling over the day's events.

Eventually Jack turned to Stella. "Why the hell did you get into this business in the first place? There are easier jobs...more satisfying jobs."

Stella shrugged. Her voice flat and weary. "Ask yourself that. I suppose we get the grandiose idea that we can contribute to the well-being of the world. Stamp out cruelty, misery and unfairness... catch the baddies and all will be well. All that sugary bullshit. But you come to realise that you catch one and there's always another that crawls out of the woodwork. It's a never-ending task and always will be. But you harden to it, Jack. It becomes just another job. You should know. You've seen it all. Me? I just get a kick out of outsmarting them... or try to, once in a while. It's a game of chess, Jack. Sometimes...most times we win and you get the satisfaction of victory but then... but then you have to watch as some booze-soaked old dodderer of a judge slaps their wrist while the victims...if they are still alive, are left to lick their wounds."

"Tell me about it," Jack said on a sigh. "Remember Church, the DCS at the Met? That's him that sent me back up north. He had a full career in this profession. He got to his retirement. He had a big party...even I got an invite back to London. He was downing the whisky, arms around everybody...laughing and leg pulling. He had booked a trip to the Seychelles for him and his missus. Five-star hotel. And he had bought a flat in Menorca. He was going to have a great retirement. At the end of the night, we managed to stuff him into a squad car...pissed but still laughing his head off. He got home ok and I presume his wife managed to get him into bed. He died in his sleep, Stella. Closed his eyes thinking what a great night he'd had and never opened them again. That was his reward for a career catching villains and making the world a better place."

Stella nodded a silent understanding. She put her hand on his thigh. "You want to come in? Let's live while we can. There's still some gin in the bottle."

He glanced at his watch. "It's nearly nine. I'd better go…"

"There's time for one drink and a… a quicky," she said seductively.

Jack gazed at her. There was something alluring about the shadow of her in the darkened car, her closeness and the sudden awareness of her perfume. He looked at his watch again, though for a moment, then opened the car door.

CHAPTER 8

It was almost seven thirty the next morning when he got to Robert's Hill. Stella was already there, coffee cup in hand reading a post-it on his desk. She looked up and smiled. "Good morning," she said brightly. "Sleep well?"

He tried to disguise a smile. He got home at ten after ten, a smattering of guilt hit him as he opened the front door but all was silent. Clare was in bed and from the muffled wheeze coming from the small bedroom, he knew she was asleep. He knew also that she was desperate for the latest developments but he presumed that her ire at his lateness had overcome her hunger for news. Tomorrow night he promised himself he would be able to get some definite progress after his visit to the other coast and feed it to her ravenous journalists ears.

He poured himself a large whisky, sipped it slowly then showered and slept almost immediately.

He was up at six. He heard Clare making noises in the kitchen and braced himself for some icy grumbling but it didn't happen. "Any joy?" she said without turning away from the toaster.

"Some. That Melrose guy certainly has it in for Nicholson. It seems our ace nuclear engineering firm is up the proverbial creek, money wise."

She turned. "I'll do some independent digging. I might come up with something else about the firm that's relevant."

"Great," he said as she passed him some toast, "if you can get some background on Nicholson that would be really useful as well."

Stella passed him the post-it. "It's from Colin Forrest he wants you to ring him."

Jack glanced at it. "Later. We need to get over to Sellafield. We've got a whole new day of revelations to winkle out of the ten thousand that work there... but we'll start with the main contenders. Then I need to see what tales McManus' computer can tell. Then there's Colin Forrest and that survey...and the inventory from McManus' car. Shit, we've got some work to do. Come on let's get going."

The journey to Sellafield was different to his trip on Monday. Low cloud hung heavy in the sky and as they got to higher ground, the cloud became hazy fog and through intermittent breaks, light snow had spread a patchwork of white across the top of the fells. Stella made the appointments on her mobile then Jack ran through his encounters with McManus junior, Butterworth, Millie and the C.N.C sergeant, Bob Driscoll. "I think we'll get more out of Millie and Butterworth. As far as Seaward's concerned it remains to be seen."

"He certainly sounded agitated on the phone. As though we had no right to be bothering him."

"We'll sharp kick that idea out of the prick's head." Jack barked, changing down a gear.

They reached the highest part of the fell road then as they descended, the fog was left above them. In the distance the iconic site of Sellafield came into view, ever mysterious, with a benign quietness but shielding weird and wonderful nuclear metamorphoses.

The main gate was as busy as on his last visit. A queue

of fifteen waiting to check in. The ever-present armed guards; expressionless, eyeing anyone and everyone that dared to approach the sanctum sanctorum without legitimate business.

Driscoll was behind the desk. A sarcastic gaze went from Jack to Stella." Well, well. If it isn't Batman…and…" he turned his eyebrows up, "Robin?"

Stella had been primed. She leant forward and placed her forearms firmly on the desk.

"And I suppose you're the fucking Joker…eh? You certainly look like him."

Jack gave a mocking laugh.

Driscoll forced a smile to his face. It was plain he hadn't crossed swords with anyone like Stella. He sniffed, rolled his tongue around the insides of his cheeks then conceded defeat with a nod. "OK what's the programme today? Any leads on the murder?"

"Some," Jack said. "We're here to see Seaward and Butterworth but before that we need your help."

Driscoll looked surprised. "What sort of help?"

"Can you fish out your files on McManus, his son Billy and Seaward. I just want to get an idea of their background. And I need a list of the dates Henry Nicholson of N.N.S signed in over... say the last six months. Can you do that? It would be a great help."

Jack had already sussed what made the man tick and knew a little smattering of involvement in the case would have him mellowed and cooperative.

"Christ… are they the main suspects?"

Jack shrugged. "You know how it is. Everyone's a suspect at first. That info will help."

"I'll see what I can do. When?"

"When we come out."

Driscoll nodded. He turned his head to the little adjoining office. "Joe, sign these two in and ring Seaward to come and get them. I need to go to the main block."

Terry Seaward appeared at the inner door with a forced smile on his face. The first thing Jack looked for was a tan. It was fading but it was still there. Seaward looked to be about mid-thirties. He was tall and slim with a fashionable three-day beard of fair hair which made up for an extremely high forehead and a thinning thatch of blond locks that had been vigorously combed from ear to ear. He was dressed smartly in a brown suit, cream shirt and vividly patterned tie. He introduced himself and shook hands while giving a small deferential bow of the head. Both Jack and Stella registered his unctuous act as someone anxious to appear guiltless of everything. There was a swagger to him; a subtle signal of cockiness and a hint of amusement at his being asked to cooperate.

"You're here about poor Albert, I suppose," he said as they walked to the office block. "Terrible business. He was not only my boss but my friend. I cannot believe he's gone. I cannot believe he's actually been murdered. I hope to God you're wrong about that."

"We intend to find out if he was, why and... more importantly by whom. We hope we're not inconveniencing you," Jack said with a touch of sarcasm. DC van Kirk thought you sounded a little irritated at having to speak to us."

Seaward pursed his lips and shook his head. "No... no, not at all. Pressure of work I suppose. Now that Albert's gone, it's all on my shoulders."

"Well, this little chat is necessary if we want to get to the bottom of it all. I intend to make this case top of my priorities. Whoever shot Mr McManus will grow old in jail, believe me. And if I had my way he wouldn't have the chance to grow old, he would wind up swinging gently by the neck in the breeze."

Seaward nodded. He cleared his throat. "I hope you catch him... and soon."

His office was next to McManus' and similar. The ubiquitous dark green metal filing cabinet. A whiteboard with a spaghetti of lines and scribbles in red marker. An untidy desk and piles of files, technical magazines and books scattered over the floor. They sat down and Seaward suddenly became serious. He picked up his phone and punched in one number. "The police are here now." He replaced the phone slowly. "Mr Butterworth is coming along shortly. He has a meeting at eleven thirty. Hope that's all right."

Jack nodded. "Now Mr Seaward, what can you tell us about why Mr McManus hightailed it to Newcastle last Thursday? You know, don't you, that he was planning to see a journalist."

Seaward shrugged. "I didn't."

"Nicholson hasn't told you?"

"No... no he hasn't."

"Sure?"

He nodded quickly. "I know he was worried about the site contamination...we both were. Albert was frustrated to say the least. He was getting fobbed off by the M.O.D. They thought he was overreacting. They wanted him to manage it and put it on the back burner. Take temporary measures and concentrate on the safety procedures for the decommissioning of piles one and two...you know... under those tall concrete chimneys. They've been shut down since the fifties. It's one hell of a task getting them back to ground level without contaminating the whole of Cumbria, and a repeat of the pile one incident."

"Yes, we know. Mr Butterworth gave me the details. But, back to McManus. Why do you think he needed to go to the Press? If the situation is as bad as he thought, going to the Press instead of the authorities would have probably cost him his job. As it happens, it cost him his life. Now who do you think would go to that extent to keep him quiet?"

Seaward shook his head thoughtfully. "I honestly haven't a clue."

"How about someone pretty close to him, workwise? You know, someone who knew the potential danger and that it could close the place down and cause a major redundancy situation. Not to mention a devastating deduction of income for the Government. Could that person be you, Mr Seaward... or even McManus' son. Mr Butterworth perhaps... or who?"

Seaward spluttered. "Jesus no! None of us. That's absolutely ridiculous. I was here in the office until after five last Thursday. Check out the movements record. I would say that whoever shot him maybe had other reasons."

"Like what?"

Seaward seemed to deflate. His shoulders sagged. He looked forlornly at the solemn faces of both Jack and Stella who knew how to intimidate a suspect merely by silence and a cold, wide- eyed disbelieving stare.

"I don't know... I just don't know."

"Are you not afraid of the contamination on this site? Surely if it is as bad as your late boss thought it was, everybody should be crapping themselves."

Seaward gave a mirthless smile. "It can be contained. It can be controlled. Albert thought the situation was getting beyond a solution. Maybe it was and maybe not. He had a full site survey instigated but he hadn't finished it. Even I didn't have all the salient facts. I had some... a few disjointed bits and pieces. He kept the whole thing close to his chest. No matter what the final outcome of that might have been, if the environmentalist yobbos had got wind of its very existence the place would be swamped with demos, banners, mock funerals and skeleton outfits."

"How was the survey going? Were there any readings that would ring any alarm bells with you?"

"Some, but like I said, from the bits I saw of the survey I believe it can be contained and controlled." He took a deep breath. "Albert got paranoid about it I'm afraid. I'm sure that's why he was on his way to blow the situation wide open."

Jack nodded. He glanced at Stella. He could tell she had the same feeling that was beginning to creep into his mind:

that they were going round in circles and getting nowhere. There seemed to be no direct link to the killer. The motive appeared plain enough but getting the vital lead to a person who might be desperate enough to waylay McManus and blow his brains out, was as remote as ever. Jack tried another tack.

"Tell us about Nicholson. He's your friend, is he not? You went over to Newcastle last Monday. A few days after McManus died to see Nicholson. Why did you do that?"

"Well, he's also a friend... we were all friends. Played golf together. We had just got back from a week in Cyprus. Two rounds a day, most days. When I heard the news, I just... just had to see Henry and wonder between us why the hell he had topped himself. But of course now it's different. Now we know he didn't. Or that's the latest rumour. Billy was devastated... so were we all."

"What about the fall out?"

Seaward looked surprised. "What fall out?"

"Nicholson and Mr McManus. We believe they had some form of row."

Seaward struggled to answer. Both Jack and Stella felt a crack forming in his composure. He waved it away, suddenly finding words. "Which row? They were always biting at each other. Mostly leg pull but sometimes it got out of hand, nothing serious, but enough to have the pair of them hunting for mild insults and the like. You know what I mean," he said with a forced chuckle.

Jack stayed poker faced.

"Three trips to Cyprus since June I believe. You must be keen."

Seaward shuffled himself to another sitting position. "Yes...yes, we're lucky. Henry has a sister over there. She and her husband have a hotel near the golf course. We love it... and it's cheap. And of course the weather... the weather is great for golf."

"They must be generous people," Stella said, "Mr Nicholson tells us you get free board and lodgings."

Seaward frowned as though hunting for a suitable reply. "Well, yes but we help out at the hotel at times…you know behind the bar and repairs… it's not a big hotel."

"Did Mr Nicholson tell you about McManus' brother?"

"Yes, he rang me… he told me. We had no idea."

Suddenly the door opened and Roger Butterworth bustled in with files under his left arm and a coffee cup in his right hand. "Good morning… good morning. Sorry I'm late." He slumped into a chair at the side of Seaward's desk, slapped the files down, took a mouthful of coffee and sat back. "Well, I hope Terry's managed to help you. I've got a meeting shortly so you must excuse the rush." He smiled at Stella. "You must be the lady who rang this morning."

Stella nodded.

"Glad you could make it Mr Butterworth. Mr Seaward has been giving us some background on his boss." Jack said. "Now I'd like you to explain to me…in simple terms please, what is Plutonium oxide."

Seaward's face drained of colour. Stella could see through the gap in his desk, his right leg vibrating; heel off the ground; his hand on his knee trying to control it.

Butterworth gave an amused frown. "Good God, sergeant you really have got Sellafield into your system. Plutonium oxide… what makes you interested in that?"

Jack waved a casual hand. "Just interested. I've been doing a bit of reading about this place and…and well it just is a sort of unusual name. Uranium I have heard of and plutonium. I know those two levelled Hiroshima and Nagasaki but what does Plutonium oxide do?"

Butterworth took a deep breath. "Well, let's see. Have you any idea how much plutonium levelled Nagasaki?"

Jack shook his head.

"A sphere about the size of a baseball. Weight… under fourteen pounds, including various bits and initiator pieces. That's what plutonium can do, sergeant. Do you know how much of it we have stored here? Over one hundred and thirty tons. Enough to blow the whole world to kingdom come. But it's a strange substance. It's what's known as an alpha emitter. You can contain it in a sugar bag. You can handle it if you're careful not to get it into a cut or breathe it in. It's warm when you pick it up because it's constantly in alpha decay. Seems almost like a gentle benign living thing. But... but oh boy, put just enough together and bang! Now Plutonium is a metal and when it's exposed to oxygen it oxidizes, that is, it turns to powder. Plutonium oxide. That's all."

"Is the powder dangerous?" Stella whispered, overawed by the information.

"It can be. It can be turned chemically back into a metal. But that's not an easy process. Here at Sellafield when we reprocess spent fuel we get uranium and a small amount of plutonium and other isotopes, but believe me the process is strictly controlled. We can never be sure exactly how much we can achieve out of any one batch but whatever it is, it is measured to the milligram, recorded, and what is not utilised in the MOX plant is stored in a repository under onerous security conditions."

Jack was tempted to jump in with the altered inventory sheets but stopped himself. To mention them would have sounded alarm bells and he needed first to clear his mind of any possible link between the murder and the papers in question. He glanced at his watch. "That's fascinating... frightening but fascinating. Well, gentlemen, thanks for your time. I don't think there's anything else to discuss at the moment."

"How's the investigation going?" Butterworth asked as they all stood up.

"Getting there. We're following some definite leads. Unfortunately, these things take time. Nothing happens overnight in a murder case unless it's a relative or a close friend that's under suspicion. That seems to get rid of a lot of the donkey- work. We'll be in touch." He turned to Seaward. "Any plans for another trip to Cyprus?"

Seaward swallowed. "No...no, not at the moment. It

won't be the same without Albert."

Jack tried his disbelieving stare but it didn't work. Seaward forced a smile to his face, ushered them to the door after Butterworth had dashed out. There was a half- hearted attempt at friendliness, similar to Nicholson's gushing greeting, as they walked to the main gate. He talked at an excited speed. He mentioned the weather and what a great job the police force did, despite their much-maligned actions against rioters and other rabble rousers. How brave they were to confront terrorists without weapons and all police should be armed. Their response was clipped but polite. He left them at the gate office, turned and strode quickly toward the main building. He glanced back once but they were already inside.

Driscoll was waiting for them. There was an air of satisfaction to him as he led them into the side office. "Got what you wanted. Any impending arrests in there?"

"Not yet. Still putting pieces of the jigsaw together." Jack muttered as he took three sheets of paper from him.

"That's Nicholson's visits to the site since last February," Driscoll said pointing to the top sheet. "Had it typed out for you."

"Jack ran his eye down the list. "Quite a regular. Bet he's on Butterworth's Christmas card list. What about McManus?"

Driscoll sneered. "That twat... Couldn't run a winkle stall. He had a half share in a new fishing boat up at Whitehaven. Cost him a packet. He thought he would have himself a nice little sideline. There was a big storm last winter and the bloody thing sank in the harbour. Not even finished... and not even insured. That's how clever he was. Put him way into debt. Then there was the new nightclub in the town. He decided to get himself involved with a couple of cronies from Carlisle. Put money up front. The place was going to be the talk of Cumbria when it was finished. What happened? They ran out of cash. Couldn't pay the rent. The place is now a fitness centre. Of course on site here, he thought he was King Dick."

"And McManus junior?"

Driscoll sneered again. "Billyboy is another loser... literally. That bastard was courting our Amy. He's a gambling addict. Internet roulette, horses, bingo, poker...you name it. He spent a fortune losing then blamed our Amy for egging him on. Other than a couple of speeding offences, there is nothing to report. He's been here since he left school. And let's see... Seaward, huh, he's had two wives and gearing up for another with a tart from Workington who's had enough cock to put a handrail around the entire site here. Fast cars and loose women, that's his lifestyle. He's driving a Porsche at the minute. Used to be a red Aston Martin. He fancies himself as James Bond and no mistake."

"A big spender." Jack said with an understanding nod. "Well, thanks for this. It might be useful. We'll get on our way and sniff out some more suspects. By the way, where were you last Thursday evening?"

Driscoll recoiled in disbelief. "Christ Almighty, I'm not on your list, surely. I hated the twat but I wouldn't kill him."

Jack smiled. "Just pulling your leg... I think."

"Well," Stella said, exaggerating the word as they returned to the car. "I get the feeling we're onto a loser ourselves. Nothing seems to lead directly to the murder. Where do we go from here?"

Jack rubbed a hand over his mouth. "You're right, Stella. There's nothing much to go on. All three of the remaining Nicholson golf society have reasonable alibis. But... but, there's something else. There's something else going on here which may or may not be related to McManus' murder, Stella."

"Like what? Did you notice Seaward's face when you mentioned Plutonium and the way his right leg started off with a major tremble. What's going on there?"

"Like some money-making scheme they are all party to.

The whole bunch of them are, or were, living above their means. There's a rabbit away and we need to catch it somehow. We'll see what little Millie can tell us then we need to do some serious work on the lap top, the survey and what's just become really significant are those Plutonium oxide lists."

Before they had cleared the car park Seaward was making a phone call.

"Hello Henry, it's me Terry."

From the tone of his voice, Nicholson knew there were problems. *"Yes, what's wrong Terry?"*

"Everything. Your favourite cop has just been here."

"Who? Shaftoe."

"Non other. With a female detective."

"I know her. She's been here twice. What did they want... are they suspicious?"

"Suspicious...maybe. The bastard wanted to know about..." he hesitated.

"About what, Terry?" A wave of fear ran across him.

"About Plut. That's what. And bloody plutonium oxide."

Silence.

"Henry, are you still there."

"I'm still here. We're going to have to speed up the schedule Terry. Get hold of Billy and don't let him think that things are about to turn to rat shit. I could see he was listening too much to his father. We can't let him take in water at this stage."

The Cat Inn in Egremont was easy to find. A grade II listed sixteenth century hostelry in a prominent position in the main street. Its white painted façade stood out like a signal between a car rental shop and a wine store. It was typical of the Inns scattered all over Cumbria and the Lake district. Small; cosy; intimate and revelling in dark wood, open fires, shiny horse brasses and real ales.

They arrived early. The bar was empty except for three

old timers playing dominoes in the far corner. A large hairy buff-coloured dog was stretched out at their feet. There was the odd grunt, a rasp of shuffling and the slap of the pieces onto the table but other than that, the place had a calming peace to it. It was just after two and they ordered drinks and ham sandwiches that came two inches thick. They had just finished when Millie poked her head shyly around the door and smiled when she recognised the detective.

Jack stood up. "Hello Millie, good of you to come." He introduced Stella to her then bought her a sweet sherry.

"Now Millie, we've come back to see you because I think you might be able to throw some more light on the contamination on site. We're looking into the site survey you gave me and some papers found in Mr McManus' car."

Millie looked over to the far corner of the bar and studied the domino players for a second.

"I'll try."

"What did you mean when you said to me you were scared… that a lot of people are scared?"

Millie took a sip of sherry and hung her head. "Mr Shaftoe, I am a widow at forty-seven years old. My husband worked at Sellafield. He died last year. He had leukaemia. My friend Gladys is a widow. Her husband died of lung cancer… he worked in THORP and he never smoked in his life. I could go on. We get scared Mr Shaftoe, because we think Sellafield is causing it, but the authorities say they cannot find a definite connection."

"What is THORP," Stella asked.

"It's the thermal oxide reprocessing plant. Don't ask me what goes on but it must be dangerous. The whole site is dangerous."

"Do you know anything about plutonium oxide?"

Millie nodded and took another sip of her drink. "I type up the lists for the records when they come in from the reprocessing plants. I know plutonium oxide is on the list. That's all."

"What happens to them then?"

"They're filed ready for any audit."

Where?"

"In the records office."

"Do you know who might tamper with them?"

Millie frowned. "Only Mr McManus… or Mr Seaward. They have keys to the big filing systems… and me… and a couple of other secretaries. And Mr Butterworth of course."

Jack took a breath between clenched teeth. "Thanks Millie. Is there anything else, anything at all that might give us a clue to who murdered Mr. McManus. Anything unusual or just something that puzzled you especially on the day it happened. Because you may not have heard this, but he was on his way to a newspaper reporter. We presume to tell all about the leak and the state of the site."

Millie was silent. The dominoes were shuffled again. The dog rolled over and started scratching its belly with a back paw. Millie took another drink. Her eyes suddenly lit up as a memory came back to her.

"I know Mr Seaward and him had another argument late in that afternoon… at Mr. McManus' house."

"At his house?"

"Yes, at tea time… at the garden gate. Their voices were raised. I live in the street at the top of their road. It's not far from here. I have to pass where they live. I had been to the butchers here in the high street for some sausage before they closed. I was on the other side of the road. It was dark but if they saw me, they didn't stop. They were angry."

"Did you hear anything, Millie? Could you hear what they were arguing about?"

Millie frowned and shook her head slowly. He could see her trying to drag out memories that had just been fleeting unregistered sounds. She took a deep breath and massaged her brow.

"I think… I think I might have heard… 'I can't'."

"From McManus?"

"Yes, then Mr Seaward shouted at him… 'you can, Albert. You can do it'." She lowered her head. "Then there was a swear word, then I was past. They still had raised voices but I couldn't make out anything else. To tell you the truth I wasn't really listening. They had been arguing a lot since they got back from their golfing trip."

"Well what do you know," Stella said, glancing at Jack. "He didn't tell us that."

Jack nodded, deep in thought. "Millie, are you sure you knew who was saying what?"

She nodded. "Yes. I know their voices well enough."

"Another thing. Do you know anyone who has a gun or is a collector of guns?"

She thought for a moment. "My neighbour, Mr Smeeton has a shotgun. He gives me a rabbit from time to time."

"No-one else?"

"I can't say. Only the police on site."

"Thank you for that. That might come in useful. In the meantime Millie please go about your business as normal, but will you ring me if there's anything else that you think might be relevant."

Millie nodded and finished her drink. The bar door opened and a woman came in. Millie looked alarmed but then relaxed. The woman was not known to her.

"We'll go now," Jack said, standing up. "Don't worry, your concern about the site has been noted. If I can get some action for you I will."

She smiled. Stella put her arm around her frail shoulder as they walked to the door and thanked her again, quietly before she made her way furtively up the street.

The return journey to Newcastle seemed to pass quickly with their conversation unending about their visit, possible suspects and the front gate argument.

"I'm confused," Jack said, as they neared Newcastle. "If McManus was coming over here to blab to Clare why did he say to Seaward 'I can't', surely he would have said, 'I am...or I will.' Then if Seaward was trying to stop him, he wouldn't have said 'you can do it...' or words to that effect.

Shit, this gets more complicated by the minute. I hope you're taking note of this Stella for when your promotion comes up."

"Note taken and what about this as a possibility?"

"What?"

"From that snatch of conversation, what if McManus was coming to see Clare, but not about the leak. What if he was coming to see Clare about a different matter. There was something Seaward wanted him to do but McManus didn't want to. That would fit the conversation, would it not?"

Jack hummed an admiring note as the possibility hit him. "Christ, Stella you'll have Charteris' job one day."

"Hah, hah, that *will* be the day. I'll probably wind up being a social worker when I get sick of this lot and realise I'll never win."

"For God's sake don't do that. They've got a chequered history of success and some major failures over the years. When Clare was at college, all the sociology students were either pot smokers or ragged arsed revolutionaries… or both. She told me she once saw a scrawled message in the women's bog next to the toilet roll. It said 'sociology degrees please tear one off.'"

Stella laughed. "Well maybe a private eye. I could fancy that. I used to love those old Chandler movies with Bogart as Philip Marlowe."

"Now there's a thought."

Jack stopped the car at Robert's Hill. He glanced at his watch. It was just after five. "You get home Stella I'm going to try to catch Colin Forrest. See you in the morning and we'll get our heads down with those papers and see what Bridget's come up with on the computer. I've got a feeling we need to lean on Seaward again. That prick is guilty as hell… guilty of what? I don't know… but something."

Colin Forrest's phone purred for twenty seconds. Jack thought he had left the office but he answered just as he was about to ring off. "*Hi Jack, sorry for the delay. Just ushering a meeting out the door. Now, your man, Dimitriou. Got some history and he's on our watch list. Nothing serious, just level four. There's another potential problem that could involve him."*

"What that?"

"The Russian mafia are slowly infiltrating the place. You know… the usual, protection rackets and the like. They're probably not on Putin's Christmas card list but they may have leant on Dimitriou for a payout to keep his hotel from going up in flames. Hopefully, they haven't linked him to any other country outside Greece or Cyprus. Our man out there just keeps an eye out and reports back if needs be.

"Sounds like he's pretty harmless."

"Looks like it. Seems his real name is Ibragim Viskhan. A Chechen from Chechnya. That area has had one hell of a history of war and all the suffering that goes with it. It would take all night to go over the unbelievable complicated political regimes that caused all the recent bloodshed. It appears Viskhan was a university lecturer in Grozny, one time capital of the state of Ichkeria. He had a wife and two kids, one seven the other eleven. They managed to survive what was known as the first Chechen war, when Russia just about levelled the city. That was a terrible conflict even by today's standards. It was estimated that there was up to one hundred thousand civilian casualties. Then came the second Chechen war, which started in 1999. The republic of Ishkeria ended when the Russians had another go. There was what's known as the winter siege of Grozny. Mr Putin initiated it and made sure the Chechens were hit hard and quickly; shock and awe they call it now – not like their first effort.

"So he would get himself involved in retaliation?"

"And then some. Listen to this. A scud missile hit the market place in Grozny. Over one hundred and forty people were killed including Viskhan's wife and kids. That was it for him. He joined a growing band of resistance fighters. They were dedicated to kill any Russian on sight… no questions asked. Guerrilla attacks are still going on today, but Viskhan decided to hightail it when Putin threatened to track down all rebels and exterminate them. He got to Turkey then Greece. He even had a spell in the UK before settling in Cyprus. We thought he might be useful."

"In what way?"

"He was a lecturer at Gozny University."

"Lecturer? In what?"

"Theoretical physics. We grilled him about what the Russians were up to in that field. Gave us some interesting tips. We had him at Cambridge for a couple of months then he did six at Oxford. He finished up doing a stint at the National Nuclear Laboratories."

'Where's that?"

"Sellafield. Do you know it? Over on the north west coast. Is that enough info for you?"

If Colin Forrest heard the sharp intake of breath he didn't remark on it. If thoughts were metal there would have been an audible clatter as a piece of the jigsaw dropped effortlessly into place.

"Yes," Jack breathed. "That's fine. That ties up some loose ends. Thank you Colin, you've been a great help."

"Oh, by the way, his wife in Cyprus owns a half share in a Newcastle company called Neutron Nuclear Services. I've checked it out. It's a relatively small straight forward engineering company specialising in nuclear installation work and the like. They've never been involved in anything that comes under the top security banner, but that's why we keep an eye on the Cyprus connection. Just in case, you know. I suppose Viskhan keeps the Newcastle outfit advised on technical matters. Does that place come onto your radar?"

"Yes…we know it, Colin. Thanks again."

"All in the service of the Crown old boy… and Jack let me know if there's any cause for alarm. Know what I mean? Don't get involved in anything that might… how can I put this politely… that might be out of your league, security wise. Cheers

The phone cut off. Jack sat back, his head alive with new possibilities. "Jesus H. Christ," he whispered to himself, "Wait till they all hear this."

CHAPTER 9

It was nine thirty when Bridget made her grand entrance. She strode into the office and with a flourish, placed the laptop on Jack's desk. "There you are sir, as ordered. Open for the whole world to see. It took what we call 'brute force cracking' but our little army of anoraks and an array of machines managed it."

Jack looked up from his frustrating examination of the papers from McManus' car. He had a suspicion that needed to be checked, but the beginning of the day's work involved a report to Coulson. He was sure he would give it only a cursory glance once he realised that it was all theory and maybe coincidence. Coulson needed hard facts. Even the sudden revelation that Nicholson's brother- in- law fitted in to a possible link would not impress him. Then he needed to give a word for word account to Stella of his talk with Forrest. He anticipated the look on her face and he was right. Eyes widening; jaw dropping and a gasp as the implications ferreted into her brain. Clare had had a similar reaction. It didn't take any more stimulation for her journalists mind to conjure up the growing possibility of some major conspiracy. The connections that had been nebulous were now strengthening by the day, and she couldn't contain her excitement. But as yet there was nothing conclusive, only conjecture and supposition. She found herself warming to her husband and his dogged approach to the case. She had done some poking into N.N.S herself but all she could glean was some background on Nicholson and the company set- up.

"Nicholson's sister owns half the company," she told him.

He nodded. "I know."

"He's got a Masters degree in chemistry and did a post grad. in physics. Heriot Watt Uni. up in Edinburgh. He worked for a while at Aldermaston, in Berkshire. That's where they manufacture Trident nuclear warheads. He moved from there to Burghfield. That's another nuclear weapons establishment. They assemble the warheads there. He also did a year up in the wilds of Scotland at Dounreay. They've got what they call a fast breeder reactor up there on the North coast. All experimental I'm told. It's long been shut down. It was supposed to produce more radioactive fuel than it consumed. But for some reason the whole idea fizzled out. The powers that be stuck it up there in case of a major nuclear incident. If it went haywire the number of human casualties would be … hopefully, few. Damage limitation they call it. Not many people up there, but a lot of sheep. He came back to Newcastle and set up his business with a legacy from his old man. It was split between him and his sister so she partnered him. It was doing OK until a couple of years ago. He landed a big contract doing a complete refurbishment job on the reactors at a nuclear power station in Scotland. He lost a packet on it. That's when the rot set in."

Jack winced. "Christ, the prick is no dunce when it comes to mass extermination, that's for sure. The more I learn about Nicholson, the more he scares me. That's really useful info, Clare. You haven't lost your touch."

She found a morsel of satisfaction in his praise and envied his meticulous and forensic approach to the whole jigsaw of clues and peripheral information. Privately she was itching to get back to Sellafield herself. Even to interview Nicholson. But she fought against it. She knew if there was a conclusion to the affair Jack would engineer it and would supply her with all the salient facts that would set the country, if not the world, on its heels. They had talked well into the late evening, lounging on the settee, Clare with her gin and tonic, Jack with his Scotch. The TV was switched off and the atmosphere was warm, the conversation soft and drowsy with subdued friendliness. Jack ran over all the developments and all his theories and the reasons for them. He saw her excitement at the Cyprus connection, and her subduing of it when he mentioned Stella's supposition that McManus' ill- fated odyssey was for something other than the leak. He made a mental note not to mention her again that night. He poured her another gin and tonic. He wanted her mellow and receptive. He sensed she might, just might submit to his subtle seduction.

"Anyway," he whispered, touching a strand of her blond hair. "How's your investigation into council corruption going?"

"There's more fiddling than the whole string section of the London Philharmonic."

Jack smiled. "Keep at it. That's something I'd really like to get involved in."

"Of course." She finished her drink and eased herself slowly off the settee. "I need a shower," she said wearily.

"Will you be sleeping on your stomach?"

She turned, and looked at him, puzzlement on her face, as he sat back with an expectant grin and eyebrows raised.

She frowned. "Sleeping on my stomach? No, I don't think so... why?"

"Well... if not... can I?"

She tutted gently. "What an optimist... see you in the morning."

"What's in it, Bridget. Anything interesting?" Jack said,

anticipating some revelation as he opened the lid of the laptop.

"Nothing much that I can make out. There are things that might strike a chord with you, but as far as I can see just normal general traffic. A few visits to the 'Eager Beaver' porn site. Orders from Amazon. Irrelevant e-mails... you know, birthday greetings and the like. Some flight reservations. Nothing really that jumps out at you. Lists and innocent looking technical stuff...you know. There might be something in there that is relevant to you, but nothing that sets off any alarm bells with me. We've managed to by-pass any random passwords. It's all there, so fill your boots, as they say."

Jack nodded. "OK Bridget, that's great. Thanks for your help. You're a star."

"Have you any more flattery up your sleeve?"

"Flattery...why?"

"Because, a few more endearing words and I could have told you that all the mats in McManus' car were slightly contaminated. I mean radioactive contamination. So were his shoes. We've had the specialists in, in space suits to cart the stuff away. His house needs a good going over, Jack. It could be contaminated... and everyone in it. I didn't mention it to the powers that be but it needs attention, Jack."

Jack took a deep breath. "Shit, I've been in there!" He thought for a moment. "No, that'll have to wait until this whole pantomime develops. We've got a thing going on here Bridget and we can't afford to spook anybody. There're bigger threats than that looming. Thank you once again. If I wasn't married I'd be after you like a shot."

Bridget smiled. Then the smile turned into a sad frown. "As if that would stop you, you rogue. Such is life," she whispered.

Father Joseph McManus woke from a troubled sleep. The conflict of social conscience against religious dogma had him in a turmoil. His mind see-sawed between the sanctity of the confessional and his moral obligation to Christ's creatures. He dressed slowly, deep in fretful thought. His breakfast of Muesli and toast was tasteless. All his senses battled within him about what was civilly right and what was thought to be correct in the eyes of the organisation he had given his life to. All that, in exchange for deliverance from the torments of hell and the delights of heaven. He sat for an hour, slowly stroking a black bible. Then, with a sigh, he stood up. He had decided on a compromise. He would hint at what had been his brother's predicament, then leave it to the experts to interpret it to whatever conclusion they could. He hoped it would be the right one.

It was another frosty morning as he stepped out. He held his black cloak tightly against himself as he walked to the road and turned into Stella's drive. The car was not there, but it didn't register with him. The bell chimed from somewhere down the passage toward the living room and he waited, but there was no blurred image coming toward the glass door. He rang again. Nothing. He peered into the living room through the window on his right. No-one. A great wave of relief ran through him. It was as though it was meant to be. It was a divine intervention. He was not to stray from the cramped edicts of his faith. He turned and walked slowly away, his mind suddenly untroubled. It was a sign, he resolved. The Church had won. The mental battle dismissed as a victory over temptation.

On the other side of the main road, a white van slowed to a stop. The driver's window slid slowly down. A broad-shouldered swarthy man with a thick black beard, watched the priest as he walked with his head hunched into his shoulders and unsure steps down Stella's drive and onto the roadside path. He watched as he turned onto the church driveway and the faint crunch of his feet on the gravel continued as he walked toward his sanctuary. The man picked up his mobile and dialled. The voice was deep and guttural. "Hello, Henry?"

"Yes."

"Henry, it's Khasan. I have him spotted."

"Good man. When?"

"As soon as everything perfect. Soon. You will hear about it when it's done."

"Will you ring me?"

"No. I think it will be reported."

"Don't delay, for Christ's sake."

"No…no delay."

Khasan Ismailov dialled again, this time to Cyprus. "Hello Ibragim, it's Khasan. The priest… I have seen him. He looks an old man. Do you want him silenced… for good?"

"Is there any other way? The project is too near completion Khasan. Remember what happened to our families and friends. You have let nothing stop you in the past. Remember looking into the dead face of your mother and your daughter. Remember your wife confined to that rotting asylum for the insane… there is no other way."

Khasan nodded to himself. "I will arrange."

Stella studied the list of entries for Henry Nicholson into Sellafield. There were many over the previous six months. They were timed. Some showed him to be on site most of the day, others, for two or three hours. Jack was suddenly engrossed in the contents of the laptop and he had asked her to see if any link could be made between Nicholson's visit and the lists of altered numbers. It was boring repetitive work but there was always a sliver of anticipation that suddenly something would gel and click into place. Jack poured over page after page of computer visits. He smiled to himself at the 'Eager Beaver' porn site. He imagined McManus in the privacy of his office having a clandestine peek at the uninhibited naked flesh spread all over the screen in contortions his wife would never even contemplate or be capable of, even in her wildest moments of passion. The latest purchase from Amazon had him wondering. It was for four golf bags. All identical.

Purchased in February of that year. Delivery to N.N.S. He assumed they would be for McManus himself and his three golf buddies, but he thought it strange that McManus would be acting as a shopper for all of them. The flight bookings were also bought on his credit card. Four seats in June, August and October. The reservations were in all four names. There was also another booked flight. January 6th in the New Year. Again, in all four names. Jack called Stella over.

"Look at this. Seaward said there wasn't another golf trip booked. Here's one for January. But it's from Manchester. Most Newcastle flights to Cyprus stop after the end of October."

Stella gave a grunt. "That man's as bent as a dog's dick. He also underestimates the power of team Shaftoe. What has he got to hide by lying about another trip to Cyprus?"

"Not sure yet but we're getting there. It's slow but it's starting to come together. Like I've said before, there's more to this than just one murder. The Greek or Chechen or whatever you want to call him could well have been a plumber or a schoolteacher, but no, he had to be a goddam nuclear physicist. That's too much of a coincidence, Stella."

"So is this." She brought over the PuO2 lists. "See what's beginning to show up. I've checked Nicholson's visit dates so far only from March to May. On the days he was there it coincides with the days the PuO2 weights were altered."

Jack blew a low whistle of surprise. "I had a hunch that might be the case. Another coincidence? I very much doubt it. Stella, keep checking those lists right up to the last. I need to nip out to see someone."

"Who?"

"Professor Samuels, head of the physics department across at the Uni. He's waiting for me. I need to clarify something… something about PuO2."

Professor Charles Samuels was a typical intellectual. If there was a stereotyped mould for academics he was the template it was formed from. A small man; bald except for an untidy crop of white hair that grew wildly above his ears and well below the realms of both the collars of his shirt and thick tweed jacket. He sported a matching moustache that bore the faint stain of nicotine from a pipe, which poked out of the breast pocket of his jacket like a miniature periscope. He had rimless spectacles, which were always perched above his bushy eyebrows until he needed to examine something at close quarters and even then, his squinting eyes were only inches from the object in question. He looked up and smiled when Jack entered his office, which was heavy with books, scattered manuscripts, a desk top anglepoise and a Newton's cradle of five shiny balls suspended from a chrome frame.

"Jack, how nice to see you." He stood up and they shook hands. "What brings you into this temple of enlightenment?"

"Just that… enlightenment." Jack said as the professor gestured for him to sit down.

"Ah ha," he exclaimed. "At last someone who might believe what I tell them about the weird and wonderful workings of this world that we live in. It's all maths you know. Everything in this unending

Universe of ours is governed by some miraculous mathematical formula."

"I'm sure," Jack said. He had heard it all before from the same man. Whenever they needed some learned explanation of things scientific the Professor was always more than delighted to oblige. Jack often wondered just what attitude his students had and whether their reaction to his lectures was just one of bored acceptance of everything he said. Outside the university realms, he seemed to sense that his knowledge was gospel, and revelled in anyone who took a genuine interest.

"Prof, what can you tell me about Plutonium oxide. I mean I know it can be dangerous… but can it be made to explode? And if so how much would it take… any ideas?"

The professor sat back and he stared at the ceiling, a look of amusement on his face. "Well now, there's a thing," he said emphatically. "Plutonium oxide...eh." He tapped his chin with a forefinger. There've been some papers written on it in the past, that I know, but I'd need to investigate... dig around a bit. Might take a while. I've got a lecture in ten minutes. Can I get back to you later this afternoon?"

"Of course."

The Professor's face suddenly darkened. "Can I ask why you want this? You're not about to become an anarchist are you?" he said with amused concern. Someone from your section was asking questions about this the other day."

"No... no, that would be my assistant. D.C. van Kirk. It's just something I need to understand." Jack tapped his nose and winked. "You know how it is, Prof."

The Professor stood up and nodded, tight lipped, falling immediately into the role of conspirator.

Jack drove back to the station. Sleet began to fall; big wet flakes drifting lazily down from a dark sky and melting on the road. It matched his mood. He had a premonition that the professor's news would be the harbinger of some dreadful event.

Back at Robert's Hill, D.I. Coulson was waiting for him. "Jack, I've read your report. Now listen. You're taking your eye off the ball here. If there's a murder...and we half agree there is, we need the culprit. You're getting sidetracked. Look for the bastard that killed McManus. We'll think about all this Sellafield bullshit later, OK?"

Jack could feel a red mist coming down. He fought to control himself. There wasn't time to count to ten. He slammed a fist down on the desk top. A pen shot up and clattered onto the floor. An empty coffee cup followed. "Boss, I'm on to something here, for Christ's sake! The murder, Nicholson and the Sellafield duo are all connected. I just need time to get all the bits together and the whole thing will gel. Jesus, Boss, you saw in the report what they do across there. I'm waiting for Professor Samuels to get back to me on just how dangerous that Plutonium Oxide is. We could be on the brink of a major... and I mean major, heist. Not in money. Not in piles of gold bullion or diamonds. In fucking egg-cups full of powder that could...I don't know...blow the whole fucking world to kingdom come. It could be that McManus was coming to see Clare about those altered Pu02 figures. Why would he have those papers secreted away and not the site survey? For Christ's sake give me some encouragement!"

Coulson stared at him, his annoyed frowning face deep in thought. His false teeth started to move like a storm-battered dingy. It seemed like an age before he replied, his voice low and menacing.

"Jack, you'd better be right or Charteris will have my bollocks on a pole for all to see."

He slapped the report down on the desk. "What goes on over there at Sellafield is their problem. We shouldn't get involved in anything other than the murder... but from what you say, well, too many cooks and all that bullshit." He poked a finger at the report. "And so is that. No hard evidence, not even a sniff of a probable suspect. All bloody theory. All 'maybe and what if'. Get some goddam hard facts, Jack so I don't have to go into Charteris' office with a book down my pants. OK?"

Jack nodded quickly. "OK. Thanks for the vote of confidence," he muttered with gentle sarcasm.

It was after three when Stella came back with the Plutonium list and the record of Nicholson's visits.

"Well it all fits. All the altered figures coincide with the days Nicholson was on site."

Jack nodded. "I could have put money on it."

"What does it mean?"

"It means he was spiriting away that Pu02. I'll bet my life on it. Whatever he took came off the recorded weights and the record was adjusted accordingly."

"For what purpose?"

"I don't know but I will shortly. Can you tot up all the altered amounts? I'm waiting for the Prof to ring back. Have we any info on that call McManus made to the Ministry of Defence in London? And we need to speak to Seaward again about that teatime phone call to McManus. Let's see what lame excuse the bastard comes up with this time."

"The trace just came in while Coulson was spitting his dummy out. Somebody called Drummond, Ralph Drummond. Apparently he's well up the slippery Civil Service ladder."

"Hmm, I think I need to give him a call."

His phone rang before he could dial. It was Professor Samuels. *"Hello Jack, I've managed to find some information for you. There was a paper produced in 1998 by an American called Richard L Garwin. He was a Senior Fellow for the Science and Technology Council on Foreign Relations in New York. He warned then that stored plutonium in any form poses a serious risk of nuclear proliferation. There are two main grades, weapons grade and reactor grade. Both of course could be made into bombs. Then there are quality factors which could be many and varied, so critical amounts can differ immensely."*

"So there's nothing exact. It's all vague."

"If we are considering Plutonium oxide there was an American physicist, not well known, but brilliant in his field called Ted Taylor. He was a genius in nuclear weaponry. He specialised for a while in producing what I would call tiny nuclear bombs. He designed one called... would you believe 'Davy Crockett.' It weighed only fifty pounds and the whole bomb only measured about twelve inches across. Now we get to the crux of the matter. Peter Zimmerman, another physicist, experimented on a proposal by Taylor and demonstrated that a one kiloton nuclear weapon could be made relatively easily with plutonium oxide.

"How big is a kiloton?"

"One thousand tons of TNT. It's a big bang. And a big radioactive fallout."

"And how much would you need?"

"Well according to Zimmerman, more than if it was bare metal, but it seems like it all depends on the quality or the purity. That would be to make a nuclear device. And that's a complicated and highly engineered piece of kit. You can easily make a dirty bomb with any amount."

"Hell, Prof, what's a dirty bomb?"

"Get some conventional explosives and tuck some plutonium oxide powder in there somewhere. The bomb goes bang and does damage but the powder flies way off in to the air, contaminating crops, water, food and a poor man miles away sitting enjoying himself gets an invisible sprinkling in his beer. Nasty, Jack. Death will certainly follow. It's called Alpha radiation, you know."

A cold sickening feeling of dread gripped at Jack's stomach. It was as he had imagined. "Thanks, Prof. Thanks a million," he breathed.

"Think nothing of it, Jack… and Jack…"

"Yes?"

"If you've got any… well let's say… possibilities about this, I'll say no more than that. You need to get the appropriate authorities involved. Radioactivity with all its many and varied forms needs specialist attention… you know that don't you?"

"I hear you, Prof. At this moment in time it's nothing but I'd appreciate it if you treat this as confidential. I'll make sure you get mentioned in despatches."

Professor Samuels laughed. *"You know me Jack. I love a bit of intrigue. My lips are sealed."*

The phone went dead. Stella was hovering, waiting for the news. "Stella, this is getting bigger by the minute. I'm tempted to call in the big guns but… but fuck it, we're going to follow this to a conclusion if old shagnasty Coulson will let us. What started as a simple suicide has turned into a possible international bloody incident and I'm going to be in the front row when the photos are taken. Are you with me?"

Stella nodded.

"Right. Let's get Mr… er, Drummond on the phone."

There wasn't time. Coulson strutted up to his desk.

"Jack, what the fuck have you been up to?" Charteris wants to see you pronto at HQ. Like now! No explanation, just get him over here now. He's crapping himself and so am I. Get over there and get straight back to me. OK?"

Leslie Charteris had his back to the door, staring out of the window, hands clasped behind him. Jack knocked and walked in. Charteris kept on staring. He was a tall man, broad and prematurely bald. He had a curious round, childishly smooth face with piercing blue eyes and puffed red cheeks. He was forty but looked like the artist Raphael could have used him as a model for one of his cherubs.

Jack stood, waiting for him to turn but he didn't. All the way over to Force HQ Jack had poured over his whole involvement in the case. He was sure he hadn't overstepped any protocol or given anyone any cause to complain unless it was to undermine his investigative position. He was ready for the worst.

"Sit Jack," he said in his usual soft menacing voice.

Jack sat.

"You know something Jack," he said to the window. "When Church sent you up here he warned me you were a good detective, but a loose cannon. He wasn't exaggerating on the first point. Your devotion to this godforsaken cause has not gone unnoticed. The second, I thought I could control by keeping you away from the gunpowder, so to speak. And up to now I have…" He finally turned around. "But it looks like you're upsetting people in high places, Jack. I've had a Mr Drummond on the phone from London. He is apparently a big noise at the Ministry of Defence. Says he wants you off the McManus murder enquiry. Says he wants the case dropped. Says you're making too many waves at Sellafield; upsetting too many people. Telling them they're all suspects. Even the bloody security police."

"That's bullshit, sir." Jack spat vehemently. "It was standard interview practice. I asked them to confirm where they were at the time of the murder… and that's all."

Charteris sat down. He studied Jack for a moment, his brow furrowed in thought; his forefinger pressed against his lips. He sighed. "I've read your report. All this conjecture about… what is it called? … plutonium oxide. I agree there's more to this than meets the eye and I should… I should be alerting the appropriate people."

Jack leaned forward. "Don't. Please don't. Give me more time. Let me pull all the bits together first. If you get the C.N.C involved, they might go in en-masse and the whole illicit operation, whatever it might be, could dissolve without a trace. I can handle it together with the murder investigation. I'm investigating a possible murder related to a radiation leak, that's all. No one has an idea about any other aspect so there shouldn't be any alerts go out."

Charteris was silent again. He scratched the back of his head. Then he spoke, his voice no more than a whisper. "I don't know if I can be a part of this Jack. There are too many big guns getting involved and getting too agitated. This Drummond guy wants to see you Jack. He wants you down at Whitehall in the morning. I suggested I come with you but…" he shrugged, "but he said no, he just wanted to meet you. I said you were my responsibility and so was the McManus investigation, but he was adamant. 'No need' he said. 'Just want to meet him and see what makes him tick.' We'd better humour him, Jack. I'll clear it with Coulson. I'll ring Drummond and tell him you'll be at his office before lunch. Get your arse down there on the early train tomorrow OK?"

Jack nodded OK, sir. Will do. Do you know that McManus phoned this Drummond bloke early on the day he died?"

"No it's not in your report. Why would he contact him?"

"I was about to find out before I came over here. And there's something else I didn't get in the report because at the moment it's just a wild stab in the dark."

"What?"

"Maybe McManus wasn't heading to the Press about the

radiation leak. Maybe he was blowing the whistle on something else. Something more sinister, involving Plutonium oxide."

"Something else… Like what?"

"I don't really know. It's just a hunch from a conversation he had before he left for Newcastle and those documents found in his car. But what needs unravelling is why McManus didn't have the site survey with him as evidence, but he did have Plutonium oxide lists secreted away in the pages of his car service book. I think there's the possibility of a major crime here, sir. Bigger than one murder and it involves Plutonium oxide and that's a big radioactive nasty."

"He was coming to see your wife, wasn't he?"

"Looks like it. Clare had interviewed him a week or so before the murder about the leak. Tip off from one of Nicholson's workmen."

"Ah, yes. Nicholson. He's got that business near here. Down by the river. Hope you're not giving the Press any forward knowledge of all of this. We don't want them twisting and exaggerating… well not yet anyway."

"Clare's just waiting for arrests then she'll publish. Nicholson's brother-in-law, in Cyprus just might be a leading man in this saga."

Charteris went back into thought mode then said suddenly, "Right, Jack. I'm going to hold back. I'm letting you off the leash unless this bugger Drummond leans hard on us. Like I said, he wants you off the case and wants the case dropped altogether. I need a bloody good reason why, Jack. When you see him, find out. Ring me as soon as you're out of his office."

Coulson was waiting for him. There was an anxious look of impending doom on his face.

"Well… well what did he say? He's been on the phone. All he told me is you've got to go to London… alone. First thing tomorrow."

Jack took of his jacket and draped it over the back of his seat. "Some big noise wants the case dropped. I have to go to MOD headquarters in Whitehall tomorrow. There's a high-flyer called Drummond wants the whole case closed down. He was the guy McManus phoned early on the day he died."

Coulson paled. "Christ what have you done, Jack. You've upset a few in your time but... fuck me... the MOD... in London."

Jack shrugged. "I've upset no one and neither has Stella. It's been a normal investigation with plenty of possible answers and a few possible suspects but it looks like they're just not interested in catching a murderer."

Coulson blew out a noisy breath, his cheeks puffing up, his head going slowly from left to right, blinking rapidly. "Is Charteris all right about it? I mean he's not blaming the unit for this, is he?"

"No, he's O.K. He wants me to stay with it until Drummond gives a good enough reason why we should pull the plug."

Coulson relaxed. A glimmer of relief came to his face. "Ring me as soon as, Jack. I want to know what's huffed this prick Drummond and what's going on in that civil service brain of his."

"Charteris wants me to ring him first."

Coulson moved closer to him, a broad smile putting vertical wrinkles down his face. He fondled Jack's tie for a second. "Do me a big favour, Jack."

"What?"

"Ring me first. Let me, for once, get one up on the bastard."

Stella laid a couple of sheets on his desk. "Weights totted up. Total just over one kilo."

"That's an amount," he whispered, his mind suddenly crowding with wild, frightening possibilities. *Enough for a nuclear bomb or a dirty bomb? Was there more taken before the current lists or more planned after?*

"Thanks Stella. We need to move quickly. Heard the news? I'm off to get my arse kicked down in the city tomorrow."

He told her the story.

"Now this stinks. When does a murder carry no consequences?"

"Exactly. I think we've stirred up the proverbial hornet's nest. Tomorrow will tell. I'll try to get back here before you leave and we'll go over the whole lousy saga."

"I'll wait anyway. I want to bum a lift home. The car's in for a MOT and service. The garage will give me a lift in."

"Right. Tomorrow will you go through all that crap on the laptop in case I've missed something? And ring Seaward will you? Just mention we picked up his call to McManus. So why did he ring him? Play him a bit. Get him sweating…OK."

Stella smiled. There was a satisfying feeling of control, both from her position and the ability to have someone who broadcast an outward invincibility to feel vulnerable. She rested her buttocks against the side of his desk. She folded her arms and looked down at him.

"We make a good team, don't we Jack. Pity you're spoken for. We could have taken this relationship a grade or two higher."

Jack gave a sad smile. "Yes…yes I think we could."

CHAPTER 10

It was an eventful journey. The 8am train should have arrived at King's Cross at 10.49 but malingered just outside Peterborough while they prised a dead cow off the track. It eventually rolled in at 11.05 as a metallic voice apologised for the delay. Jack couldn't wait to free himself from the carriage. A woman sat opposite him who got on at Durham. Fiftyish; suicide blonde; overweight; wrapped in a beige faux fur coat and reeking of some cheap perfume. By the time the train ground to a halt near Peterborough, he felt as though he knew both of her late husband's intimately. He could give a lecture to medical students on the progression of emphysema in her first and write a novel based on the predilection of her second for whisky, greyhound racing and loose women. She was meeting her sister who lived in Gillingham and if the train had another half hour to run past London, he would have known her sister's life story past the age of twenty and the convoluted saga of how she went from Durham to Kent via Abu Dhabi, in minute detail.

He bid her a grateful farewell and took a taxi to Whitehall. The city was buzzing as usual: cars, buses, taxis and commercial vehicles in an endless noisy nose to tail parade. The massive grade 1 listed off-white building came into view as he passed the Cenotaph and the taxi turned into Horseguards Avenue. Across the Thames he could see the London Eye, still revolving in slow motion. He had been back to London several times since joining the Northumbria Force and the yearning for all the action such a gigantic cosmopolitan city could offer on both sides of the law seeped into his mind on each visit. He paid the taxi fare and stood facing the imposing columned entrance of the Ministry of Defence. He looked up past floor after floor of small paned windows and he imagined the hive of intense subdued activity that took place seven days a week within its high walls and down in the three- storey underground complex. No let-up in a world of uncertainty and never-ending friction. He wondered what Drummond would be like; what his attitude would be; whether he would get a reproachful lecture or a lame excuse to drop the case. Whatever it was, he resolved, he would stand his corner. He knew he was on the righteous side of the affair and to drop the case was an affront to justice.

He walked up the steps and into the large busy reception area. He showed his ID and asked for Ralph Drummond. He stood for five minutes watching the human traffic coming in and going out and wondered what they were all about; their business and destination. Eventually a young black woman approached him with a smile and an outstretched hand. "Detective Shaftoe. Pleased to meet you. I'm Sharon, Mr Drummond's P.A. Please follow me."

He passed through an airport-style security sensor and they took a lift to the sixth floor. On the way up she didn't speak. The lift doors slid open onto a short corridor of offices that seemed to reflect the status of their inhabitants. Large glass windows looking out into the corridor; polished wood doors; brass nameplates and expensive looking furniture. At the end, a big open office of thirty desks or more, each one occupied; heads staring at computer screens and between them an eclectic mix of men and women distributing and collecting papers. The recipients did not look up. The deliverers did not linger. Sharon stopped short of the main office. The nameplate on the door said 'R Drummond.' She knocked and opened it. "Detective Shaftoe, sir." She moved to the side to let him in. Ralph Drummond stood up from behind a large mahogany desk, smiling. He was a person that would be hard to describe in an identity line up. Average height and build; about late forties and dressed in a blue double-breasted pin-stripe suit. He had a head of black hair, parted at the side and combed flat. If there was one feature someone might remember, it was a prominent dimple in his jutting chin that reminded Jack of Kirk Douglas. Not the usual requirement for special staff. No tattoos; no birthmarks; no recognisable features were all on the application form.

"Ah ha, Shaftoe," he said with enthusiasm, in a perfect BBC voice, "good of you to come."

Jack rankled immediately. He did not like to be called by his singular surname. Mr. Shaftoe or Jack was fine no matter how well he knew the person. To him, addressing someone in that manner gave the impression of superiority to the deliverer and inferiority to the recipient.

"Pleased to meet you... Drummond," he replied with distinct emphasis on the name.

If his reply had hinted that Jack was not overawed in his presence, it didn't show.

He signalled him to sit. Sharon appeared with two coffees and Drummond sat back studying his visitor. "Well now...Jack... Can I call you Jack?"

"Sure...can I call you Ralph?"

Drummond was intrigued with the man in front of him. He had been in the Civil Service for over twenty years. For the last ten his position was such that as soon as he entered the building he was 'sir' or at the most familiar, 'Mr. Drummond'.

"Yes," he said with some amusement. "Yes, call me Ralph. Now Jack, I wanted to meet you for two reasons. First, to see what sort of man you are. By that, I mean I'm fascinated that your investigation into the McManus death progressed from a suicide to a murder. And second, how you came to make big waves at Sellafield. By the way, Jack, I'd better caution you that this conversation comes under the official secrets act. Do you understand that?"

Jack nodded. "Whatever you say. Now can I ask you why you want me off this case...of which I am sure *is* murder... and the investigation scrapped?"

The traffic past the office door was never ending and had him constantly glancing through the glass as people, some in military uniform strutted by, carrying files, boxes and briefcases.

"Busy place you have here," he added.

Drummond sniffed. "Always busy, Jack. The world is in constant turmoil. Sometimes I wonder why we cling on to our Victorian image of trying to involve ourselves in every skirmish that crops up in the world. But we do, so we act, thanks to our being joined at the hip with the U.S." He took a sip of coffee and leaned back in his chair. "Now, first let me clarify something. You are aware of the situation at Sellafield. The leak from pond five and McManus' paranoia about safety?"

"Yes. I've had it explained by Mr Butterworth."

"Good. Therefore, you know the consequences of an immediate shut down. The job losses and revenue will be gone forever. Not to mention awkward...really embarrassing questions the bloody politicians will come up with in the House."

"Yes."

"Believe me, Jack, we have the problem in hand... and we are dealing with it. There was no need for the drastic action that would have resulted in McManus going public as he so often threatened."

"He rang you, didn't he, early on the morning of the day he died?"

The voice was monotone and robotic. "Indeed he did. He was calm and in control. He rang to say his site survey was nearing completion and would consult and report when it was finished. He reassured me that there would be nothing done until then. He was so positive on that. We spoke for at least fifteen minutes and he gave me no cause to doubt his word."

There was a quick tap on the office door and it swung open. Jack turned automatically. Drummond's face took on a look of pained horror. The man stared for an instant at Jack. The door slammed shut in a second but already Jack's mind had recoiled in shock. He turned to look at Drummond. He had his eyes shut and his arms folded tightly in front of him, as though in pain. Memory shunted into memory. The facts all came together in a flash. Jack instantly recognised the man, squatting against the lorry wheel, bathed in the blue-white beam of a floodlight, crying in anguish at the sight he had just witnessed. He remembered the concave scar running from his hairline to the bridge of his nose; his olive skin and black hair. It was the Spanish lorry driver.

Jack leapt to his feet. "You killed him...you bastards killed him!" Jack spat out the words. "It's no wonder you want the fucking case dropped!"

Drummond desperately waved him back down to his seat. "Sit, Jack. Please sit! You were not meant to see that," he breathed. "Let me explain. Please let me explain. Now you need to know the facts."

"Facts...facts! I already know the fucking facts! Your man shot McManus. But he didn't make a very good job of faking a suicide. He didn't realise McManus was left-handed...or that he left him holding the gun like a two-penny lollypop. What's his code name? double oh seven, brackets apprentice! Oh Christ...you know what comes straight to mind? David Kelly and the Chilcot enquiry. Remember that Mr. Drummond? Mr. Kelly was found with his wrists cut and an overdose of Co-proxamol inside him, back in 2003. There were no fingerprints on the knife and no fingerprints on the sleeve of tablets. Official verdict suicide... I remember the case well. One of your proper professionals then?"

Drummond lowered his head. "No comment," he whispered.

Jack shook his head in desperation. "The bloody lorry driver. Whose half-baked idea was it to have the prick stay at the scene? He should have been halfway down the country by the time someone discovered the body. Anyway, how come Scarface there is one of your goons? He stands out a mile. I thought you guys had to be anonymous and blend in with the crowd."

Drummond cupped his head with both hands. "The fact that he looks like that has its advantages, Jack. A scar like that rules him out of the club... or so our adversaries would think." He pointed to his chin. "Me likewise but I've always been safely deskbound. But it wasn't the lorry driver, Jack. He was there to make sure the police got there first. We didn't want McManus undiscovered until dawn...or later. Our man did what he had to do and was... as you so rightly assumed... halfway down the country when the police arrived. You see... we have our ways, Jack. Some quite unique, don't you think? It fooled you didn't it?"

"Who did it had me fooled but not the crime itself. Why? Why for Christ's sake did you have to kill him?"

Drummond took a deep breath. "Your coffee's getting cold. Let me tell you a few things."

Jack took a sip. Drummond sat silent and deep in thought for a moment then spoke with quiet determination. "Remember Jack, this conversation is still under the official secrets act."

"I haven't forgotten. It sure needs to be."

"Mr. McManus was classified as a P.S.S. That is a Potential State Subversive. Sounds nasty but it's a very broad term covering a surprising number of people in this country of ours: From all walks of life: from the top to the bottom. Even some who... if we as a country were in a vulnerable situation might turn to our enemies for succour.

Are you with me? Most of them lead exemplary lives, but it includes anyone from a budding terrorist to people with even a little classified or useful information that might be used, given circumstances, to the detriment of the nation. In other words, McManus was a person who could do damage to the country's wellbeing, whatever that might be. You already know what that damage could have been. His attitude about the safety at Sellafield was getting more obsessive by the day. He constantly harangued us about the state of the site and our supposed lack of action. He contacted the International Atomic Agency and Euratom, who…" he shrugged "… leaned heavily on to us. We went through the motions and managed to convince them that a threat to health and safety was not a pressing issue. We kept trying to convince McManus but he wasn't having it. We examined his proposal for a complete and comprehensive survey to nail it once and for all and told him we would act on his findings. That seemed to pacify him. When he rang on the morning he died, as I said, he sounded totally satisfied with the situation. We arranged to meet as soon as the survey was finished. I promised a full team to find a solution to the problem. He was overjoyed. He thanked me. Said it was a great relief and he could now sleep at nights. We left it at that… and then…and then Seaward rang me… Terry Seaward. That's McManus' second in command, by the way."

Jack nodded. "I know him."

"What had happened between early morning and early evening God only knows but Seaward was frantic. He said McManus was planning to go to the Press that night and had just left. He said McManus was intent on giving the world the complete story with all the inherent dangers that would affect the workforce and Cumbria…and farther afield." Drummond dropped his head and sat staring at his desktop. "He had to be stopped, Jack. Even Seaward agreed he had to be stopped without even thinking how."

"So how did you manage that?"

He looked up. "We had a suitable agent...who was...qualified, in the area. He had a pending, less onerous assignment in Sunderland. It didn't take him long to get to Newcastle or thereabouts. I asked Seaward if he could suggest a place that McManus could stop...make some excuse to get him to break his journey. He came back ten minutes later. He said he had convinced him to wait in the lay-by east of a town called Corbridge."

"How... and for what.?"

"Seaward said he told McManus he would bring him the site survey documents and some other readings to back up his story; that he realised what he was doing was right and he would support him all the way. I contacted our man and our lorry driver who... who was intending to meet up with the said Sunderland visitor. He had certain items for him in the lorry."

"What sort of items?"

"Just...items. Let us leave it at that. I briefed the pair of them ... and he... they..." Drummond gave a quick shrug, "got to the lay-by and there he was. The Sunderland assignment was postponed."

Jack hummed a note of disbelief. "Did you really fall for that bullshit from Seaward?"

Drummond frowned. "I believed him...yes. Why should I not?"

"Firstly it's a piss poor ruse. How did he know that McManus didn't have copies of the survey with him. Secondly, from our investigations... Ralph... a few words of an overheard conversation led us to believe that McManus and Seaward had been arguing at around about five or six that evening. We think that McManus was heading to Newcastle about another matter, which was plaguing him. It could be that you killed him for nothing. It seems strange that his attitude after his phone call with you had changed so dramatically. Why? What could possibly have caused that?"

Drummond scratched the top of his head, then

smoothed his hair down with a slow flat hand. "I don't know," he whispered.

"How's this for a theory. Seaward was using you as an excuse. He knew you would do something drastic to keep him quiet. He conjured up that half-baked story to get you to act. McManus was heading to the Press to reveal some illegal scheme that was going to make him, Seaward and McManus junior a lot of money, together with one Henry Nicholson, boss man of a contractor who's regularly on site. McManus chickened out and was hell bent on telling the Press."

A frown of alarm creased Drummond's face. "What sort of illegal scheme? And why go to the Press? Why not the C.N.C if his conscience suddenly began to bother him?"

"I reckon he thought it would be just another cover up. He didn't want to give them any kudos for stopping... or should I say hiding, a major breach of security. McManus had a big gripe against the C.N.C in the shape of one Sergeant Driscoll. If the story broke in the Press he...and the rest of them would have egg on their faces, big time."

Drummond paled. "Hold on. What are you saying here? You're talking about an illegal scheme and a

major breach of security. What the hell do you know, sergeant?"

"I know nothing. I think plenty. Now I don't have a murder inquiry, I want to nail those bastards to that big dome they have up there." Jack shook his head slowly. "I still can't believe McManus needed killing."

Drummond hunted among his teeth with his tongue. Then he spoke. The words were slow; his voice low and meant to emphasise his statement: "Jack, you were in the Army. An exemplary record...except for a few breaches of discipline. I've seen it. Did you shoot anyone in your line of duty?"

Jack stared him straight in the eye. "A few...in the Middle East. None in Northern Ireland."

"Why? Why did you point your gun at a perfect stranger

and kill him?

"Because he… all of them, were a threat to me and… and my colleagues."

"And on a greater scale, a threat, however minor, to your country."

"I suppose so."

"Did you have any qualms about pulling the trigger?"

Jack thought for a moment then nodded. "Some… but it was necessary."

"Exactly, Jack. In this weird civilisation of ours you get jailed for murdering a civilian but a medal for killing a declared enemy of the Country. Forget McManus, he's now history. Maybe a mistake…but these things happen as they do in all conflicts. Now for God's sake tell me what you think is going on up there." His voice became gruff; urgent, demanding an answer.

Jack shuffled in his chair. His instinct was to not trust this man. There was something of an automaton in his attitude. Cold and bloodless; without ethics or the concept of mitigation. He wondered what he was like at home; whether he had a wife who he treated with silent tolerance or subtle ridicule and children who he might have browbeaten into subservience. It was hard to imagine him being capable of a normal loving family relationship. Yet, Jack imagined, he might change once down the steps and into Horseguards Avenue; become a mild-mannered and tolerant pillar of the community who, among unsuspecting friends and neighbours, was all things good and honourable.

"Come on, Jack, I need this information," he said. "A breach of security is a bigger fish than radiation problems at the moment. What the hell is Seaward and Co. up to?"

Jack didn't want to tell him. His instinct told him that Drummond would be straight on the phone and he would be muscled out of the whole operation. He suddenly realised he had said too much already but if he left Drummond wondering, alarm bells would ring all the way from London to Cumbria in a trice anyway. He knew he had to bring him up to date on his investigation so far.

"We still under the official secrets act?" he said raising his eyebrows.

Drummond sat back, panic creasing his face. "Of course. Of course."

"I believe… and at this moment in time it's only a possibility, but a strong possibility, that our suspects are planning to…or already have removed Plutonium Oxide from the Sellafield site."

Colour drained from Drummond's face. His head was pulled back in disbelief. He blinked rapidly as the consequences of such an act echoed around his reasoning. "No. No! Jack, that's impossible! How? How could they do it? The security is top of the range. The operations are monitored constantly. No Jack, that can't be correct."

Jack folded his arms and inched himself closer to the desk. He gave him a verbal précis of the case from day one and explained his suspicions gleaned from the interviews and the scant evidence he and Stella had so far managed to accumulate. "They're guilty, Ralph… guilty as hell. All I've got to do is get some cast iron proof."

Drummond reeled backward in his chair. He put his right forefinger between his teeth and gazed out beyond Jack and into the communal office. "I need to get the C.N.C. involved now… immediately," he snapped, "and Special Branch… and Scotland Yard's Counter Terrorism Command."

"No! No!" Jack said as an order. "Don't! … think! The operation needs to be done quietly…no suspicion aroused. They get spooked and the whole thing could turn to chicken shit. Ralph… Mr Drummond… I now have no murder to chase up, but I'm up to my neck in the case. Let me sort it. One suspect is on my patch. As far as anyone at Sellafield knows, I'm still looking for a murderer and nothing else. Clear it with Charteris and whoever else you need to deal with and let me finish the job."

Drummond thought for a moment, tugging gently at the

loose skin under his chin. "You're suggesting a good old fashioned Hollywood style covert operation? This isn't the movies you know," he whispered with some ridicule in his voice. "Although we have however, had plenty of experience of such things Jack, as you can well imagine."

"Call it what you like. That's just what this little shindig needs. But as far as McManus goes, Charteris needs to know the truth. You realise that don't you."

Drummond nodded. He took a deep breath "I'll give you a week, then it's more than my inevitable gong from Buck house is worth not to involve the correct authorities responsible. My wife will kill me if being Lady Drummond doesn't materialise. I can see you've done an excellent job of detection on this, Jack. Even to the extent of sussing out the mistakes of our so-called expert...shall we say... 'laundryman'. But remember what you're dealing with here. Plutonium Oxide. If there's any off site already and pray that there's not, it needs to be handled by experts... you understand?"

"Yes. I know. I've had it all explained."

"I thought you might. Now it was my intention to take you for some lunch but I'd appreciate it Jack if you get back up North and sort this out now as a matter of extreme urgency."

"I'll be on the next train."

They shook hands. Drummond looked him straight in the eye. "Good luck. God knows what will happen if we don't put a stop to this."

"We will put a stop to it. It's a pity when we do, your... 'laundryman' as you so fondly call him, couldn't get to them before the judge."

Drummond gave a sickly smile. "And Jack... if any of the McManus case happens to become common knowledge, you realise that we already have comprehensive plans in place. There will be a total denial backed up with whatever it takes to keep our reputation pure and clean. Are you clear on that?"

"Oh yes. Very clear. I would have expected nothing less. By the way I'll see you get your Luger back."

Drummond's face twisted into a pained grimace. He nodded, picked up the phone and called for Sharon to escort him out.

When she returned, he beckoned her in through the glass. She opened the office door. "Yes sir?"

Drummond's face was pale and his eyes wide and blinking with shock. "Get that bastard, Miguel in here, now!"

CHAPTER 11

Stella drove her car to the garage. It was a typical late November morning. A weak dawn hovered in the East with low, dark clouds threatening rain into the cold, damp air. She hated the winters in England and longed for the hot sunny days in Curacao that were not exaggerated by her childhood memories. She could still remember palm trees swaying gently in the warm breeze. She could see ocean going oil tankers nosing slowly in from the open sea at Willemstad, past the pontoon bridge and into the wide, sheltered Schottegat to moor at the refinery. She could still smell the vague ever- present aroma from its workings and the brightly painted Dutch style wooden houses remote from the Island's industry. It always flooded her memory on such days and left her with a pipedream to return, walk across that bridge at Willemstad and immerse herself in her idyllic carefree childhood life once again.

Her Mini was due its MOT and overdue a badly needed service. "Tomorrow afternoon," the mechanic said as he took her keys and tried not to mentally undress her. He whistled down the garage littered with bald tyres, the debris of crashed vehicles and two cars suspended in mid-air on hydraulic jacks. A young, fresh faced apprentice in grease-caked coveralls walked up grinning and wiping his hands on an oily rag.

"Fred, take this young lady to Robert's Hill Police Station and get me a cheese and onion pasty on the way back."

She was tempted to ring Jack, to make light of his impending meeting with Drummond but decided against it. She thought he would be preoccupied with his own thoughts on how to respond to whatever the mysterious Mr Drummond threw at him in the way of excuses for cancelling out a murder. Besides, she had work to do. A clinical examination of everything on the McManus laptop; a delicious call to Seaward and the delight of a subtle interrogation that would have him squirming. She hoped she could glean something meaningful from the laptop; something Jack might have missed; something that would give him a smile of satisfaction and initiate some positive action when he returned.

She sat at her desk for a few minutes, gathering all the strands of the investigation so far and drank a coffee. She checked the time. Eight fifteen. She decided to wait until the afternoon before contacting Seaward. It would give him a chance to settle down to what she thought he imagined would be a normal working day. She finished her coffee and opened the laptop.

It was two thirty in the afternoon when the white van came to a halt opposite St Cecilia's. It had stopped twice already that morning and Khasan Ismailov had sat for a few moments each time, wary that he was on double yellow lines and watching for the priest. He noticed that there were people arriving on foot at the church; couples; what looked like small families; an old man struggling painfully with two walking sticks. Cars drove onto the side of the wide gravel driveway to the church and he imagined a service was imminent. He glanced in his rear mirror to check for a warden sneaking up on him, then ahead. For the moment he was satisfied that he could observe without disturbance. A long shining black hearse came slowly around the corner from the main street followed by four mourner's cars. They turned into the church drive and stopped outside the heavy doors. Khasan watched with unblinking eyes and as the cars stopped, he saw the priest appear. "Now…now it must be done," he said to himself. "A funeral. A catholic funeral." He knew the service would take time. He knew he could do what he wanted to do without the stress of being interrupted. He sat watching as the coffin was lifted from the hearse and carried into the church. He noted the polished wood of the coffin and the brass handles that shone even in the dank light of a winter's afternoon. His thoughts went back to his homeland and the terrifying onslaught on Grozny and his country that winter in 1999. He tried not to bring his mother and his daughter back into his memories but he could not stop their grey lifeless images filling his mind. He could not stop the sound of the screaming disbelief of his wife as she stood, mouth wide open and tearing at her hair. He could hear the roar of the Russian bombers as they flashed overhead. He could see the vivid bursts of colour as the cluster bombs opened and sprayed a carpet of explosions across his village of Elistanzhi. Thirty-five civilians died in the attack. Five children died the next day. Some of the devices did not explode until they were picked up from the ground. One of the curious was his daughter. There was no shiny coffin of wood or ornate Muslim shroud for her. Only a soiled sheet. Since those days, his profession was forgotten. Revenge consumed all of his time and his senses. He became adept at snuffing out life. He had relished the demise of every Russian that happened to be in his sights whether it be by bullet or explosion, until he was forced to flee and engineer remotely, his sworn task. He joined a legion of Chechens hungry for vengeance, now scattered across the globe and was glad he was part of Ibragim's select band. He and the man in Cyprus were resolute in their dedication. The priest was expendable to ensure Ibragim's ultimate revenge. He had no qualms. His determined actions lit no spark of compassion. It had to be done.

He waited until all the mourners had filed into the church. The undertaker's pallbearers reappeared and stood together talking. Two lit cigarettes and leaned against one of the cars. Khasan started the engine and drove his white van slowly across the road and onto the gravel drive of Amen cottage. He opened the van door and rummaged among a pile of spanners and tools. He selected a few and slid them into the deep inside pocket of his jacket. He was calm and determined. He knew precisely what he had to do. He walked past the front door and around to the far gable end of the cottage. It backed onto Stella's small garden and a boundary stone wall with the far section of the graveyard beyond. He was aware that the house could be alarmed but his practiced eye had seen no external box and he knew, even if it was, the sudden sound of an intruder would probably go unnoticed or ignored as was the case so many times. He peered through a window into the small kitchen, waited a moment for signs of any possible unexpected guest, and then examined the internal window catch. He smiled; there was no need for a drastic assault to gain entry. He reached inside his coat and produced a spanner and a glasscutter. He drew a small arc across the corner of the bottom pane and tapped with the spanner. The glass broke, leaving jagged edges held in the frame. Quickly he knocked out enough for his hand to reach in and lever up the window catch. The window opened outward. In a second, he squeezed his big frame through and was on his knees on the kitchen bench, then standing on the floor. No sounds. No alarm. He smiled again when he saw the oven hob. He would not need to use his tools to loosen pipes. The hob was not recent and did not have a flame supervision device. A battery- operated gas lighter lay beside it. He knew his task would be an easy one. He peered from the kitchen, down the passage to the front entrance. There were closed doors on either side. Quickly he opened each one and glanced around. Radiators; no open fires. He slammed the doors shut. He looked up to the ceiling in the passage. A single bulb hung down from a pink lampshade. He found the light switch near the front door and flicked it on for a second, satisfied that it worked. He reached up and held the bulb gingerly in his hand. With his other he gently tapped at the thin glass with a small spanner until it broke into tinkling shards, revealing the filament. He brought a pen torch from his pocket, shone it into the remains of the bulb and checked the filament was still intact. He returned to the kitchen and held a hand on a small radiator that was positioned opposite the cooker. It was warm. He turned to the wall-mounted boiler which gave out a low buzz of activity. He flicked the control panel open and turned both the heating control and the hot water control to the off position. He lowered himself until he was at eye level with the control panel and could see the copper service pipes that supplied both water and gas underneath. He selected a spanner from his pocket and turned the gas valve to the off position. After a moment, the pilot light indicator turned from orange to red. He gave a short grunt of satisfaction then pressed the electric switch to off. He turned to the fridge freezer and pulled the plug out of the socket. He turned back to the oven hob and slowly turned the four dials on to maximum. The gas hissed benignly. Quickly he grabbed a towel, which was hanging on a rail next to the kitchen basin and climbed out of the window. He pushed it shut and stuffed the towel deep into the hole in the glass. He looked around for any sign that he had been seen. He saw no one. A dirge filtered through the afternoon air and he knew the funeral was still in progress. It would surely be the last of the day. He strode casually to the van and smiled again as he turned on the ignition. Ibragim would be pleased with his work. He pushed the gear lever into reverse, swung the van around in the drive and drove out into the street, heading for Sheffield.

Jack caught the train at two o'clock. His mind still reeled with the McManus revelation. State sponsored murder was usually the thing of novels and spy movies, yet in a way he should have guessed. He well remembered the Chilcot enquiry and the controversy over the death of David Kelly. It could have happened. This time it had happened. He and Stella had done the rounds, questioned the possible suspects and got nowhere. Now he knew the truth he could concentrate fully on the other crime that had reared its head almost since day one. He had time to grab a sandwich and a beer at King's Cross and rang Charteris, knowing full well that Drummond would have already given him all the details. He wasn't wrong. Charteris' voice was low and strangely despondent. *"Well Mr Shaftoe, you have friends in high places. Drummond wants you to finish what you started. I'm worried, Jack if you…we foul up on this we're in deep shit. When you get back brief your boss. I've spoken to him already. This McManus thing is a mess, Jack. Christ, I could hardly believe what he nearly admitted. See me first thing and let's get everything clear and in perspective. OK?"*

"Will do, sir. We won't foul up. I'm just about ready to nail the bastards."

"You'd better be right. Coulson has nightmares about his balls being removed without anaesthetic. You'd better start having them as well."

He rang Coulson from the train. Knowing that Charteris had already given him an outline of his meeting, it took the edge off the blasting he knew he would get for not contacting him first. Coulson was subdued, probably in awe of Drummond's decision and almost polite when Jack rang. *"Charteris has been on to me. This guy Drummond rang him. I know what happened. It stinks Jack, but we have to go along with it. We're getting all the support we need. All eyes are on us now. What time are you back?"*

"Gets in at 16.50 if it's on time. I'll be straight to the Station. Stella's been doing some more digging into the laptop but I'll bring you right up to date on everything.

153

Too…too contentious to discuss anything more just now."

"You can say that again. See you later."

He punched a number into his phone again and Clare answered. *"Well, how did it go?"* she said urgently.

He knew she would be desperate to hear the news. When he told her the night before that he was ordered to London, she was full of cautious doubt. "Watch it, Jack. They're ruthless down there. They don't want to see you for tea and a sticky bun."

When he added that they wanted him off the case and the case dropped, her caution turned to suspicion. "There's something amiss here, I'm telling you. It looks like you've upset someone, big time. Jesus, Jack this is going to make one hell of a story. Ring me, will you, as soon as."

The previous evening they had once again lounged on the settee, drinks in hand. He tried to put an arm around her but she pushed it away. It was a gentle push and it gave him a glimmer of hope that with another gin inside her she might just warm to his advances. But it was not to be. Since her return, her attitude had mellowed to an affable but sterile routine. After moving north, a sourness and fault- finding atmosphere had again slowly filtered into their lives without either of them realising it as their two professions collided. It had happened on occasion in London. He always felt that he was the one who was wronged and that Clare should understand the demands of his job. But it seemed she had not been in tune with that and it was only since the McManus case and their mutual interest in it, that she began to appreciate the genuine commitment required to carry out his job. Her feelings for him were returning but so far, she could not muster any intimacy that would let him into her bed.

"Clare, I'm on my way back…"

She interrupted him. *"What happened?"*

His mouth went dry. "Can't say too much over the phone…but it's big, Clare. Sensational. I don't know how much I can tell you at this stage."

"Jack! Come on. I need to know everything! For Christ' sake don't clam up on me now."

"I don't intend to but we need to do some serious talking. I'll see you tonight. I have to see Coulson first. Not sure what time I'll be in. I'm not sure how long he'll take."

"Get back as quick as you can. I'm on hot bricks here."

"Promise."

"As soon as?"

"Yes."

The phone went dead. Jack sat back and closed his eyes. Mercifully the train was not packed and the seat opposite unoccupied, so he was allowed to be alone with his thoughts. He ran over all the events in his head. The links between Nicholson and the Sellafield trio. Their trips to Cyprus. What had stopped McManus on his journey if it wasn't the situation at the site? If it was something else, was it the Plutonium oxide list? What was the connection with the Greek cum Chechen? The fact that he had spent time at Sellafield in the National Nuclear laboratories was intriguing. What was the significance of the altered documents? What about Plutonium Oxide and its potential? It all rolled like an unbroken wave in his reasoning without any real resolution. He could fit matters together in his imagination but he needed some hard evidence to get the urgent action Drummond was expecting. Maybe it was time. Maybe he needed to instigate warrants and search Nicholson's offices and workshops. A simultaneous swoop on Seaward and Billy McManus, would, hopefully, produce the goods. Then there was the priest. First thing the next day he resolved to persuade him to overcome his skewed religious beliefs for the good of the nation instead of hanging on to some ancient dogma designed for the Church to know all, the *laity* to be overawed by its power to speak to God and its ability to cleanse the soul, ready to sin all over again.

He dozed off watching the fields and naked trees flash by in the dull winter light. The sun, now a large tangerine globe, hung weak and low among the clearing clouds, promising a cold and frosty night.

He woke as the train rolled to a screeching halt at Durham. He stretched himself and prepared to get off at Newcastle and his meeting with Coulson. He looked at his phone. Missed call from Stella. He would see her at Robert's Hill. After Coulson, he would give her the details as he gave her a lift home. He wondered if she had managed to speak to Terry Seaward and it occurred to him that she might have been too forceful in her conversation. At this juncture he did not want any of them getting suspicious and busily covering their tracks.

Stella looked up and smiled when he appeared. "Well are you still gainfully employed?"

He nodded. "Still got a job and then some. I've got to see Coulson. I'll fill you in on the way home."

"OK. By the way, I've been dying to tell you. Got some info from the laptop. McManus has visited a dozen or so pages about…"

He cut her off. "Tell me later. I have to see Coulson, pronto."

Coulson seemed overawed at the situation. He spoke in low monotones over his desk as though conscious of a great conspiracy. "Did Drummond really admit to killing McManus?"

"Not in so many words. He would have said nothing except his Spanish lorry-driver stooge poked his head around the door then he had to admit their involvement once he realised I recognised him."

Coulson massaged his chin. "Christ…hard to believe. No wonder he wanted the case dropped."

"Figures, doesn't it. God knows what excuse he would have thrown at me if Speedy Gonzales hadn't appeared. Of course, Drummond's got us on the official secrets act. The whole thing about McManus is now wiped off the books. We might as well release the body and admit it was suicide."

Coulson nodded, deep in thought. "Can't do anything else now," he murmured. He sighed, "So…what's our next move? We need some hard evidence, Jack. Charteris will be watching us every goddam minute from now on."

"Search warrant. I'll get it tomorrow. Straight into Nicholson's home and factory. We should get one organised for Seaward and McManus junior at the same time in case they tip each other off. And we need to alert the Cumberland boys about possible contamination. They're going to have to have personnel in the proper gear. But first, tomorrow I'm going to lean hard on the priest. He knows the whole balls-aching scenario. If I can get him to talk, we can move in a positive direction."

Coulson's lips thinned. He rubbed at his chin again. "OK Jack but don't get too heavy on the priest. We can't have him bleating to the Press, squawking police brutality."

Jack smiled. "You know me boss. Ever the gentleman."

Coulson stood up. "Bullshit," he spat. "Now I'm going home and pretend none of this is happening."

"Well, what's the great revelation from the laptop?" Jack said as he strode toward Stella's desk.

She looked up. "You'll never believe this. I found out he's visited page after page about…" she hesitated, enjoying the impatient curiosity on his face.

"Come on," he barked, "don't piss about."

"Airport security."

"Airport security?"

"Anything and everything about X ray machines, sniffer dogs, all kinds of detection equipment including…get this… a scheme called Programme Cyclamen designed to detect radioactive materials coming into the country."

Jack whistled as the implication hit him. "So they could be planning to get that Plutonium Oxide *out* of the country. But that's crazy. If they've got detectors they must know they're taking a risk…a big risk."

Stella nodded. "I don't need to remind you, desperate

men take desperate risks. Except as far as I can see the detectors are for incoming goods only. I can't find a mention of the same for taking packages out of U.K. X ray, of course. Sniffer dogs for drugs, yes, but you'd need this super special equipment to detect radioactive stuff."

"Are we talking about all airports?"

Stella shrugged. "Don't know. We can check with Newcastle and say Manchester. But where would they be taking it? And how? Not in a suitcase surely."

Jack closed his eyes and covered them with a weary hand. "I've got an idea. How about Cyprus?... in golf bags. Did you speak to Seaward?"

She shook her head. "No. Not in his office all day. Got his home number. No answer."

"Mobile?"

"Not answering."

"Christ, I hope he hasn't done a runner."

"Don't think so. I spoke to Millie. She saw him in Egremont this afternoon. And get this. I checked with Sellafield personnel department. We knew Billy McManus worked in the MOX plant…"

"And?"

"He ground and polished fuel pellets that go to form fuel rods. And what does he grind and polish?…Plutonium."

Jack smiled. A warm, satisfying glow flowed over him. The bits of the jigsaw were still fitting perfectly. "Good work, Stella. We'll get on his tail as well tomorrow. Everything is leading to the same conclusion."

He drove her home. The evening had turned from a cold, damp afternoon to a crisp night with frost beginning to form and a bright bitten- off moon hanging at an angle in the black sky. He went over the day's events and the reason the McManus case had been dropped. The news was met with the same dark foreboding that had gripped Jack and his superiors. It was as though some inviolable decree that was ever present in Britain and essential to human chivalry had been swept away in that one blunt action.

"What are we doing here, Jack," she whispered. "What is the point of it all? We're pissing into the wind."

"We are, I know it. But…but," he shrugged, "what the hell. What else can we do?"

He pulled onto the broad drive of Amen cottage and spun the car around to face out into the street. The icy air seemed to magnify the crunch of the tyres on the gravel. He pulled on the handbrake and turned to her in the silence. "Tomorrow morning we'll lean on the Priest again. No need to get a taxi into work. I've got to see Charteris first thing then I'll pick you up and we'll go next door and try to drag the confession details out of that bugger. You can pick up your car after that."

"You're in your terrier mode again," she said softly. "You need to relax. Forget this evil world for a few hours. Can I help? Let me help, Jack. I need you tonight."

He stared at her in the darkness. The question ran through his mind just what she found in him to like or to allow him the uninhibited familiarity of her body. He knew he was far away from handsome. He knew he should lose a stone or two to bring his figure into some semblance of normality. Was it that she thought of him as just a good lay? Was it a strange chemistry? God only knew how much that had been to the fore in the last few days. With the lights of the main street behind her, she was almost a silhouette and her gentle words became an alluring invitation he was finding, as usual, hard to ignore. He found her right hand and squeezed it. "Sorry Stella. Not tonight. I'd better get home tonight. Clare's anxious to hear the latest. She'll be waiting up for me. She'll be pacing the floor waiting for the news from London. She'll ask too many questions if I'm late."

Silence. Then he saw her nod slowly and whisper OK as she sat beside him in the gloom. Both her outline and her rich dark voice were like something from an exotic dream and her hushed acceptance of his answer seemed to lend itself to even greater temptation. She became a mysterious seductress who in his imagination would lead him to unknown and untapped ecstasy. The warmth of her hand and the knowledge of her body had him in a sweat of beguiling submission but he fought it.

"Sorry Stella. Not tonight…not tonight." He leaned toward her and kissed her cheek. "Christ you're lovely. Get some sleep. See you in the morning," he whispered in her ear.

She opened the car door, staring straight ahead. He could almost feel the thwarted desire running through her as she eased herself out and closed the door without speaking. He watched her through the rear mirror as she walked slowly through the crackling gravel up to the front door. He started the car engine as Stella placed the key in the lock. He engaged first gear, dropped the handbrake and began to move forward. Stella opened the front door. She smelled gas immediately, but her hand was already on the light switch before her mind registered danger. Amen cottage instantly erupted into a violent deafening white-yellow blast that lifted the rear of Jack's Volvo two feet off the ground and reduced the cottage instantly into a pile of debris, bits of stone, wood and household detritus that rained back to Earth over two hundred yards away.

CHAPTER 12

It was after two in the morning when he got home. Clare was asleep on the settee and woke when he entered. She knew immediately there was something wrong. The way he slouched forward silently into the room; the look of utter despair on his dirt smudged features. She sat up. "What the hell happened to you? Where have you been all night?"

He dropped down into the armchair opposite her and cradled his head in his arms. "There's been an explosion. A gas explosion…"

"Where?"

"Stella's… Stella's house. Did you not see it on the late news? All the cameras were there. Your pal from the Paper, Colin Rhodes was there…everybody was there."

"No. I've been writing up a piece on the Triads. An explosion. How?"

Jack rubbed his hands over weary eyes and shook his head. "Don't know. Gas leak they think. Stella's …dead. She's dead, Clare."

The vision of it all ran vividly though his mind. He had leapt out of his car and stared back unable to believe the scene of carnage in front of him. The smoke: the flames; the utter wreckage and the noise of debris that had been blasted

161

skyward and was still raining down onto his car and onto the ground around him.

"*Stella!* he bellowed, as he ran forward. *Stella!*"

He could not see her among the tangled remains of Amen cottage. Suddenly he was back in Northern Ireland surrounded by the nightmare of shrieking civilians stumbling blindly around what had been an instant before, a busy street bustling with shoppers. Then in a flash of noise and blast, there was death and severed limbs, pain and destruction. But this wasn't an image of the past. This was the here and now. "Stella!" he yelled again, turning frantically in a circle. "*Stella!*"

Then he saw her in a direct line from her front door. Thirty yards away. Another semi- silhouette against the blue streetlights. The blast had carried her straight out of the passage like a bullet from a gun. She was upside down, hanging from a naked elderberry bush as though she had been stapled to it. He stood staring at the rigid still body, her blackened clothes holed and smouldering gently. He didn't need to pull her down to examine her for life. He knew instinctively she was dead. Her face was covered by her dress but that did not hide her lifelessness. There was still a slight twitch from her fingers that signalled the final demise of her nerves. Yet he knew he had to hold her but he couldn't move. Somehow, his legs were not part of him. Somehow, his mind had shed his body. All he could do was stand and stare. People began to collect in the street in shocked silence. Soon there were the sirens of police cars, ambulances and fire engines; blue flashing lights that were so familiar to him came from all directions. And then the sudden hubbub of action. People running. Hoses rolled out. Orders bellowed. Among it all he stood in blank confusion and disbelief until he was ushered away, silently and without resistance.

Clare stood up. "Dead? Stella died in it! She died in it but you're Ok. How the hell are you not dead?"

Jack looked up. "Clare, I wasn't with her...not in her

house. I gave her a lift home. Her car's in dock. I dropped her off and...and it just exploded when she opened the front door."

Clare nodded silently. For all her suspicions over the last year or so, it seemed a logical explanation. "An accident?" she asked with a hint of sarcasm.

"What else? But she never mentioned problems with her gas supply. Jesus, Clare... the blast. It lifted the car off its back wheels. It blew Stella clear across the front lawn. Killed her stone dead...stone dead," he repeated, shaking visibly, still in disbelief.

Clare stood for a moment looking down on the dishevelled figure, his head buried among the arms of his dust- smeared coat, hiding from the reality of his trauma. She had seen it before. In the early days of their marriage when he would sit bolt upright in bed, a hoarse cry of anguish coming from an open mouth as his mind had him locked in visions of hell. She managed to calm him then. She had felt the desperation melt away from him as he returned to the safety of her embrace and the warmth of her body.

"I'll make you some tea," she said softly. "Get yourself a shower."

Slowly he unfolded from his hunched position. He looked at her and nodded. He stood and shuffled unsteadily out of the room as though his legs were attached to a ball and chain and his shoulders, like Father McManus, had all the troubles of the world resting upon them.

When he reappeared, he was in his dressing gown and the tea was steaming in his black and white striped mug. Clare waited until he drank it, saying nothing; watching his far away gaze and wide bloodshot, lifeless eyes.

"Come on," she said softly. "It's your bedtime."

He followed her up the stairs and onto the landing. They went their separate ways. He took off his dressing gown, climbed into bed and switched off the table lamp. He lay down and as his head touched the pillow, he felt the duvet lift and Clare slipped in beside him. He wrapped himself around her, clinging on to her as though to leave the safety of her closeness, he would drown. Then the tears came and the uncontrollable sobbing. Somehow, she knew it was not only for Stella but also for her and their intimacy that made him immune from a wretched world and bound them together as one.

Henry Nicholson sat in his living room, his slippered feet resting comfortably on a pouffe; a whiskey and soda in hand and watching the late news on Sky TV. His wife was in bed, unaware of her husband's criminal plotting and his forthcoming visit to Cyprus. She was quietly pleased when he went off on his golfing trips. It freed her from his domineering attitude to everything in their marriage and his ever-present depression about the state of his company. To him, everything was wrong in the world. There was some jinx on him and all his efforts to be rich and influential. He craved some meaningful status. He had withdrawn into a grumbling petulant rage when he was defeated in two council elections. He often voiced the cruel injustice of it all but she had learned to let all his prophecies and woeful anger dissolve into the ether as an incoherent drone as they reached her ears.

For all his efforts that day there was still a dull feeling of dread in him. He had fought it since morning and still it was nagging at him; clinging to his innards; trickling through his mind like a cloying misery. He had returned from Sellafield at six after a hurried meeting with Terry Seaward and Billy McManus. It had been called urgently by Seaward. He was in a mild panic. Billy had been starting to throw doubts and imagined hurdles into their plans. He was wracked with foreboding about the manner of his father's death; the reasons why and by whom and whether by suicide or murder and it had him suddenly aware of the enormity of their illicit scheme. At the beginning, it seemed so easy; the rewards so tempting and satisfying. But he confided in Seaward with hand wringing apprehension that he knew things could go wrong. His father had said as much. He had watched his father's confidence slowly evaporate with their third dry run to Cyprus. There were arguments and threats even though the flight had been trouble-free, as had the first two but January was looming and the reality of possible capture had him in turmoil. What would happen to his mother? How could she cope? Other than himself, she now had no one except an older frail sister in Carlisle. Seaward knew it needed Nicholson to add some forceful reassurance before Billy backed out altogether and left the team of four down to two.

Nicholson arrived at Egremont for the meeting at Seaward's house. He was confident he could ease Billy's doubts just as he had done with his father in Cyprus. Then, there was further forceful persuasion after their return. Even though the hex had worn off, Seaward had managed to have him silenced. Billy was full of apprehension; scared, but he had not become paranoid like his father. He laid greater importance on the good life. The vision of wealth and what pleasures it could bring always brought him back under control. Nicholson was armed with the news that their next trip to Cyprus might be brought forward and that as soon as the delivery was made their individual payments would be deposited into anonymous safe deposit boxes deep below the busy streets of London. Nicholson had reminded Billy of the amount they would earn. Five hundred thousand pounds each. Life changing; a carefree hedonistic future for him and Terry. A sizeable cash injection into N.N.S. to keep it afloat. For what had proved to be an achievable operation. Three times, they had passed through security without a hitch, the radioactive source from smoke alarms undetected in their golf bags. He saw Billy visibly relax. He watched as his eyes widened and his imagination again took over. He had him calm and even though he was lacking his initial enthusiasm, back on track. There was one thing however, Nicholson was reluctant to tell him. Billy was unaware of his father's confession. He was also unaware of his uncle's impending fate. Khasan had rang him as he returned from Sellafield.

"It will be today," he said. *"The priest will be silenced and it will be an accident. No repercussions. No suspicions. No criminal investigation."*

"Are you sure?" Nicholson said, immediately wondering how the act could be that precise and a chill of the inevitability of it all ran up his spine.

"Yes. Sure."

"How?"

"Wait and see. You will know when it happens."

He sipped his whiskey fighting to convince himself that everything was now in order; that their next golfing visit to Cyprus would render them clear of any suspicion regarding Albert McManus. And even the more remote possibility of any involvement in the smuggling of Plutonium Oxide to his Chechen brother- in- law. What happened to the powder after the delivery was of no consequence to them. The reason why they wanted it so desperately seemed just and honourable. It was retaliation for all the suffering of the Chechen people. The outcome of their own successful operation meant security for all three of them and that was the imperative driving force; the satisfying result of their action for financial impunity.

The news flash came as a moving strip along the bottom of the screen. Above it, two journalists playfully harangued each other over the day's political chicanery. Nicholson sat upright, reading the words as they appeared. *Jesmond, a suburb of Newcastle. Violent gas explosion. Adjoining St Cecilia's church. One killed. A female police officer.'* Nicholson's jaw dropped. A nauseating fear gripped at his stomach. How could it be a police officer and not the priest? It had to be wrong. Surely it had to be Khasan's work and that involved the priest. After two minutes of anxious wondering, the phone rang. It was Cyprus.

"Henry, Khasan's been on the phone. He thinks he fucked up. He thinks it was the wrong house."

"Jesus Christ Almighty, I guessed Al. It's all-over national TV. But the stupid prick killed a cop, for crying out loud…A cop…a female cop! How could he do that?"

The Chechen was silent. Nicholson could hear his noisy breathing. He could sense his mind galloping; tumbling with possibilities. Then he spoke, his voice low and deliberate. *"Henry, we must now forget the priest. We must rely on his religious convictions… for the moment…that is all we can do. I need to see you Henry, you and the others. I need to come to England. I will try to get flight tomorrow. It is after midnight here…"*

He was stopped by Nicholson's sudden soft cry of pained anguish. "Oh no!… no…no."

"What? What is it, Henry?"

The TV screen showed the smoking remains of Amen cottage and a female reporter. She was wrapped bulkily against the cold night with vapour billowing from her mouth, telling the country that the victim was a detective with Northumbria CID named Stella van Kirk.

It was after just ten on Saturday morning when Jack Shaftoe arrived at Charteris' office. He looked up from a pile of paperwork, his face solemn, and his hands gesturing uselessly.

"Didn't think you'd be here, Jack," he said softly. "Didn't think I'd be in at all today, either. Christ, you look rough. Not much sleep last night I take it. That's a hell of a blow to the unit. Lucky you dodged the blast."

Jack shook his head slowly, "Still can't believe it, Sir. One minute she's there… the next she's… dead…"

Charteris pointed to a chair. "Sit, Jack. She'll get the full treatment, rest assured on that. It'll be a full Force ceremony, believe me. I understand she had no close relatives."

Jack nodded and slumped down as though every ounce of energy had left him. Nobody close… an aunt in Groningen and a cousin in Enkhuisen. That's all she ever mentioned to me."

"We'll make sure they're contacted. We'll need a formal identification. From what Coulson tells me she was everything you'd want in a good detective."

Jack nodded, inwardly sneering at Coulson's synthetic appraisal. "She was good. She had a good intuitive brain. She's been great on this Sellafield case."

Charteris sat back. "Ah yes, the Sellafield case." He pulled at his bottom lip, deep in thought for a moment. "Jack, we're getting into the murky waters of national security on this one. I'm just a bit scared it's going to put the whole Force under the Government microscope especially if it turns to rats. You sure you can handle it? Drummond thinks you can. Looks like you sold yourself to him. If they saw off McManus, you know the power we're dealing with, here Jack. They've got carte blanche on everything. They're above the law, Jack. They can do what they like and get away with it."

Jack hung his head, staring between his legs at the floor and said nothing. Yesterday had been a day that would be etched in his mind forever. It was the shock of Drummond's disclosure that had erased all the basic principles he had devoted himself to since joining the Force. He knew he himself had bent the rules when he felt it necessary. But the reason behind that was to engineer an outcome that overrode the stifling edicts that masqueraded as fair justice. Edicts that allowed criminals free reign to do their dirty work with laughable and impotent deterrents. He would lie, steal and cheat for a just cause, but murder, as they called it for killing a fellow countryman, cold blooded murder, was beyond his moral capabilities. Then there was Stella. He was still trying to convince himself that it was all a hellish nightmare; that she would be back at Amen cottage and she would be waiting for him. Together they would grill the priest until he confirmed what they had already surmised. Then there would be the satisfaction of the arrests and the sick look of defeat on their surprised faces. But he knew it was not to be. The absolute finality of a death was something he had known so many times but when it was someone he had lived life with, the awareness of it all was shattering. He looked up and stared at Charteris.

"I'm going to do this, Sir," he mumbled. "I can do it and I will. I need today to finalise a few things, then a couple of search warrants then, I think…some arrests."

Charteris nodded. "Sure? I know what you're like Jack. You're a bloody Rottweiler and don't care who you bite. I knew that when I took you on. Stick to the rules."

Jack nodded. He wasn't sure he would, but he knew whatever happened he was going to see the saga through to some conclusion.

"OK, Jack. Get cracking. I'll tell Coulson you've got my blessing on any move you make… and as many bodies that's needed on the case, but Jack, for Christ' sake, don't fuck up. Drummond's been on already this morning. He wants results."

Jack stood up. "He might get results he doesn't want to hear."

"How do you mean?"

"It depends how far these suspects have got with their little scheme."

He was on his way to St Cecilia's when 'Blaydon Races' chirped out of his mobile on the passenger seat. It was Harry Lockwood.

"Jack, it's Harry. Heard about Stella. Jesus, Jack, I can't believe it."

"You and me both, Harry. A fucking gas leak… can you believe that?"

Harry's voice dropped a tone. *"Jack, that's one reason I'm ringing. Can you come to the Station?"*

"When…now?"

"I think you should."

"Why, what's up?"

"I'll tell you when you get here. I've got something to show you."

"What, for fuck's sake?"

"Better I show you Jack. Don't argue. Get your arse to Robert's Hill."

He ignored the turn that would have taken him to Jesmond and continued through the city and on to the main road heading west. In a way, he was glad of the diversion. He left Force headquarters in Wallsend and it had suddenly dawned on him that he would have to pass the remains of Amen cottage before he turned into the church. Already the vision of it lanced through his memory. The flash; the noise; the blast and the image of Stella, a ravaged figure seemingly suspended against the elderberry bush, arms and legs open wide like some grotesque inverted crucifixion. Her ragged smoking skirt hanging downward covering her face and revealing white scorched underwear. But he steeled himself. He knew it had to be done. He had, at this crucial stage, to wring some facts out of the priest for his own satisfaction; for the Forces satisfaction; for the Government's satisfaction and also, he thought, if Stella was looking down from God knows where, hers too. And then there was Clare, chomping at the bit for her story. He had managed a slice of toast at breakfast time and told her all, her eyes widening with each salient fact.

"You're telling me McManus was a Government sanctioned execution," she gasped.

"Yes. He was…so called, a potential danger to the Country. But Clare, I was told this under the official secrets act. You cannot, and I mean it…you cannot breathe a word of this at this time. If you do," he stared into her face, "you could wind up dead in a lay-by…if you know what I mean. None of the old 'publish and be damned' bullshit. Not yet anyway. Promise me, Clare. Take it all down but do not go into print until it's all done and dusted."

She thought for a moment then nodded sullenly. "OK Jack, I hear what you say."

Harry Lockwood was waiting for him. With his hat off, his wild grey hair seemed in a frenzy to release itself from his broad head, while his pock-marked face still carried the expression of total angry boredom. Jack made his way across the office, his colleagues silent, staring solemnly at him as he past them. Some whispered a subdued hello. They knew the fate of Stella and they knew, however vaguely, the relationship between them. One day she had been a dynamo of a detective and the object of secret silent lust. Suddenly she was gone forever.

"Jack, plug this into your desktop." Harry held a flash drive between thumb and forefinger. "This is going to interest you. There was an attempted robbery in the high street at Jesmond, yesterday. Some young smartarse tried to hold up the bookies shop waving a knife about. Of course, all the bells and whistles went off and he took fright, jumped on a motor bike and roared off in a cloud of exhaust fumes. We've just gone through three CCTV cameras to see if he's there and get the number plate of the bike." He passed the stick to Jack. "As usual the quality of the video is crap to say the least but it does throw up something you'll be interested in."

Jack sat down, switched on the computer and stuck the flash drive into the USB port. The high street in Jesmond came to life in grainy black and white. Coulson walked over. He said nothing but patted Jack's shoulder, a scant gesture of sadness and reassurance at the absence of Stella.

"Look Jack," Harry grunted. We've edited this to get rid of the boring bits but the first few minutes might just stir your curiosity."

Jack looked. There was normal traffic; cars, bikes and pedestrians. Commercial vehicles stopping and starting. "Well," he said. "What am I looking for?"

Harry leaned over his shoulder. "See that? See that white van?"

"Yes I see it," Jack said with a hint of irritation in his voice.

Harry pointed at the screen and the digital time displayed in the corner. "Ten twenty-seven am. Watch the van. It goes up the high street and turns right. You can just make it out stopping before it disappears off the screen. Right opposite St Cecilia's church and what's more significant opposite Stella van Kirk's house. It was there for four and a half minutes."

"So what does that tell us?"

"Nothing except nobody got out or got in. Hardly earth-shattering I suppose, but watch. Twelve seventeen. Same day. Look, there's the twat that tried to rob the bookies. That's him parking outside the shop. Two minutes later he's out, back on the bike, and away like a bat out of hell, but look at that white van."

Jack looked, beginning to take a curious interest. The van drove up the high street, turned and stopped again opposite the church and Amen cottage. It appeared to be the same van. The digital timer showed it was stationary for six minutes and twenty second. Nobody got out and nobody got in.

Jack grunted, a sudden suspicion beginning to claw its way into his reasoning. He needed Harry to quench it. He shrugged. "Coincidence…surely?"

Harry shook his head. "We took a statement from the manager at the bookies and his CCTV footage, which incidentally only showed the prick wearing his crash helmet and a blurred face. Later the manager rang us back, saying he was out in the street and thought he recognised him walking, this time. He recognised his leather jacket with a lion on the back, looking in shop windows."

"So?" Jack whispered.

"So we ran the whole day's street video. Fast forward Jack till I tell you to stop."

The action speeded up.

"Stop!" Harry barked. "Back to normal. Now let it roll for a second or two… now look. Look what's driving up the high street. A white van."

Jack looked. It appeared to be the same van. It moved up the high street. The number plate, in keeping with most

amazon.co.uk®

A gift from **Miss L R Niblock**

Just like Vera...Mark's friend he used to work with. Check out the acknowledgments. Hope you're feeling better. Lots of love Sis xxx From Miss L R Niblock

Gift note included with The **Priest** and the **Whistleblower**

CCTV quality, was unreadable. It was, like before, a plain van. Plain white and anonymous; no visible signs on its side advertising the offerings of its owner. It turned right and parked opposite the church. Timed at two thirty.

"Now watch," Harry growled, a hint of triumph in his voice.

Jack watched. He saw the funeral cortege drive slowly up the high street. It turned right then left into the church grounds. It was another seven minutes before the van moved. Jack watched with eye-widening disbelief as the van drove slowly across the road and into the entrance of Amen cottage.

"There now, Sherlock. What do you make of that?" Harry whispered.

"Fuck me," Coulson breathed. "How long was it there?"

Jack was silent, his imagination galloping through a torrent of wild and implausible possibilities.

"Keep watching." Harry snapped.

They watched. Everyone in the office sensed some great revelation and silently gathered around the computer, all eyes on the top corner of the screen where the first twenty yards of the drive were visible. They saw the van door slide open and the figure of a man plant his feet on the gravel. He was tall and broad with a forest of black hair and a prominent beard. He wore what looked like a workman's site jacket and his trouser bottoms appeared to be tucked into stout boots or folded against his ankles with bicycle clips. He moved to the back of the van, opened the double doors and rummaged for a moment, putting things inside his jacket. He closed the van doors, walked toward the front of the van and disappeared off the screen.

"Shit," Jack hissed.

"Hold on." Harry grunted again. "He's there for just under twenty minutes. We've chopped out the interval. Here he comes again. Cool as a fucking cucumber."

The man reappeared on the screen, walking casually. He stopped at the van door and looked around. They watched him ease his big frame into the driver's seat and reverse in the drive. They gazed at the moving van, willing the video to clarify the small grainy image of his face through the windscreen but it was too vague; the front number plate a blur of black and white and too far away from the camera.

"Now that's not all," Harry said as he poked another flash drive in front of Jack's nose. "Stick this in. We ran the CCTV back a couple of days to see if we could spot Dick Turpin casing the bookies. Look what shows on Thursday."

They looked. Again, the white van was opposite the church and Amen cottage. "Now watch," Harry whispered with triumph in his voice. "Look who's coming toward the road from Stella's house."

There was no doubt who it was. The stooped, careworn gait and the flowing robes of office. It was Father McManus moving slowly down the drive of Amen cottage and turning left into the church grounds. The digital clock showed ten seventeen. Stella was at Robert's Hill.

"Jesus. H. Christ" Jack breathed. "He was after the priest but mistook the house… he rigged Stella's goddam house! He wanted the priest…he wanted the priest dead, for Christ' sake."

Harry's mobile buzzed before Jack could even dare to get some agreement for his suspicions. The possibility was incredible, almost beyond belief. Harry had a brief conversation punctuated with grunts and hummed agreements then lifted his chin ready for a major pronouncement.

"The site is crawling with inspectors from the Health and Safety executive, the Gas supplier, Forensics…you name it. It's now a crime scene. You're right Jack. They found Stella's gas hob propped up against a gravestone. All four control knobs were in the full-on position."

CHAPTER 13

Jack drove to St Cecilia's as if on autopilot. His mind was seething with the probability that Stella was a case of mistaken identity, and the priest was the target. As the action of the video had unfolded he searched his mind trying to find a logical reason why anyone would want to eliminate her. The local mafia came to mind. He was aware of her involvement in their protection racket, which had the owners of half of the quayside bars paying out to save having their livelihood from being burned to the ground. She had been deep into the investigation with D.S. Harvey, and Jack knew only too well their capabilities when mafia feathers got ruffled. The action was mainly among themselves when trespassers from another district dared to encroach. Jim Hakimi had been a recent example. A big noise Arab in the sleazy underworld of drugs and prostitution, he was standing nonchalantly outside 'The Jolly Riveter' pub in South Shields, smoking and king of his domain, enjoying the evening air and a bulky wallet of takings for the night. Then a car pulled up and the passenger window came down. A bullet from a Webley Mk V1 .455 went straight through his sternum. Jim had ventured north of the Tyne in search of new customers. He needed to be taught a lesson. The gunman was on the train back to London within an hour. There was a possible sighting at Newcastle Central Station but whoever it was, was never apprehended.

But that was turf war tactics. They and their kind were fair game but not the Law. The Law was there only to be outsmarted. Then the second video played and it all became clear. It was not Stella, it was the priest who had stoked someone's ire. It was the priest who required silencing. It was yet another case of a tragic meaningless death. But this time Jack was sure he knew why and who had initiated it.

He tried not to look as he passed the remains of Amen cottage but he couldn't help a glance at the war zone, still issuing wisps of smoke; still host to inspectors and forensics, like scavengers, picking over the piles of stone and shards of household rubble. He quickly looked away as the vision of the blast and the mayhem shot through his memory again. He turned onto the church grounds. He was determined to get the information he needed before he initiated search warrants and arrests. He was unsure how he would approach the priest, whether to lean hard on him or try some sympathetic persuasion. He decided he might need both. He turned up the broad, church drive and onto the narrowed section that led to the priest's front door. He stood for a moment staring at it, gathering his thoughts. There was no bell, just a large ornate knocker that could have come from some gloomy Transylvania horror movie. The impact as it struck the door, echoed, as though behind the ancient wood there was enclosed emptiness. Father McManus opened the rectory door. He gave no visible sign of recognition, just a mournful, troubled stare. "Detective Shaftoe," he croaked, his throat still producing phlegm, "Your colleague," he said, "so sad… so very sad."

"Father McManus, we need to talk," Jack said softly, choosing a gentle opening gambit. "Can you spare me a few moments? There has been a serious development since I saw you last."

The priest stood to one side. "Come... yes please come in. I saw you last night. I saw you standing there. The rectory shook. I feared for the church windows. I prayed for...for your colleague. I hear she was taken."

He led Jack to the same room where they had talked before. There was the same smell; the same atmosphere of being frozen in time and absolute sanctity.

"Sit... please sit," he said. "Can I offer you something...some tea...or something stronger?"

"No Father," Jack whispered. "Thank you, but no." He took a deep breath. "Father McManus, the explosion last night..."

The priest adjusted his spectacles and bowed his head. "A terrible business, detective. Miss...er...?"

"Stella...Stella van Kirk."

"Ah yes." He nodded. "How could that happen?"

Jack leaned forward. "I can tell you how it happened. It was not an accident."

The priest frowned. "Not an accident?" his voice a tone higher in surprise.

Jack shook his head. "We know it was a deliberate act. We know someone tampered with the gas supply to her house."

The priest held a hand to his mouth. He closed his eyes then sagged as though the news had robbed him of the last smattering of his belief in human morality. "But why? Oh Lord, why?"

Jack stared into his tortured face. "She was not meant to be involved...or die, Father...you were. You were meant to be blown up...killed." Jack sat back quickly, waiting for a reaction.

The priest recoiled in shock. He gave a nervous laugh. "No detective Shaftoe. No, I have no enemies."

"You may not have enemies in the normal sense but you have enemies because of what you know."

"What I know? What do I know?"

Jack hesitated, unsure if he was pacing the meeting too

177

quickly. "You know what your brother and your nephew and Seaward and Nicholson were doing. You know the nature of their crime."

The priest's face crumpled again in painful recollection. He removed his spectacles slowly and laid them on a closed bible in front of him. He pushed the book gently to one side with the back of his hand and lowered his head, deep in thought.

"I need to know, Father. I need you to tell me everything," Jack whispered, undisguised desperation in his voice. "Unless you told someone other than me about your brother's confession, there was only one other person aware of it." He nodded ruefully. "In the course of our investigation I told Henry Nicholson. Now it is possible… in fact, it's probable that Nicholson and his friends were worried that you might just break your vows and tell all to someone… such as me."

The priest cleared his throat. He appeared unconvinced that Jack's theory was anywhere near the truth. "No… no, detective, surely not. I am only too aware of the evils of this world but to… to…"

Jack took in a noisy breath. It was time to bend the truth. "Listen, Father, nobody knows about the evils of this world more than me and… and please believe me, if what I think is true, I know… I know what desperate men are capable of doing. I think I know what Nicholson and the Sellafield mob are up to. I need you to confirm it. Your brother was brutally murdered because of it…you saw the damage they did to him. You know what happened to my colleague, Stella. She was mistaken for you. You were the one they wanted to silence. You have got to believe that. You must, for once, if you have any conscience, look beyond church rules and let me eliminate these villains from society. You told me your brother had demons in him; that he was a very troubled man. Let me catch the ones that put those demons there."

The priest looked beyond him, staring for a moment at

the wall of dusty books, his eyes blinking and Jack could see the inner turmoil that tore at him. He seemed to deflate as a decision locked itself in his mind. He toyed with the crucifix that hung around his neck then nodded. "Detective Shaftoe... tell me, do you believe in God? Do you believe that there is a heaven for those that deserve it?"

Jack thought for a moment. He rubbed a forefinger under his nose then shook his head slowly. "No Father McManus... no. I wish I could but I can't. But you do and I admire you for your faith. But what if there is nothing... if there is only oblivion. You will not even be able to sense the utter disappointment knowing that you and two thousand years of believers were wasting their time."

"But what if we are right? What will you find yourself feeling if the gates of heaven are there for you?"

Jack smiled. "Then I'll know you were right and I was wrong. But if I'm right and it's total wipe-out, I won't have the satisfaction of knowing that I was right either."

The priest nodded sadly, "One day we will see... or not see." His cleared his phlegmy throat and sat up straight. "I will tell you all I know," he whispered. "You realise that in doing this I can be excommunicated, detective Shaftoe. There was a decree from the holy office way back in time...back in 1682 and even before that, forbidding revelations from the confessional. Canon law 938.1. There are no exceptions. No one and no edict can force disclosure. That, in itself, is a sin the church will not and cannot tolerate."

Jack nodded. His lips thinned; inwardly he had no interest in the historical precepts, but he forced a look of respect and gratitude to form on his face. He realised the priest's devout faith and the authoritarian directive he had decided to ignore.

"I'm sure your God will understand, Father. Maybe He will understand even if your church cannot." Jack whispered, pleased with his sudden burst of religious philosophy.

He waited as Father McManus stared at his desk, his right hand holding the crucifix, his left slowly chasing a paperclip with his forefinger around scattered documents in front of him.

"This has been troubling me ever since your first visit. I thought I might help your cause, detective Shaftoe by... by at least giving you some hint or some direction however vague, without violating the principles of the Holy Church. I tried to see my neighbour, Miss van Kirk. I made a decision to give some... some direction to your investigation... for my brother's sake. I wanted revenge, detective Shaftoe. Revenge... revenge is a sin and I was ashamed of myself. Yet it forced me to her door. But she was not there. No one came to the door. It was meant to be."

Jack's head moved slowly up and down. "So Father, tell me... tell me everything."

The priest leaned forward as though there were invisible ears waiting to hear and damn him. He spoke in a hushed, hesitant voice. "When my brother came to see me he was in a state of torment. There was a haunted look on his face. He crossed himself then embraced me. I could feel the tremble in his body. 'I need absolution' he said. 'Brother, help me' he pleaded. I sat him down and poured him a brandy. Never had I seen him in such distress. 'Forgive me Father, I have sinned' he whispered. He was involved with an act of theft from his place of work... Sellafield. He was involved with his son... my nephew and his colleague, Mr Seaward. There was also Henry Nicholson who I gathered was a driving force, controlling my brother... controlling them all. He told me they were to smuggle some dangerous substance out of Sellafield and deliver it to Cyprus, to Nicholson's brother- in- law. This man, he had a Greek name, but was originally from Chechnya, intended to use it for..." the priest hesitated, "to... to make a bomb. To kill people."

Jack leaned forward until their heads were almost touching. "A bomb... for where? What people? Where was the bomb to be used?"

"It was to...to get revenge for all the killing and maiming of the Chechen people. They were going to explode it, in...in Moscow."

A prickle of shock ran up Jack's spine. The consequences of such an act of terrorism would reverberate around the world. He remembered Professor Samuels' information. A bomb, whether nuclear or 'dirty' as he had called it, would cause immeasurable damage physically and politically. Blame would scatter across a dozen or more factions. There would be retaliation. There would be escalation.

"Fucking hell," Jack breathed.

The priest ignored the remark.

"When, Father? When was all this going to happen?"

"In January. They are planning to deliver the substance in January. But my brother began to have doubts. My brother had a conscience. He told me he was wracked with both fear...fear for what he would be a party to, and fear from being caught. The shame, detective. The shame and the consequences. Many people would die. He was a tortured man. I took his confession, and I begged him to stop his involvement; to cleanse his soul and his mind and God would absolve him and give him peace."

Jack sighed. "He tried. He was on his way to tell the Press because, I'm guessing, he assumed the others would not listen. He was desperate, Father."

"He said at first he was blinded by the rewards. They were to be paid a fortune. They travelled to Cyprus three times this year. Each time they carried some other substance in their golf bags and it was never detected. They thought it would be the same in January but as it got closer he became more nervous and aware of the dire consequences if they were successful... and also if they were not."

"How much were they to be paid?"

The priest shook his head. "I'm not sure. Many thousands I think. Money really is the root of all evil." "Do you know where this substance is now?"

The priest massaged his brow with his fingertips. "I think Nicholson has it. Albert said it was always carried out in his briefcase."

"And it was to be smuggled in their golf bags?"

"That is what he said...yes, somewhere in their golf bags."

Jack nibbled at the edge of his forefinger, his mind racing; thoughts crowding into each other as he mentally ordered his priorities. Search warrants for Nicholson and the two at Sellafield. Simultaneously, so they couldn't alert each other. Specialists to handle the Plutonium oxide. Colin Forrest to get his men to descend on the Greek in Cyprus. He stood up.

"Father McManus, you have been great help on this case. I know how hard it was for you to disclose this information, but believe me, it will save many lives. I hope you realise just how much of a Christian act you have delivered here."

The priest gave a sad smile. "I do detective Shaftoe but... but I will now regret it and forever ask God for forgiveness."

"For being a true Christian?"

"Sometimes the Church and Christianity are at odds with each other. What's wrong is right...what's right is wrong." He shrugged. "It was ever so. But that is faith, detective Shaftoe...that is what defines our calling and governs our actions."

"I understand, Father. Nevertheless what you did in this instance was one hundred percent right in the eyes of humanity. And just for the record we have not had this conversation. No one need know you have broken some ancient religious law."

The priest slowly rose to his feet. "I know... and that's enough." He led Jack to the front door. "I have also committed my nephew to prison. He was always a wayward child; headstrong and out of control. A problem to his parents. He has been another victim of avarice."

"He, Father, could have been a player in your planned execution, although I'm betting on Nicholson and his brother- in- law as the instigators."

The priest shook his head, still unsure of Jack's theory. "And my brother? Have you made any progress on his murder?"

Jack was tempted to tell him. The whole clandestine atmosphere of their meeting had been an uneasy but positive outpouring of truth and to tell him the facts seemed almost natural and automatic, but he resisted. "We are making progress, Father. I believe his body is being released for a funeral any time now."

"Thank you. I will speak to his wife. She may want me to officiate."

It occurred to Jack that the woman, if she was innocent herself, would have both the ordeal of a funeral and the trauma of her son's arrest. But, he concluded, such was the penalty for straying outside the law. He turned at the door. "Father, whatever you do, do not mention my visit here today. What you have told me will lead to arrests but I do not want Seaward and your nephew alerted. Do you understand the importance of that?"

The priest nodded. "Of course, detective. Do your job. I will do mine and pray for your success."

Jack offered his hand. "Thank you, Father. And can I say I hope your beliefs are right…so you can say 'I told you so' and I can say 'thank the Lord'. And until there is some positive action and arrests, you must be careful… very careful and wary of everyone and everything. Do you believe me?"

The priest nodded. His fingers were cold and bony. Jack eased his normal assertive grip. A feeling of sadness came over him. He walked to his car, started the engine and looked out at the forlorn figure in the doorway. He waved. Father McManus held out an open hand no higher than his shoulder then the big wooden door closed slowly.

Jack sat for a moment staring at it. He felt an affinity with the man. He had a sense of the unfairness that the priest would have to take upon himself and the hopeless and unrewarding task of putting mankind into a state of utopia. In a way, his task was similar but without the ritual of faith and conversion. Good outsmarts bad; right overcomes wrong. That is what it was all about. That was it in its simplistic form. He sighed, summing up in his mind all the work he had now to do. There had to be positive important and significant actions that would have major consequences on so many lives. He was about to move off when 'Blaydon Races' stopped him.

"*Hello, Jack?*" It was Wilbur Coulson. "*Where are you?*"

"Just left the priest's house. Got the full confession. I'm heading straight back to the Station. We need warrants Boss, and quickly. I'll give you all the details in fifteen minutes."

"*Good work. Got some news for you. The whizz kids have been at that CCTV footage. They've managed to read the number plate on the white van. Registered in Sheffield to a car hire company. We've checked it out. It was hired to some foreign bastard called Khasan Ismailov. We've got his address. I'll get the Sheffield Force to round him up.*"

"No, not yet, Boss. He might have time to alert his mates. Let's get them all in one big action."

He heard Coulson hum as he thought. "*Yes…yes OK Jack. On your bike.*"

Jack felt a burst of elation. It was all coming together. "See you in a jiffy."

He turned the car out of the church drive and past the still smouldering ruin of Amen cottage. "This is all for you, Stella," he yelled joyously. "We're going to nail the bastards. It's for you…just for you."

It was Saturday and Neutron Nuclear Services was quiet. The staff and workforce had left on Friday evening for the weekend. Other than a cleaner who mopped and dusted and hummed a tune from 'Phantom of the Opera', there was only Henry Nicholson sitting ruminating in his office. He sat staring sightlessly at the wall, fighting off the cold prospect of possible defeat. He tried to persuade himself that their actions would now leave them rich and without incriminating evidence. It was only a matter of time before the police came knocking again. It was hard for him to imagine they could assume any direct link between him and the explosion, but just their interest in him and his association with Sellafield and the McManus death was enough to unnerve him. Now, with the priest still alive it was possible, just possible that McManus had told all to his brother in a fit of righteousness. There again, he tried to convince himself that a catholic confession was sacrosanct and Shaftoe would not be able to extract it from the priest. Otherwise it would be the end of a glorious dream. He glanced at his watch as he had done two minutes before, checking and calculating how much longer he would have to wait for the arrival of Alessandro, Terry Seaward and Billy McManus. His brother- in- law had rang him, waking him from a troubled sleep at six in the morning.

"Henry," he said urgently. *"Get organised. Get Terry and Billy over to Wallsend now. I will arrive in Manchester at noon. Will be with you at about four or five at latest. We must move fast. Get the stuff ready to transfer. I will take the spare golf bag. We leave overnight and fly at 05.30. I need passport details for you all. I arrange tickets this end. We cannot wait. The bastard priest should have been dead. Khasan fucked up really good. But if the priest talks, now there will be no evidence... right? You will return on Monday evening. Then little suspicion at your absence and no evidence... only words, OK?"*

Nicholson was instantly wide- awake. He grunted, suddenly aware of their imminent trial of nerves and their heart pounding suspense as they passed over the golf bags and waited anxiously to board the plane.

"Henry. I say OK?"

"Yes... yes Al." he whispered. "Two minutes. I have all the passport details here... somewhere. Albert gave me copies. They're downstairs."

"Sure?"

"Sure. Let me ring you back."

"Straight away. Not much time. I go to airport now... and whatever you do, do not let those two at Sellafield forget passports... and golf clubs... Albert's as well. OK?"

Nicholson's wife stirred. "Who's that?" the dreamy question came muffled from the depths of her pillow.

"It's Al. He's in England. He's coming to see me today. He wants the golf team to go back with him tomorrow. Just for a couple of days. Er... he says the weather is great... getting past 18 degrees and sunny."

His wife turned over and buried her head into the pillow again. She groaned. "And he rings in the middle of the night. Hope it rains, you bastards," she said in a low drawn- out muted mumble.

He rang Terry Seaward. "Get over here this morning. Get Billy. We're taking the stuff out tomorrow, before the priest decides to tell all."

Terry Seaward was instantly excited. *"T...today?"* he stuttered in surprise. *"Wow, that's good Henry. Leave it much longer and Billy boy will chicken out. He kicked off again after you left. Sooner the better. He's calm at the minute but,"* he put a whine in is voice, *"How many years if we get caught?' What happens to my old man's share of the money?' and 'What if they find out when we get back?' He's had me pissed off, Henry. I never told him the female detective that was killed was linked with the visit he had from Shaftoe. Jesus, that was a cock up and a half. If he had known it was meant for his goddam uncle, it would have really spooked him. That would have finished the whole thing off. I'll get him roused now and we'll be over there as soon as. He's got to come with us. We can't carry four golf bags between us."*

"Al's taking Albert's, so we can shift the whole lot as planned. We could have got more in the next few weeks but what's there will have to do. There's over a kilo, so that should earn the pay off."

"OK. We just need a holdall if we're only there with the delivery and straight back. Anyway, it will look like a genuine golf trip if we're

carrying a cabin bag. The security cameras won't get suspicious."

"For Christ' sake don't say that to Billy." Nicholson snapped. "If he takes fright we're shagged. We need him for placing the goods in the correct positions. I didn't spend all those sunny days cooped up with Al and Billy working out the physics and the methodology for nothing."

Nicholson glanced at his watch again. Ten past eleven. He had reckoned on an hour for Seaward to organise himself and contact McManus junior, then another half to get to his house and pick him up. That made it about eight for them to set off. "Any minute," he whispered anxiously to himself.

It was eleven thirty when he heard a car pull up outside the office. He breathed a sigh of relief. He was on his third cup of coffee, his mind a whirl of reasons why they should be late. He had visions of Seaward having to drag Billy into his car. Then he wondered if there had been an accident or a breakdown which could put a halt to the programme. He walked to the reception desk, pressed the button and opened the glass door. He knew it was Seaward's silver Porsche. He felt all the tension drain away in an instant.

"Where have you buggers been?" he yelled. "I've been crapping myself here."

Seaward eased himself out of the driver's seat. Billy McManus appeared at the other side. It was obvious from his slow actions and his sullen face he was not a happy man.

"Accident near Haltwhistle," Seaward said. "They had us diverted at Greenhead up onto the military road."

Nicholson nodded. He knew the B road. It was a legacy from the Romans that ran parallel with the remains of the wall. "You alright Billy?" he said, trying to be cheerful. "Today's the big day. You'll be coming back on Monday a bloody rich bastard."

Billy's face twisted into a rueful grin. His shoulders twitched as though easing an itching back as he walked into the reception. "You'd better be right Henry. I've got a feeling about this. There's something not right. I've got this fucking feeling…"

Seaward grabbed his arm and ushered him into Nicholson's office. "We're fine, you daft prick. We went through with no bother… three times. The way we've got the stuff configured will not cause the slightest interest. They are golf bags, golf clubs, and all the paraphernalia that goes with them. When we get back you can do what I'm going to do… tell Sellafield to take a flying fuck."

Billy slumped down in a chair. "That was Newcastle. Manchester might be different. We should have waited until March when the flights from Newcastle are regular again. I told you January was too soon. Now it's even sooner. And I've got a father still in the morgue."

Seaward frowned. "He's got a point, but let's do it now and get it over with. We've been waiting months for this."

Nicholson tousled his red hair. "Billy, for Christ's sake stop worrying. If there was anything to detect they would have done it at Newcastle. Now come on… let's get fucking rich. Just think, you could be off to Las Vegas shortly."

"And lose it all," Seaward said with a sarcastic grin.

Billy sneered. "And you'll waste yours on that cow from Workington who's had more pokes than a Victorian fireplace."

Seaward's face twisted into a scowl. "Ha, fucking ha. Just wait and see. Jealous twat."

Nicholson stood between them. "Enough," he snapped. "We've got better things to do. No leg pulling. No aggro. Right?"

He shouted up the corridor. "Sadie, you might as well go now we're going to be busy."

Sadie looked up from where she manoeuvred her mop. "I haven't finished the drawing office."

"It doesn't matter. Leave it today."

She dropped the mop and ran her hands down her pinafore. She sniffed. "You're the boss."

Nicholson waited until Sadie had let herself out. He checked the entrance then walked back to the office. Billy sat with legs open, his forearms resting on his thighs and his head down. Seaward sat next to him, legs crossed reading a magazine.

"What time will Al get here?" he said without looking up.

"He said about four. Did you two remember your passports and the golf gear?"

"In the car," Seaward said nonchalantly, again with his gaze on the magazine. "Stuffed in like sardines, we were. Cars like mine were not built for freight." He patted his chest. "Passport in here."

"And you Billy?"

Billy raised his head. He looked pale and heavy eyed. He nodded.

Nicholson took a deep breath. "OK boys. Let's get going and get the stuff ready for our friend and golfing partner to arrive."

He led them past a row of offices and into a large room with desks, computers and drawing boards scattered around at various angles. Beyond it, was a locked door that led to a workshop. He opened it, flicked a switch and the place fluttered into bright light. It was big and airy, cold and surprisingly clean. It was full of engineering equipment; a blue painted overhead crane and gleaming valves and pipes in weird and tortuous shapes lying in taped- off sections. Rolls of bubble wrap, filing cabinets and assorted tools neatly held in clips above a line of seven workbenches. It had the smell of industry and the air of the precision demanded by the environment it was meant to work in. At the top corner of the workshop there was a small brick-built room with a sliding metal door. The door carried a large iconic sign in yellow and black. '*Danger X rays.*' Alongside it another sign, a standard no entry notice in red and black. '*Do not enter when red light is on*'. Nicholson turned a key in the robust lock, pulled at the handle and the door slid open with a rumble. He turned around and smiled. "Industrial X ray bay. We check all welds here. It also doubles up as our own little Cyprus radioactive store. I've got everything ready in here. Nobody gets in this place but me… for most of this year, anyway. There shouldn't be a problem but just in case there's any chance of butterfingers, we've got surgical gloves, masks and plastic coveralls." He opened a large cupboard. "The golf bags are here, just as Albert ordered. I've doctored them ready to take the stuff. And look…special treat. Baseball caps with our own logo 'Aphrodite Golf Club' just for extra show."

"Where's the Plut?" Billy whispered.

Nicholson pointed to a small refrigerator in the corner. "Keeping cool," he said with a satisfied smile. "It doesn't need it but… a little bit of pampering. Just making sure it's comfortable."

He opened the fridge door. On the top two shelves, there were small, lidded Petri dishes in orderly rows. "There's the sherbet, ready for installation," he pronounced with pride. "Reminds me of lemon crystals I had as a kid. I used to dip a liquorice stick in it. Each dish is 54 millimetres wide. Four fit into a bag. I've got the lead discs and the spacers ready to fit into the golf bags as well." He turned to the cupboard and pulled out three A4 sheets of photographic paper. "Look, Billy. That's what the airport will see. I did a mock up with the lead in place and this is what the X rays look like. Similar to our other trips. You did the configuration so it will be safe and invisible."

Billy gazed solemnly at the images. He sniffed and passed them to Seaward.

"You see," Nicholson said with soft persuasion in his voice, "when the lead disks encase the Petri dishes all the X ray shows is a black image about an inch thick which is the base of the golf bag. All the clubs will be in there as well. Exactly the same as the other three dry runs. No problem. OK?"

"No problem." Seaward said. "Looks foolproof."

"And you Billy?"

Billy thought for a moment then nodded reluctantly.

Nicholson looked at his watch. "Right. We're on track. It's a quarter to one. Al will be here at about fourish. Get your clubs, balls, tees and all the rest of your golf gear out of the car ready to load up when he gets here. Then it's up, up and away. Come on boys, for a nice pub lunch on me."

CHAPTER 14

Coulson listened, his thumb between his teeth. "Jesus Christ" he whispered after each facet of the priest's revelation came to his ears. "This Nicholson bloke actually carried the stuff out in his briefcase."

Jack nodded. "A bit at a time, probably in a lead lined false bottom, just to be sure. Those altered lists show just over a kilo. He was such a regular there, I imagine any security was lax where he was concerned. It would be an easy job anyway. I understand that plutonium oxide is safe if it's contained in just a plastic bag or something similar."

"And they are heading out to Cyprus in January?"

"So the priest reckons. We've seen four plane tickets booked for January on McManus' laptop. Manchester, not Newcastle. Only a few winter flights from Newcastle until the spring."

"So, let's nip it in the bud. We'll piss on their chips right now, before they know what's happening to them." Coulson stared at the ceiling and juggled his false teeth, a sign his mind was in overdrive.

"O.K," he snapped. "Jack, get down to the magistrate's house and get those search warrants signed off. It's Saturday and he'll be at home. I'll brief Charteris. I think he'll want

Drummond to know. Christ, it is Saturday. Everybody will be at home with their feet up or at a football match or out shopping with their bloody wives. Do we have mobile or home numbers? If not we need to get them. We need warrants for Egremont as well."

Jack nodded. "I need to ring Colin Forrest in London. I'll break the news to him and he'll have his boys straight into that hotel near Paphos. We need to coordinate the times. Cyprus is two hours ahead of us. It's Sunday tomorrow. It's unlikely that Seaward and young McManus will be on site but just in case, let's organise the entries at say...seven in the morning, just in case they are working. Same for both Nicholson's house and offices. That makes the Cyprus action at nine, their time. We all go in together on the dot and surprise them before they start punching their mobiles. The Sheffield Force needs to be alerted to go in at the same time and arrest the van driver."

"You've been into the Whitehaven station, haven't you?" Coulson asked.

Jack nodded. "Checked with the Inspector when I first went over there."

"Contact him and get him to do the arrests and search over there. Better alert him to what they might find. But Christ, don't tell him the full story. Cook something up... anything. They'll need the special squad and so will we."

Colin Forrest was in his office. The phone rang.

"Colin?"

"Speaking."

"Colin, it's Jack Shaftoe. Newcastle CID."

"Jack! Hello again. You've just caught me. I'm off in a minute. Taking my son to his first rugby match. I had a few papers to check before one thirty or I wouldn't have been here."

"Glad you are or I would have been chasing you on your mobile or had someone searching for you at the rugby ground."

The voice in London suddenly went low and dark.

"What's up, Jack?"

"You know that Chechen cum Greek I asked you about the other day?"

"Yes…" came a cautious reply.

"Colin, we need your help. This Alessandro Dimitriou as he's now calling himself… we have reason to believe he is involved in subversion or sedition or whatever you want to call it. Major act of terrorism, Colin. We need him arrested and his hotel tooth-combed."

There was silence. Jack could almost hear wheels spinning in his brain.

"You still there?"

Forrest's voice was even lower and darker. *"I'm here Jack. He's got history, we know that. He's…he's, how can I say this, he's…or was until now, a minor potential problem. With his knowledge and experience, he could be trouble to the East or the West. Like I told you, he's on the watch list but as far as I can gather from the latest reports he's kept his nose clean and his hotel occupies most of his time."*

"Would you call him a P.S.S.?"

"Christ Jack, you know the jargon. Yes, I think he's got that accolade to his name. Now tell me what you know."

Jack told him the story from the beginning. There was no sound from Forrest during the telling.

"Are you still with me?" Jack said, interrupting the convoluted tale.

The voice at the other end of the line took a moment to answer. It was slow and doom laden. *"Yes Jack, still here. Stella was killed…murdered… go on."*

Jack continued until all the information had been passed over. Again a long silence.

"Is that everything?" Forrest said eventually. *"I need to get some people here into gear Jack, and like immediately."*

"No! For Christ' sake Colin…no!"

"There're people who need to be in on this Jack. I mean big people. This is major stuff. This could be… this could mean…shit, I'm scared to even think."

"Colin, contact Ralph Drummond at M.O.D. headquarters. He knows the score. He'll fill you in on the details. If he's not there I'm sure you've got his mobile number. We have the OK from him to land these creeps, but it's got to be undercover. We are organising a coordinated swoop on all of them. We need you to join the dots in Cyprus. Are you with me?"

'I understand. I know Drummond. He's a big noise in the firework factory. I still need to inform a host of people or my neck'll be on the block. I'll make sure that nothing is done until the arrests.'

"That's it, Colin. We'll need a simultaneous operation. Bang on 9am Cyprus time.7am our time. Still dark here at that time in the morning. We can have a conference call after the deed is done…and Colin you'll need some specialist radiation guys to go in with your men, just in case. God knows what he's got stashed in that hotel of his."

'We have a couple at the Akrotiri air force base. I'll put them on standby. And Jack, thanks for this. If it had got as far as Moscow…well it doesn't bear thinking about. He's got pals there…undercover. We know that, but until now they were all relatively harmless.'

"Still going to the rugby match?"

'You're joking. I now have a thousand and one things to do and phone calls to make.'

"For Christ' sake don't let anyone get too excited and fly off on a tangent. We cannot afford to let anybody get spooked or they'll go to ground."

'Understood. Speak to you tomorrow after the sortie. Good hunting, Jack,' he said with dread in his voice.

It was a quarter after six when the Cypriot arrived at Neutron Nuclear Services. His journey had been rushed, with little time to formulate any contingencies should there be snags to his sudden plans. That in itself unnerved him. He was a man who left nothing to chance. Their precise and exact operation that had been well-rehearsed and thought out over months, had suddenly been shunted into panic mode. His wife had tried to persuade him to wait; that the priest would not talk and the police would be focussed on the explosion. His determination frightened her. The successful conclusion to his plotting, scared her even more. There was a quiet savagery in him that she tried to dilute but her words were just noises in his ears. But for the first time, the possibility that the operation could fail had a flutter of dread in his innards. He knew he had to move fast. He knew he had to cajole and present a confidence that would have them all moving with a carefree nonchalance. It was the secret to a successful mission that would have Russia staggering from the enormity of it. He ignored his wife and made the flight bookings and tried to counter the sensation in his gut, a sensation he had not felt since his desperate departure from Chechnya.

Nicholson heard the car pull up and walked quickly to the reception and pressed the unlock button. He watched as the driver's door of a black hired Kia Sportage opened and Alessandro Dimitriou's legs both hit the ground together. He stood up and slammed the car door and turned for a second, admiring Seaward's Porsche before waving at Nicholson and striding forward. He was a tall man; thick necked and beefy; clean shaven but with a shock of wiry greying black hair that tumbled down to his ears and covered most of his brow. He had a patriarchal face that was stern and careworn at the same time. His eyes carried the rheumy look of sleeplessness, and traumas that seemed to tell the story of his past in one glance. He was dressed in jeans and a red polo necked sweater showed under a padded dark blue anorak. "Henry!" he growled loudly, his voice carrying a gruff pleasure as he hugged Nicholson. "Jesus, it fucking cold here. Your sister…my poor suffering wife, she says hello." His voice lowered. "I see they have arrived. Is everything ready?"

Nicholson tried to smile. "Yes…thank God you've got here, Al. We've been worried sick in case something happened."

He gave a throaty laugh. "Happened to me! What could happen to me?"

Nicholson shrugged. "Don't know. We're all just jumpy and thinking anything could happen, you know what I mean?"

The Cypriot gave an exaggerated sigh. He put his arm around Nicholson's shoulder as he led him up the corridor and toward the workshop. "Nothing will happen to me, Henry. And nothing will happen to you or the boys. Soon we will all be happy…yes?"

Nicholson stopped. "Al, Billy is getting more anxious by the minute. All the fear and anxiety his father started is rubbing off on him. He's OK but only just."

The Cypriot grunted. "Henry, this operation of mine must not fail. I would not be feeling this cold winter if the priest had been silenced. Kahsan is an idiot. I carry the revenge of all of Chechnya on my shoulders. Russia will pay as we all paid. They need to feel our pain. I will speak to Billy again. He'll smile when he gets his money."

Nicholson turned to face him. "Al… the money is…is definitely there isn't it?"

"Of course," he said as though the question was preposterous. "The money will be waiting for you. Separate safe deposit boxes in the London bank. No sweat. Our friend in the City will be doing all the inquisitive and involved paperwork. The money will be in small denominations as we arranged. Spend it how you like."

"Where's all that cash coming from? It's a lot of loot, Al."

Alessandro's face broke into a benign smile. "Henry, you have no idea who supports our cause and supplies everything from guns to cash. Big names and big countries. Now come on, we have work to do."

They worked in silence. It was time for positive action. Alessandro had greeted Billy McManus and Terry Seaward with bear hugs and excited encouragement. Then he grabbed Billy again, holding him at arm's length, suddenly serious.

"Billy, I am so sorry. Albert, your father, was my friend. I first met him when I worked at National Nuclear Laboratories. He was a good man. Who could have done such a thing? Why would he himself do such a thing? I do not know Billy. I am so sorry."

Billy nodded. "Thanks…thank you for that Al, but I don't know either. I don't know if he was murdered or he topped himself because of this…" He waved an arm around the workshop, "this… this fucking idea of yours."

The Cypriot frowned. "No, Billy, Albert would not do such a thing because of our plan. I know that, Billy. Now I'm telling you, everything will be all right. OK?"

Billy reluctantly nodded again.

Alessandro's face broke into a broad smile showing two gold teeth. "Good…good man. I will also tell you that your father's share of the money will come to all three of you, OK? Now let us get the cargo positioned."

It could have been an operating theatre. They were dressed in plastic coveralls, face masks and surgical gloves. The Petri dishes were carried from the fridge to a workbench and laid in a row. The golf bags were positioned next to the workbench. Nicholson produced the first lead disc. It was two millimetres thick. Billy placed a wooden former over it. The wood was ten millimetres deep, five millimetres thick and in the form of a cross, each arm of equal length and twenty millimetres from the edge. A Petri dish was placed into each of the four spaces.

"Each Petri dish has 63 grams of plutonium oxide, that's a total of just over a kilo," Nicholson whispered as though to speak any louder would activate the substance into a chain reaction. The Petri dishes were covered with another circle of lead. It was the same diameter as the first and again left a rim of twenty millimetres.

"Now," Billy mumbled. He took a pair of pliers and crimped the edges of the lead firmly together. He worked slowly and precisely, turning the disk as he worked. His three companions stared silently, almost mesmerised by this final act of containment.

"That's it," he said. "Same for the other three."

There was a noticeable atmosphere of relief at Billy's sudden relaxed comment.

"Good man," the Cypriot growled. "I coach you well. You've earned your money."

Seaward took one of the golf bags. "OK let's get it fitted." He unzipped the large side pocket on the bag. The golf club spacers had been removed as one, and the internal fabric had been cut open from the top to the base. The lead disc, now nineteen millimetres thick, was carefully slotted into the gap. It was a tight, neat fit at the bottom of the bag. The spacers were replaced, and the fabric was taped together.

"Told you," Nicholson said joyfully. "Told you it would be straightforward. I rehearsed the thing often enough. Now load it up with clubs, balls, tees and all the rest of our golfing paraphernalia and we're cooking with gas, boys. Oh, and I've got posh travel covers for the bags. With wheels. Just zip them into the carriers and put a lock on."

The Cypriot put his arm around Billy's shoulder. "See…see, Billy, everything is fine. Tomorrow you will be a rich man, Billy. Are you OK now?"

Billy's lips thinned, and then he nodded. "Yes, suppose so."

Alessandro squeezed him, his big hand biting into Billy's shoulder blade. Then he stood back a pace and cupped Billy's cheeks. "You are a good man Billy. Without you we would have no goods to trade." He glanced at his watch. "Look my friends, let's finish here. It's almost eight. We leave for Manchester now. We stay at the airport hotel tonight and away to sunny Cyprus early in the morning."

Jack got home at the same time. Clare threw down a magazine and stood up.

"Well," she said cautiously. "Any developments? You look totally shattered. You shouldn't have gone in today. Christ Jack, you're a bloody fool. You were inches away from winding up like Stella. You should have had a week off at least."

Jack headed for the drinks cabinet and poured himself a triple Scotch. "Clare, you are not going to believe this. Stella was murdered."

"What!"

"It's all on CCTV. Bloke from Sheffield in a white van. Looks like he booby trapped the house." He slumped down in an armchair opposite her and swallowed a mouthful of whisky. "And the priest spilled the beans. It's just as we thought…the whole rigmarole; all the suspects including the Cyprus connection."

Clare sat down again, opened mouthed. "But why Stella? Why was she murdered?"

"It was a mistake. They were after the priest and rigged the wrong house. I'm sure of it."

Clare shook her head in amazement. "This is going to be some story."

"There's more, Clare. This will give you the biggest scoop of the century."

She sat forward. "What…what is it, Jack?"

"The Plutonium oxide was to make a bomb…to explode in Moscow."

She closed her eyes. Her face twisted into crumpled wrinkles as the thought of that act and its consequences brutally rifled her imagination.

"Jesus Christ Almighty, that's…that's incredible."

"It won't happen. We're jumping on the whole band of villains tomorrow morning. Seven o'clock we descend on the two across on the West coast, Nicholson, Sheffield and Cyprus. It's all coordinated. It'll be one hell of a swoop. We'll round them all up and throw the book at them. Murder; theft; terrorism; attempting to smuggle dangerous materials out of the country. It's a life sentence if we're lucky."

"Can I go to Press with some preliminaries?"

"No! for Christ' sake, no Clare. Wait until the shit hits the fan tomorrow then we can talk about what can and can't be published. Remember Drummond's official secrets act caution. Normally I would have said bollocks to him, but remember McManus, Clare. You already know they can be above the law when they feel like it. And anyway, if any of this leaks out prematurely they've got their own story all ready for publication. The whole supposition will be ridiculed. A fantasy. They'll be whiter than white …and you know what? that'll be my job away up shit creek."

Clare tutted her disappointment and walked to the kitchen. "I hope all this 'wait and see' bullshit is going to be worth it," she shouted back at him. "This is big stuff, Jack. International big stuff. It better be worth the goddam wait."

"It will be Clare…trust me."

He heard dishes rattling. "There'll be food in twenty minutes. Finish your whisky."

Jack sat back. He gulped a mouthful, enjoying the smooth, smoky bite of an Islay single malt as it went down. He ran over the day's events in his mind. He had never experienced so many developments in such a short time. The priests outpouring; the white van hit man; the four-way raid planned for the next day, all arranged and coordinated with Charteris' instructions to get it all done. Then there was Stella. The vision of her slammed back into his memory. The feeling of revenge ran bitter sweet through him for a moment. He took another mouthful. It was going to be a Sunday to remember.

It was a Sunday to remember for the Cypriot and his cohort. They sat in the departure lounge at terminal 1. It was five past five in the morning and the place was already busy. The smell of coffee brewing and bacon cooking wafted around from the cafés. Loud laughter came from a table of six young men, already on their third pint and well on their way to a raucous flight before landing in Cancun for a week of bachelor debauchery.

Alessandro looked at his companions and smiled. "See," he whispered, "No problems, no sweat." He shrugged, eyebrows lifted, nodding; forcing himself to coax some confidence out of them. All three sat hunched and silent. Seaward tried to lose himself in a hefty Sunday newspaper. The check-in had been an ordeal of false jollity, playing to anyone that might be observing them, as they watched their golf bags disappear on the luggage belt. Now the gut-wrenching wait for the flight to be called.

"We're not out of the woods yet," Billy whispered.

The Cypriot put a finger to his mouth and glanced around. "Don't," he whispered. "They have long-range listening devices."

"Don't mention anything like that, Billy." Nicholson said, shaking his head.

Seaward didn't bother to lower his newspaper. "If it turns to rats, Billy boy will be to blame."

"Get stuffed," Billy muttered.

"Right… now," Alessandro said brightly. "We will board soon. We're on holiday, OK? No arguments. We are playing golf in sunny Cyprus. What could be better than leaving this cold winter behind. Now I'll buy us all a big whisky, Yes? Terry…Yes?"

Seaward lowered his paper. All three nodded, knowing the hit would give some measure of easing the awful dread that waltzed around within their bowels.

The Aegean airlines 737 roared down the runway and lifted into the air through a bank of low cloud. It was still dark outside but once they had emerged into clear sky, a faint dawn was clawing its way above the horizon. The plane was only half-full; mostly elderly couples heading for winter sunshine and near the rear, a gang of giggling females dressed as French maids; yet another pre marriage ritual.

The seat belt sign went out and Alessandro sat back,

leaned across the aisle and grabbed Billy's knee; a final reassurance. To him there had been no danger. They had passed through Manchester airport without even a second glance. Everything was to plan. Three rehearsals had stripped away any doubts that their golf bag strategy was less than foolproof. The priest might just be aware of their plan but tongue-tied by the church and its stifling rules. "*Pity he's still alive*," he thought to himself, "*pity the possible utterances of one man could ruin such a profound act of revenge.*" But now, after an anxious delay, they were on their way and the church would hold on to its secret, whatever that might be.

He shook Billy's knee. "Happy holiday. Happy holiday," he said joyously. "We are on our way, boys. Look where I booked the seats. Row two. We get the drinks first. Come on, let's celebrate."

Nicholson was near the Port window, sitting next to Seaward. Billy was in the aisle seat and the Cypriot opposite. The row in front and the two rows behind were vacant.

All three on the Port side felt an incredible sensation of relief. As take-off time got nearer, the tension in them grew. The delay had their innards churning and their eyes seeing every stranger as someone ready to pounce. As they approached the gate and waited for the boarding card check their imagination played havoc. They saw drastic scenarios where a multitude of uniformed officials descended from nowhere and manhandled them away to eternal captivity. But it had been painless. Routine; just like the three dry runs. They were now airborne and free of the suspicious confines of England. They began to relax. How to spend their reward flowed through their minds with honeyed visions of a carefree life. Billy had an uncontrolled elation in his voice as he gabbled on about nothing. Seaward told a ribald story about one of his past girlfriends and her habit of lapsing into baby- talk when close to a climax. Nicholson leaned across them and teased his brother-in-law about his sister and her liking for Ouzini and Keo red.

The drinks trolley appeared from the tiny galley in front

of them. Alessandro was happy to see them finally in a good mood. There was no need now for his burbling act of confidence. He was already formulating in his mind, his contacts, his choice of mule and the method of delivering his *present to Moscow*, as he called it.

"Coffee, tea…or some water?" the hostess asked him.

"Whisky, young lady, four whisky. "No make that doubles. We are celebrating," he said with exaggerated pleasure.

The hostess smiled. "What's the celebration?"

Alessandro opened his arms. "Life!...we love life."

"Ice?"

"Yes please," Billy shouted. "I used to make it myself but I lost the recipe."

They all laughed. It was going to be a good flight.

CHAPTER 15

He was awake before five after a troubled night, his mind racing with scenarios of the coming action.

Clare was beside him and he drew comfort from her warmth even though their closeness had not matured into a gratifying coupling. He slipped out of bed, showered and dressed quickly, stopping to listen for the gentle wheeze that signalled he hadn't disturbed her. He looked out of the landing window. It was frosty with a clear sky, a waning moon and a few of the brightest stars visible despite the streetlights. He imagined Nicholson, Seaward and Billy McManus still asleep, oblivious to the sudden descent of bellowing policemen. The shock, the uproar and their pale, downtrodden faces when the reality of their predicament hit home. Then there was the mysterious foreigner in Sheffield, unaware that a budding young thief in Jesmond could have caused his sudden arrest. He, like the others, would probably be turning over and snuggling in, expecting another couple of hours dreaming in the darkness of a winter's morning. The prospect of the instant mayhem had Jack tingling with excitement and itching for the action to get started.

He arrived at Robert's Hill just after six, his car touching seventy in the quiet sleeping streets. The place was already buzzing with activity. There were uniformed officers in the briefing room listening intently to Coulson explaining the planned routine. At seven on the dot, a detective, two police officers and two from the armed response unit, plus two radiation experts from the police special operations unit would enter Nicholson's house and a similar team would search the works and offices of Neutron Nuclear Services. The same operation was arranged for the houses of Terry Seaward and Billy McManus. Jack couldn't disguise the euphoria that built inside him. He looked at the gorilla- built men ready to act on the information he with Stella had gleaned, analysed, evaluated and caused to mature into a major exercise that satisfied his simple basic desire to out-wit criminals. It would be a delight to see them pay the price for their ill-judged notion that the law was there to be broken and money to be made because of it.

Harry Lockwood appeared and tugged at Jack's arm. "Well, today's your big day, sunshine. Christ, things have moved on a bit since that supposed suicide in the lay-by."

Jack sighed. "You do not exaggerate Harry. Are you in on this op?"

Harry grunted. "You're fucking right I am. I'm with you Jackie boy. We go to the house, is that right.?"

Jack nodded. "Coulson is in on the action. He goes to the factory. We get to see Nicholson crap himself."

"Great."

Nicholson's house was a large five bedroomed edifice on the coast. It looked out over the North Sea with a view to St Mary's island to the left and the massive ruins of Tynemouth Priory to the right, dominating the headland and the entrance to the river. In its 2000-year history which began as an iron age settlement, it became an Anglo-Saxon monastery, a royal castle and a coastal defence during two world wars. The marauding Danes had several attempts at sacking it and succeeded 1200 years before. Nicholson had bought the house with some of his father's legacy. He wanted it not only for the views but, so he imagined, its size and position reflected his own standing in the community. Looking out from the upstairs windows, he often surveyed the many strollers passing on a rare sunny weekend and imagined they glanced at his own castle with envy. And it pleased him.

On that early Sunday morning in late November there was no view out at sea other than the faint, slow moving light of a passing ship near an invisible horizon. The moon still hung low at a lazy angle in the sky to the west. The air was crisp and still and the population still slumbered on in their weekend oblivion. The hush seemed to be in awe of what was to come.

The police van rolled to a quiet stop at the roadside one hundred yards from the broad gate leading up to the front door of Nicholson's house. Jack sat opposite Harry Lockwood who had a rare smile cemented into his pock-marked features. He glanced at his watch. "Three minutes," he whispered.

"I love these fucking raids. I love the sudden mayhem, the panic and the villains crapping themselves."

Jack nodded "Me too." He could feel his heart pounding. Such operations carried danger. There was no guarantee that the occupants of the house were not armed. And on this occasion, it was not only the possibility of guns or knives but deadly radioactive crystals that could be thrown around or pushed into the faces of the intruders. It was always a worst-case possibility. Desperate men do desperate things as Stella used to always remind him. He had never needed reminding; he had seen it all before. They had to be ready for any retaliation.

"Right! Let's go." Jack said to the driver. The van engine started and it rolled forward to the gate.

"Got the big red key," Harry whispered as he pulled a metal battering ram out with him.

The party of seven walked quickly up the drive. Two

officers disappeared immediately around the left gable end, to head off anyone bolting out of the back door. The front door was black high quality German manufacture with a 3-millimetre skin of aluminium. There was a quadruple glazed vertical window down the left-hand side and five-point automatic locking. It took three blows with the ram and it buckled in the middle.

Harry kicked hard with the flat of his right boot and it caved in. The special operations men charged in behind the armed helmeted officers.

"Police!" Harry bellowed above the screaming coming from up the stairs and the high- pitched anxious bark of a small dog coming from somewhere toward the kitchen. The hall light was switched on and Molly Nicholson appeared at the landing, a loud piercing whine coming from behind fists clenched at her mouth. She stood there, her cramped blue nightdress hanging loosely and her greying hair an unkempt tangle straight from her warm pillow.

"Henry Nicholson!" Harry bellowed ignoring her abject terror. "Where is Henry Nicholson?" he repeated as he climbed the stairs. Jack followed him as their colleagues rampaged through the rooms on the ground floor.

"No!" she shrieked. "No! he's not here…he's away! What's wrong? Jesus, what have we done?"

"Where is he?" Jack barked as he squeezed past Harry and the woman, opening doors and glancing quickly into each room.

Molly let out another anguished cry. "He's not here! He's not here, I'm telling you. He's…he's gone to Cyprus. What has he done? My God what has he done?"

They ignored her. Then a sudden sickening dread hit Jack as her words gelled in his mind. He turned to the woman. "When…when did he go to Cyprus?"

She started sobbing; deep, long uncontrollable sobs as the impact of the frantic chaos hit her. "Ye… yesterday. Golf…just golf. They left last night for Manchester. They're flying this morning. For Christ's sake tell me what he has done?"

Jack looked into Harry's solemn face. Harry's eyebrows lifted, a gesture of 'what do we do now?'

Jack knew immediately what he had to do. He punched Coulson's number viciously into his phone.

"He's done a runner Boss," he said flatly. "Anything at his works?"

Coulson's voice was equally without expression. "Nobody. The boys are searching the place with their sensors. So far, nothing except there's a room in the workshop. It was locked and secured but we've got in. Plastic coveralls, masks, gloves lying around. And four golf bags that have seen some use. They're running their gear over the place now to make sure it's clean but it looks like they've been busy…hold on…"

Jack heard a short, muffled conversation then he was back. "Just had the west coast boys on. Seaward's house was empty, so was the McManus residence. Neighbours say the mother had gone to her sister's in Carlisle for the weekend."

Jack grunted. "The bastards have done a runner, Boss. Nicholson's wife says they went to Manchester and flew this morning. Can we get Manchester to check and stop the flight?"

He heard Coulson sniff. He imagined his teeth doing the rhumba. "Yes, I'll get them to check the passenger lists for Cyprus. They can stop the flight, that is if the birds haven't already flown."

Jack turned to Nicholson's wife, still standing in her nightdress, her face white and tear-filled eyes wide with shock. Her dog, a Yorkshire terrier, ran up the stairs and she gathered it up, holding it tightly against her chest.

"Get your dressing gown on and make yourself a cup of tea," he said gently.

"What have we done? What have we done?" she wailed.

Harry Lockwood wandered around the landing checking the same rooms as Jack had done. "You'll find out soon enough, love," he muttered. "Your husband's been a naughty boy."

It was ten minutes before Coulson called. His voice carried an exaggerated tone of defeat. They're on Aegean Airlines flight 109. And so is this Dimitriou bloke."

Jack sucked in a breath. "Well I'll be buggered. They're all together. We'll catch the whole nest of them. What time does it leave?"

"It already has. Scheduled for 0530 but it took off at 0655."

Jack glanced at his watch. It was 0715. "Shit," he hissed, "They've been away twenty minutes."

"All is not lost," Coulson said, his voice suddenly brighter. "Charteris has been on to Drummond. He's been up all night. He's getting the plane turned around."

Jack whistled a note of surprise. "Brilliant! But we need to get to Manchester."

"No we don't, Jack. Just rely on your uncle Wilbur. Drummond's instructed air traffic control to tell the pilot to say nothing in case our friends decide to kick off. Just turn around gently and set course for Newcastle. They're just near the German border now. They'll be landing here in about twenty-five minutes."

Jack let out a whoop of joy. "We're on our way to the airport, Boss."

"See you there... and by the way, the Sheffield force have collared the van driver. And guess what? he's a bloody Chechen. They'll have him here this afternoon."

Their drinks were no more than two sips in and the trolley up to row five when it was pulled back into the galley. They took no notice or if they did, it did not register any significance when a hostess walked slowly up to the trolley and whispered in her colleague's ear. Their conversation had mellowed. The whisky and their early morning departure brought a contented drowsiness to their minds. Nicholson glanced out of the window. The sky held a tenuous grey dawn and the clouds below were a quilt of dull white stretching to the dark horizon. Nicholson's glance was casual; almost without seeing, until his eye caught a break in the monotonous pattern below. He could see the sea. He began to take notice. Was it the sea? No, it couldn't be... it was a lake. It must be a lake. They had to be well beyond the North Sea after...he glanced at his watch...after forty minutes. He leaned forward looking past his brother-in-law and through his window. He could see that the weak light of a new day was forming beyond his vision to the right. Surely it should be ahead at one side of the plane or the other. The cloud blanket below them seemed to be closer. Again, it did not stir any real curiosity until the plane was suddenly lost in fog. Nicholson frowned. The engine noise altered. Then he relaxed. Cloud formations were often at different heights. The plane shuddered. He nudged Seaward.

"Looks like we might get some turbulence."

Seaward shrugged.

The 'fasten seat belt' sign lit up.

"It is turbulence," Nicholson said.

A hostess appeared from her tiny galley and unhooked a microphone. "Ladies and gentlemen, we have a minor problem. There is no cause for alarm. Please fasten your seat belts for landing."

All four of them sat bolt upright and looked to each other for some explanation. Alessandro ignored the order, jumped up, and stood at the galley. The two hostesses sat facing them and buckled in. "Why? Why are we landing?"

They shook their heads, faces blank, without expression. "Emergency. Nothing to worry about. Please sit down and fasten your seat belt."

The Cypriot sat. Nicholson gazed out of the window. The fog disappeared in an instant and he could see the sea. Then he could see a coastline. Then the lighthouse at St Mary's island, and with it came the sickening realisation that they were landing at Newcastle.

"Oh...Christ, no! Its fucking Newcastle!" he said from

behind clenched teeth.

"Newcastle? No. It's an emergency," Alessandro barked. "They land for help…spare part or…or something."

Seaward's knee started quivering.

They sat and waited; All of them silent. Their minds in an uproar of possibilities, as the plane taxied toward the terminal and parked at the remote end of the apron. As it swung around Nicholson watched in disbelief. He counted six police cars, two police vans, a dozen or more uniformed policemen and four men dressed in white hooded coveralls.

"We're fucked," he whispered. "There're police tripping over themselves out there. It's all over."

The others didn't answer. Seaward covered his face with his hands. The Cypriot stared straight ahead, blinking in the reality of it. Billy was bent forward, his head almost touching his legs and his forearms shielding his head as he gently sobbed.

The plane door opened. Jack Shaftoe and Coulson entered followed by Harry Lockwood and three other uniformed officers. Big men; strong and capable of man-handling any reluctant suspect.

Jack stood for a moment looking up the aisle at the silent wondering passengers, then at the four in row two. He tried to hide a smile of satisfaction but he failed. "Well, well, look who we have here. Welcome back to dear old England… Henry Nicholson, Terence Seaward, William McManus…" he turned to the other side of the aisle. "And…Alessandro Dimitriou I'm arresting you on suspicion of the murder of Stella van Kirk, contravening the Nuclear Offences act 1983, theft, initiating an act of terrorism and the illegal export of hazardous substances. You do not have to say anything but it may harm your defence if you do not mention, when questioned, something which you later rely on in court. Anything you do say may be given in evidence."

The girls at the back of the plane started cheering. Jack stepped to one side and let Harry and his officers prise the limp figures out of their seats.

"Now we aren't going to have to use cuffs…are we...? Yes, I think we'd better." Harry said, chastisingly, as though speaking to some wayward children. They were spun around. There was no resistance as their arms were pressed together behind them and handcuffs snapped into place.

As they were led down the steps, Harry turned back to the passengers. "Sorry to interrupt your holiday folks. We just need to get some bags out of the hold and you'll be on your way."

The girls cheered again.

On the apron, Coulson grabbed Jack's arm. "I've just phoned Drummond. He's chuffed to say the least. He's coming up tomorrow. He wants to speak to us all. He says to tell you, not a word of this to the Press, at the moment. He's sending out a blanket DSMA security notice to all media outlets killing the story." He nodded toward the control tower. "Somebody up there will be ringing the Tabloids as we speak and half those passengers in the plane will have their mobiles going again."

Jack nodded. He wondered how Clare would react to that development. In the car on the way to the airport, he had imagined her delight at the finale of the investigation and being able at last to get her fingers on the computer keyboard. Now he would have to stall her again. Suddenly the whole saga took on a mood of anti-climax. The team had been sparking with anticipated action. Now it was over. It had been textbook. No chase. No violence. No armed retaliation. Just straightforward submissions. He watched as the four reluctant figures were filed into a police van.

Jack smiled at the Cypriot. "Just in case you were wondering, we have your pal… what's his name again...? oh yes…you know, the visitor from Sheffield, Khasan Ismailov."

Alessandro did not react. His face was locked in a sagging look of abject defeat. Only Seaward carried a swaggering defiance. He looked over to Jack. "Bastard!" he shouted before he disappeared and Harry Lockwood slammed the doors. Jack patted him on the back. "Harry, you know that punk who tried to rob the bookies…did you catch him?"

"We did. We managed to get his number plate the same time as the van. Spotty faced little prick said his mother had her pension pinched and she needed money for food. Ha… fuckin'… ha."

"As well as getting his wrist slapped will you give him a medal?"

"A medal?"

"If he hadn't tried to rob the bookies, we would have never got a lead on a suspect for Stella's murder."

Harry gave a sarcastic grin. "I'll see what I can do."

"Coulson turned to him, putting and arm across his shoulders as they walked to the cars. "That's that. Ten out of ten, Jack. Let's get back to the Station…" he glanced at his watch. "It's after nine already. Time for a big mug of tea and a bacon sarnie."

It was after midday when Forrest rang from London.

"Jack, it's Colin Forrest. I hear your operation went well."

"Perfect. I rang earlier but you were not at your desk. How did Cyprus go? I wanted to tell you that our Chechen cum Greek Cypriot was here in the UK. We got him…we got them all."

"So that's where he was hiding. His English wife was screaming and scratching when we cuffed her. Said she didn't know where her beloved was. Wouldn't cooperate at all. Kept yelling 'police brutality'. We went through his hotel from top to bottom. We picked up some useful stuff, Jack. Frightening stuff. E- mails on his laptop. Addresses in Grozny… and in Moscow. Names…including your mates in the UK. So far, I understand the hotel is clean radiation wise. And get this Jack, a map. Just had it E- mailed to me. Five sheets. A large-scale map of Moscow with some chilling spots highlighted."

"Like where?"

"How about The National Defence Management Centre,

Znamenka in Moscow. That's the headquarters of the Russian Ministry of Defence and Russian Armed forces. Then there's a nice red ring around the homes of Mikhail Mezentsev and his boss Sergei Shoigu."

"Who are they?"

"Just the head honcho and the deputy director of the whole place. Then of course there's the Kremlin and the Bely Dom on Krasnopresenskaya. It's called the White House. Prime Minister's office and the main government building. Looks like they meant business, Jack. They had some choice targets to choose from. The controlled lines here have been buzzing all morning. Just came out of a meeting with so much brass, the floor was groaning under the strain. I had one fucking hell of a job stopping them running amok when they knew your little operation was underway. We need to see your catch. I understand you have Ralph Drummond coming up tomorrow."

"Yes, there's a meeting in Charteris' office."

"What about the goods they were smuggling?"

"Safely locked away. Nicely hidden in the bottom of their golf bags in lead shielding. The special ops unit took five minutes to suss it out."

"Christ, Jack just looking at that map and what Dimitriou planned to do, it does not bear thinking about."

"You can say that again. But thankfully they're behind bars and licking their wounds. They'll get life if we're lucky. Just heard the jailer took them some lunch. It was mince. Terry Seaward took one look at it and said 'I don't like mince' The jailer said 'would you like to see the menu?' and he said 'yes please.' Oh dear, I think the jailer's given himself a hernia with laughing so much."

CHAPTER 16

It was after seven in the evening when he got home, and he was exhausted. With all the excitement of the raid and the adrenalin rush of the unknown, its outcome had melted into dull routine. He had watched as Khasan Ismailov arrived from Sheffield, handcuffed and noisy. Jack looked into his sneering face, his beard still carrying breakfast crumbs. He tried to fathom the inner workings of his brain that allowed the clinical extermination of an innocent human being. He had eyeballed many a murderer but never one who had taken the life of someone close to him as Stella. To anyone who gave him a casual glance he was a conventional human being. Somewhat unusual; big and broad shouldered with an ebullient manner and wild growth of facial hair but nothing that broadcast an ability to kill someone so remote from his cause.

"You're a fucking bastard," Jack whispered close to his face. "You understand that English, don't you, you pig?" He had the urge to grab him by the throat, squeeze his thumbs into his windpipe and watch his eyes pop out like ping pong balls. He looked him up and down, dressed in a camouflage jacket and khaki pants and heavy army boots. Then it struck him. The boots. The boots would be removed anyway, in case he decided to use the laces on his neck. The CCTV had seemed to show he was wearing them. The boots went on priority, straight to forensics. At shortly after four the report came back. Gravel caught in the deep tread of his boots matched the gravel on Stella's drive. It was a no brainer. E-mails on his mobile and sheaves of papers harvested from his flat linking him to his fellow Chechen was enough to get him off the streets for a long time. Jack sat opposite him in the interview room. He stared into his sullen belligerent face, still wanting to punch the life out of him for Stella. The Chechen was silent. He ignored every question.

"The gravel on your boots matches the gravel on the drive of the deceased. How do you explain that?"

There was no response. He stared back at Jack with unblinking eyes.

"We intend to examine the van you were driving. What if we find matching gravel in the tyre tread. How will you explain that?"

The Chechen's face was set as though in a trance.

"Who gave you the order to rig that house? Was it Henry Nicholson? Was it the Cypriot or maybe Seaward and young McManus? You know them all, don't you? We have them all you know…all ready to spill the beans and drop you right in the shit. Because they will all deny any involvement in the murder and let you take the blame. You realise that, don't you?"

There was no spark of anxiety or concern. He sat rigid, his face cast in stone, his eyes heavy lidded and staring sightlessly ahead. Jack took a deep slow breath. He waited a second then hit the stop button on the recorder.

"Terminating the interview with Khasan Ismailov at sixteen twenty- two." He stood up. The Chechen followed, pulling his lumbering frame from the seat. Jack forced a smile to his face. "Be as silent as you like," he whispered as the guard led him away. "You're going to jail. Sure as hell, you're going to rot in jail. And boy, when they get you in there… you'd better get some Vaseline from the prison shop. When some of those randy long termers who haven't touched a woman for years see you... wow, you'll not be so quiet then."

He interviewed the others. Nicholson looked strangely vulnerable out of his business suit and dressed in a polo shirt and summer jacket. He was subdued and his face carried a shocked fear as though he was about to face a guillotine.

Jack sat back and stared into his heavy-lidded eyes. "Well now Henry what are you going to tell me about your little escapade?"

Nicholson hung his head. He blinked quickly as though in a bad dream that would not let him go.

"Tell me, how did you get the plutonium oxide past security? It was in your briefcase, wasn't it?"

Nicholson made to speak, then he stopped himself.

"Come on, Henry old pal. We know that's how you did it. But what about security? Was Driscoll involved? Was he part of your team, Henry? Did he just turn a blind eye for a piece of the action?"

Nicholson shook his head. He closed his eyes. "No," he croaked. "Driscoll was just used to my coming and going. I've been going to that site for a long time. H trusted me... I was... I was not a security risk."

"Well, well, Henry you've pissed right on his chips now, haven't you. He'll probably get the sack because he allowed himself to trust you. And that's his pension up shit creek. And that's not all. Your sister in Cyprus is in a cell at RAF Akrotiri. I hear there's quite a big bunch of illegal Lebanese immigrants keeping her company. Your little trips to the sun kissed isle are over, my friend, and your sister's cosy little hotel business with your Chechen brother- in- law is well and truly shagged. Not to mention Neutron Nuclear Services. Its financial state means bankruptcy boy–oh, and all the staff will be on the 'old king Cole.' Proud of yourself?"

Nicholson's face crumpled. He covered it with trembling hands. "How... how did you find all this out?"

"That's what we're paid to do, Henry. Suss out rank amateurs, like you lot. It was easy. It was a no brainer. Now tell me about the powder, Henry. Is there any still out there? We've been into your so-called X ray unit and found all the paraphernalia for handling the stuff. Your golf bags were holding the lot, or is there more?"

Nicholson nodded. "That's all there is." There was a pained pleading in his face. "Was it the Priest? Was it Albert's brother who shopped us?"

Jack gave a satisfied grunt. "No way, just good old fashioned detective work. It didn't take us long to have you all in our sites. Now Henry, what about the gas explosion? Did you organise that? You wanted to kill the priest, didn't you? You got your brother- in- law to fix it in case the priest blew the whistle on your enterprise. Am I right? But he balls it up, Henry. What a bunch of amateurs you are. He got the wrong house. That was it wasn't it?"

Nicholson came to life. He sat up, his face creased with fear. "No...Jesus, no! It was all Dim..."

He seemed to deflate again. There was surprise on his face as though he suddenly realised that he had been talking. "I'm saying nothing more. I want a lawyer."

"You were going to say Dimitriou... your brother- in- law?"

Jack watched as a bead of sweat ran slowly from Nicholson's temple. It meandered down his cheek and dripped off his jaw onto the dark green plastic table.

Jack was enjoying watching him squirm. He threw in another frightener, just for fun. "Who shot Albert, Henry? Was it you? Did you shut him up in case he got to the Press?"

Nicholson hung his head. "No... no never," he whispered, "I'm saying nothing more."

Jack smiled. He could read the signs. Two or three more sessions and he would be singing like a canary on a summer day. "Terminating the interview with Henry Nicholson at..." he glanced at his watch... "Sixteen fifty-five."

The Cypriot was more defiant. He sat upright in total contempt of the situation, shaking his head in answer to each question. Finally, after twenty minutes, Jack terminated the interview. Dimitriou stood up. "You know nothing," he spat. "You know nothing of my life. You know nothing of our suffering."

Only Billy cracked immediately. Only Billy poured out all the details that would condemn them to a quick and straightforward trial. When he was told that the explosion that killed Stella was meant for his uncle the priest, his words came in short urgent bursts in between long sobbing intervals. He screwed his clenched fists hard against his cheeks, the action twisting his face as the tortured words came out. He admitted to everything. The theft and the transfers to Nicholson's brief case. How Albert McManus and Terry Seaward altered the documents and how Alessandro Dimitriou had engineered the whole operation from afar. Two things had played on Jack's mind during the investigation. The minor but significant observation of their suntans and the reason McManus was parked in that particular lay-by. Billy answered one of them. He explained how on their dry runs he and Nicholson had spent most of their time with the Cypriot while Seaward and his father had played golf. It needed their nuclear expertise to fathom out the details but the operation itself needed four people; four golf bags.

"Can I go to my father's funeral?" he bleated.

Jack didn't reply.

The other answer came from Seaward. It took more than forty minutes to get anything positive out of him. He sat, defiant; arms folded tightly across his chest, demanding a lawyer and repeating 'no comment' to every question. Then Jack sensed he was wilting. Seaward's right leg started trembling. His shoulders sagged. The frown that came to his face was covered with two clinging hands.

"Come on Terry, you know the game is up. We have all

the evidence and positive statements from your friends. Just tell me one thing. How did you get Albert to stop in that lay-by?"

Seaward laid his hands on the table. Then he scratched at his left shoulder with his right hand then his right with his left. The action was desperate, as though termites were eating him alive. He blew noisily from his nose as he came to life. His eyes widened. "I didn't kill him. I swear I didn't kill him!"

Jack gestured for him to calm down. "Ok…ok, we don't think you did, Terry but…" Jack shrugged, "…but we know you rang Albert on his way to Newcastle, supposedly about the leak on site… then Mr Drummond in London… but it wasn't for that was it, Terry? Come on. Help us and help yourself, Terry. I hope you appreciate the predicament you've got yourself into here. I'll ask you again. It wasn't about the leak… was it?"

Terry shook his head sullenly. "No," he whispered. "Albert was going to spill the beans to the Press about the Cyprus trips. He had threatened all day. I couldn't rest after he left for home. I had to see him… try once again to convince the stupid prick everything would be all right. I went to his house but he wouldn't listen. He had convinced himself that the whole idea was jinxed." Seaward scratched at his brow as though his skin was on fire. "I said think about your son… think about your wife. The police won't forget about it just because you confessed. We'll all land up in jail no matter what. I said the whole scheme is foolproof. Just keep silent, I said. You can do this, Albert, I said, but he wouldn't listen. 'I can't' he said. I begged him to reconsider. I even thought about some physical way to stop him… you know, bash him over the head with a brick or something. There was panic running through him. I could see it his eyes even in the darkness. He was… he was… deranged. Then I panicked. Somehow, he had to be stopped. I contacted Drummond and told him he was on his way to spill the beans to the Press about the safety issues on site. I rang McManus after I saw his car leave and I knew I couldn't stop him. I told him some stupid story about Nicholson and that he was on his way to Egremont to see him. That he had a whole new set of plans from Dimitriou that were easier and safer and he wanted to explain them to him. I said they would pass each other on the road if he didn't stop. I told him Nicholson had suggested the lay-by just east of Corbridge. Somehow, after a load of wrangling, begging and bull shit, I got him to agree. It was a crazy, desperate idea but it worked. Then I rang Mr Drummond… told him Albert was desperate to blow the whistle on the site contamination but what happened after that, I just don't know. I told Drummond that I had convinced him he was meeting Nicholson at that lay-by. Drummond just said leave it to me. But Christ, he topped himself… or somebody shot him. But it wasn't me… it wasn't us… I swear it wasn't me. Surely it wasn't Drummond's doing."

He closed his eyes and shook his head slowly.

"So Mr Drummond really thought he was on his way to tell all about the site contamination?"

Seaward nodded.

"Well, well, that explains a lot, Terry."

"Will we get jailed for a long time? We didn't kill anybody," he whispered.

"There's the death of detective constable Stella van Kirk. Want to tell me anything about that? Who organised that, Terry? Was it you? Was it Nicholson or maybe your pal from Cyprus?"

Seaward thought for a moment with his thumb between his teeth. He stared down at the table in front of him and sobbed gently. "It was Nicholson's brother- in-law. Nicholson told me it was his brother- in- law… because… because it should have been the priest and it was a mistake. A terrible mistake. I had nothing to do with it. How long do you think I'll get in jail?"

Jack was tempted to tell him that it would surely be many years and he would get used to mince.

Clare was, as usual, eager for news. She knew it was the day of the big raid and now was the time for all the facts and all the facets of the investigation to come out into the open. She was itching to interview anybody and everybody remotely connected to the suspects. Sellafield was ripe for a full- blown expose. A proposed act of international terrorism was a rare and bountiful journalistic treat.

She assumed the police operation had been successful but she hadn't linked it to the incident at the airport. Bellamy had sent her there after a hint of something unusual on the Apron had sizzled through the ether. But when she got there, whatever had happened was over. Things were as normal. Nobody she spoke to knew anything or would say anything except there had been a host of police cars and flashing blue lights and people taken off the plane. She managed to speak to the airport manager but he dismissed her with a flustered shrug. She could tell he'd been ordered not to say anything to the Press.

She had been home only fifteen minutes when Jack appeared. "You got them locked up?"

He flopped down in a chair. "Yep, we got them... got them all, including the Cypriot mastermind. He was in England and party to the smuggling. We didn't collar them here. They had done a runner to Manchester." He gave a satisfied smile. "The stupid pricks thought they had got away with it. They were actually in the air but we got the plane turned around and it landed at Newcastle."

"Aha!" That's what caused the buzz at the airport."

"You heard about it?"

"Got there but... but nothing. All done and dusted. Nobody knew or wouldn't say what all the action was about."

Jack got up. He gently massaged his nose between thumb and forefinger. "Clare, it'll have to stay that way...at least for a day or two."

"What!"

"London has put a Defence Security notice on it until everything is assessed. Bellamy can't print even if you hand him the whole intricate shebang."

She turned and strode forcefully into the kitchen. "This is pissing me off, Jack," she shouted among the clatter of pans.

He winced at the noise. When Clare got mad, she always headed for the kitchen and it was time to slip into protective gear. "I'm sorry. It's not my fault. I was all set to give you the final chapter."

Her head appeared at the kitchen door. "A day or two you say?"

Jack nodded. "So Coulson tells me, but Drummond's coming up from London for a meeting tomorrow. I'll twist his arm then."

She thought for a moment then disappeared back into the kitchen. "You'd better," she shouted. "Better twist it good and fucking hard. I'm pig sick of Triads and Council fiddlers. I want some proper raw meat...OK?"

"OK," Jack said wearily and headed for the drinks cabinet.

Drummond arrived at Force headquarters off the BA morning flight from Heathrow. The three major players were there in Charteris' office. He still looked robotic. Dark blue three-quarter length overcoat. Expensive looking grey double-breasted suit. Flat 1940's hairstyle and eye- catching dimpled chin. He introduced himself with an officious stiff posture and single movement handshake to each in turn. He came to Jack.

He smiled. "Jack, nice to see you again."

"Ralph. Likewise."

Eyebrows went up at the display of familiarity. Charteris offered him a seat. He took off his overcoat and placed it carefully over the back of his chair, sat and took time looking at each of them in turn.

"Gentlemen, first let me say this visit and our meeting

today is now under the official secrets act. Are we all clear on that?"

They nodded.

"Let me congratulate you all on a first-class job. I had to come north to tell you that in person because... well, because of the seriousness of the crime and its possible consequences if it had not been terminated. From what I can gather so far, a major Chechen terrorist incident in Moscow could have had damaging repercussions on a world scale... are you with me? Because of the nature of it, and how it was to come about, there could be certain detrimental insights to our security system. Because of that it has been decided that there will be a full DSMA security notice on this for the foreseeable future."

Jack frowned. "You mean a total Press blackout?"

Drummond breathed in through his teeth. "'Fraid so."

"Oh Christ," Jack groaned. Visions of Clare in ballistic mode had him driving her to the train station again.

"But what about the Russians?" Charteris said. "Surely they'll tell it all."

Drummond sat back and smiled. He gave a dainty dry reserved laugh. "No they won't. The Russians will know nothing about it."

"Nothing?" Charteris said with surprise. "How can you keep it from them?"

Drummond sighed. "Way back in 1978 there was a Bulgarian defector working for the BBC. Georgi Markov. He was walking across Waterloo Bridge and was shot in the leg from a weapon disguised as an umbrella, would you believe. Ricin poisoned him. Ricin is made from the castor plant. Castor oil comes from the same plant. My mother used to chase me around the house trying to get a spoonful down my throat. It was her cure-all for everything. But process the castor seed husks and you get a lethal substance... ricin." He smiled. "Vomiting; abdominal pains; lungs fill up with fluid and you drown. A nasty way to die. Then in 2006 Albert Litvinenko was poisoned with radioactive Polonium 210. He was a British naturalised Russian defector and former Russian secret service agent. He died a nasty slow death. Then, not so long ago, you will remember Sergei Skripal and his daughter Yulia. He was a former Russian military officer turned UK agent. That attempted assassination was unsuccessful but as you know, I'm sure, Novichok, a really virulent nerve agent was used. All these, and there are others still under wraps, happened in the UK. Russia has no conscience about borders or assassinations. They are master assassins and poisoners, among other things. Now, we have just saved Moscow from a devastating incident, which would have contaminated the whole city and then some. Do we want them knowing what a wonderful job we have done? No way. We don't want them to have the satisfaction to know that the UK saved them from total disaster. They would just laugh their socks off at our gullible reaction, knowing full well that they can use us as a killing shop when the mood takes them…are you with me?"

"So, the whole thing never happened," Coulson whispered, looking at Jack's disbelieving face.

"'Fraid so. And we will want some input into the trial, which will be held in camera of course, due to its sensitive nature. Firstly, I need to send up some of our men to interview them. They'll be security personnel, special branch and the anti-terrorist brigade. That will be in the next few days. If you can do anything to… how shall I put it… soften them up, all well and good."

"And McManus committed suicide?" Coulson said.

"Of course he did."

"And DC van Kirk's death was accidental?"

He nodded.

Jack leaned forward. "But… but Russia. Wouldn't it have been a great relief to the West if Moscow couldn't function?"

Drummond smiled again. "What if they thought we had engineered the whole thing? What would their reaction be?

It's a funny old world, Jack. Wheels within wheels. We don't support things like that. That's not how it's done. How it *is* done? Unfortunately I am not at liberty to tell you."

"So what about the suspects? They'll blab for sure... probably to the tabloids."

"No they won't. The Press cannot print. We'll see they're put away for at least fifteen years; probably life...and I mean life. Not that ridiculous sentencing system that means they'll be out in eight. If they ever do get out then, well, the world might be a different place and we'll take whatever action is relevant at the time."

"You mean they might be silenced... permanently."

Drummond didn't answer. He sat back. They knew there was no latitude for argument. His face was set and his arms were folded tightly across his chest.

As Jack drove home trying to suppress the dread that held him in a sickly embrace, all the events of a few swift days ran through his mind. He found it hard to convince himself that somehow a vibrant and active case had fizzled out to nothing. It hadn't happened. Had it been a dream? Drummond would swear it had, if there was ever a whiff of the facts came to the curious. Drummond had stayed another hour before leaving for some meeting in Durham. He chatted idly about security in general, potential terrorist activity in the UK and the major task of keeping ahead of cyber-attacks. He briefly mentioned the input GCHQ at Cheltenham had for shutting down enemy communications, misinformation and its own brand of computer hacking. Sellafield was not mentioned until he made to leave.

Jack stood up and shook his hand. "There's a promise I made to a lady who works at Sellafield."

Drummond nodded, open mouthed. "Ah yes, Sellafield."

"I promised I would do what I could to get some action on that all important site survey. Will Butterworth be keeping it going?"

Drummond nodded again. "It's in hand, Jack. Butterworth is interviewing replacements for McManus and Seaward as we speak. The survey will be completed and acted upon. Seaward of course has been sacked for incompetence which threatened significant danger to the workforce. And young McManus … several undisclosed major breaches of security. As for your man, Nicholson, we'll wait and see what the boys from London say. Maybe major tax evasion or some obscure fiddle that the legal men can pin on him. We'll make sure the charges warrant their sentence. And, as I said, there'll be no 'good boys get out early'. Are you with me?" He gave a smile that lasted all of a second as he reached for his coat.

When he had gone, there was silence for a moment. Charteris shrugged. "Well, that's it boys. Close the file. Might as well burn it… but don't. Things might change sometime in the distant future."

"Come on," Coulson said to Jack. "Let's get back to the Station."

Jack turned to Charteris. "Just one thing, sir. Have we managed to contact Stella's relations?"

Charteris nodded. "Yes, they'll be here tomorrow. There'll be a formal identification and a full official funeral. Of course, following that edict from Drummond, she died in a gas explosion." He gave a helpless shrug. "Nothing else we can do."

"Can I ask a favour?"

"Yes, what is it.?"

"Ask her relatives to take her ashes to Curacao. I know that would be what she wanted. She never shut up about the place. I'll mention it to them, but it will help coming from you."

Charteris' lips thinned. He thought for a moment. "Yes, yes… OK. I'll tell them."

Somehow, the atmosphere had taken on a sombre depressing finality, and it did not feel good.

Clare stared at him wide eyed in disbelief, yet somehow as the story grew in importance she had half expected it. "So it's dead. It never happened. Are you really trying to tell me there is nothing to print? Are you really telling me I've been sitting here waiting... waiting for sweet bugger all?"

"It never happened," he repeated, head bowed and scratching the back of his left hand. "I'm sorry Clare. I know this has turned out to be a wild goose chase but I never..."

She cut him off. "I did. I fucking well did! As the goddam thing matured, I sort of knew there would be security implications. I knew they'd be trying to preserve their precious balls-aching reputation. I've thought about it ever since the MOD came into the picture. But I kept hoping that I was being too bloody pessimistic."

"But you didn't say..."

"I didn't want to tempt fate, for Christ' sake," she yelled. "This is news the world deserves to hear. This is a gigantic cover up if ever there was one. The story of the century and it never fucking happened! It's been a revelation, Jack. A fucking eye-opener. Oh God this makes me sick!" She looked at him, standing with his head down and his arms hanging loosely by his sides. She looked at his hair, long overdue the attention of a pair of scissors. His jacket was open and a roll of fat was trying to escape through the buttonholes of his shirt. But there was something in him that she had never seen before. Behind his façade of hard-boiled devotion to the cause, there was now a blatant vulnerability lurking among his invincible optimism. Suddenly, trying to quell her anger, she felt guilty for the year or more of sterility in their marriage and the need to make amends.

He was almost afraid to ask but he had to. "You...you're not going back to London are you?"

She took a deep breath and strode purposefully into the kitchen. There was the usual clatter of agitated dishes and a loud, almost hysterical curse as a pan bounced off the tiled floor. Then she was silent for a moment. Jack winced expecting missiles. Then she appeared at the kitchen door. "Oh fucking hell," she finally barked. "No…no Jack, I'll stay. I've got to stay, I suppose. The whole world's gone crazy. Somewhere out there I might find one, at least one sane sod who will give me some something to write about." She hung her head, deep in thought for a moment. "I haven't finished with those members of the massed council string sections or the Triads…yes, I'll stay." she repeated with more conviction.

"So, we're OK?"

She thought for a moment. Her lips thinned into a twisted grimace then nodded. "Yes, as OK as we'll ever be, I suppose." She nodded. "Yes, we are OK."

He wrapped his arms around her and squeezed tightly. He could feel the warmth at her neck and the smell of her perfume swam around his head. "Thank God," he whispered.

'Blaydon races' suddenly struck up on his phone. He fished it out of his jacket pocket. It was Wilbur Coulson.

Clare heard grunts and the quick hum of understanding. "OK boss," he said.

"Well?" Clare asked with emphasis.

"It's the boss. Somebody just rang in to the Station. They've found a body in a back lane up the West road. Woman…looks like an Indian or Pakistani. She's got a knife sticking out of her back. Coulson wants me to check it out." He gazed at her, eyebrows raised for some smattering of understanding.

She shook her head in disbelief, eyes closed, then she gave a pained smile. She turned and stamped loudly up the stairs. "My God, here we go again." she yelled. Then she reappeared, leaning over the landing banister. "I want this story even if it means she was the head of M.I goddam 5 or the queen of fucking Sheba. Do you hear me? and don't you bloody dare wake me up if you're late!"

END

ABOUT THE AUTHOR

Gordon Parker has lived in the Northeast of England since birth but has travelled widely. Educated at Blyth Grammar School and Newcastle Polytechnic he took up an apprenticeship as a marine engineer and later served as an engineer with the Shell Tanker Company before joining the Newcastle office of a Midlands-based engineering company specialising in power station steam raising equipment. He concluded his engineering career after 35 years in the nuclear industry as Marketing Manager for Rolls-Royce Nuclear Engineering Services and then Studsvik, a Swedish company and a world leader specialising in Nuclear Decommissioning. Gordon Parker is married to Ann and has two daughters Kim and Tracey, four grandsons and six great grandchildren.

He began writing short stories for local radio in the early 1970s and completed his first novel "The Darkness of the Morning" in 1975. It became an immediate best seller. Based on an actual local mining disaster in 1862, it attracted praise from the Country's mining community and had a foreword by Sir Derek Ezra, NCB chairman. Following publication, it had the unusual accolade of a personal letter from US president Jimmy Carter and also being reproduced as an English reader in Russian schools and serialised in a prominent Russian magazine. It was also published in the

Netherlands, and well received in Japan and Bulgaria. It was serialised on BBC Radio Newcastle with an article in the Radio Times by Playwright Tom Haddaway. It was widely reviewed in the UK as a novel that classically illustrated the battle between miners and mine owners in the 19th century. It has been likened to the writings of both A.J.Cronin and Émile Zola. Two radio plays followed: The Seance and God protect the lonely widow, both broadcast on local BBC radio stations, the latter to commemorate the Trimdon Pit disaster in 1882.

His second novel titled Lightning in May was based on the infamous derailing of the "Flying Scotsman" during the 1926 general strike. This was serialised in the Newcastle Journal to commemorate the 50th anniversary of the event. Lord Ted Willis British Television dramatist and playwright, in his foreword, described Parker as "A bright new talent". The novel was widely reviewed. His third novel The Pool was a satire about corruption in local government. At the time of writing, such corruption was headline news and his novel caused a stir among councils up and down the country. It prompted a meeting arranged by the British Council and Georgy Andjaparidze, Senior research fellow of the Gorky institute of World literature to discuss critical approaches to Post War English literature. The novel was subscribed in Russia for 500,000 copies.

Again, a factual event sparked his next novel, "The Action of the Tiger" his first attempt at a "faction" thriller was also internationally successful. This novel involved the US wartime liberty ship SS Richard Montgomery which in 1944 ran aground and sunk in the Thames estuary with over 2000 tons of bombs and high explosives on board, and remains there to this day. It was widely reviewed with added interest from the area local to the sunken ship. After a long lapse due to pressure of his engineering career and now retired, his next novel A Waking of Rooks was published as an ebook and is receiving excellent reviews. Described as a rites of passage novel and based in the Northeast of England in the 1960s it follows the convoluted fortunes of two male teenagers and their path to maturity. His latest novel titled 'The Priest and the Whistleblower' introduces a tough, no nonsense, detective sergeant based in Newcastle and is a fast-paced crime thriller involving theft, murder and a frightening threat to world peace.

Other titles from Burton Mayers Books:

Can a small Royal British Naval fleet repel the might of Napoleon's navy? £9.99 rrp

1980s Britain. A young reporter uncovers police corruption but becomes the target of a local crime family when he tries to publish. £9.99 rrp

Ingram Content Group UK Ltd.
Milton Keynes UK
UKHW010840180723
425342UK00004B/170

9 781739 367503